Think of it, the Hand hissed, its power moving through him now, filling him with the slightest taste of the incredible strength it could give him.

A perfect world, one in which you and your beloved Buffy could be together because you would be a mortal and there would be no need for a slayer.

Go to hell, Angel thought, avoiding the temptation to reach into his pocket, draw out the Hand, and toss it as far away from him as he could.

He had accepted the responsibility of keeping this thing out of Lillith's hands, and besides . . . what if there was something to what it was saying? What if what it described could be made to happen?

You can picture it, can't you? the Hand asked. *I know you can. I can see what's in your head and your heart.*

What the Hand proposed was a daydream. A fantasy. Angel knew that.

Despite himself, he wanted to hear more.

D0226587

Angel™

City of
Not Forgotten
Redemption
Close to the Ground
Shakedown
Hollywood Noir
Avatar
Soul Trade
Bruja
The Summoned
Haunted
Image
Stranger to the Sun
Vengeance

The Casefiles Volume One
The Essential Angel Posterbook

Available from Pocket Books

ANGEL™

vengeance

Scott Ciencin
and Dan Jolley

An original novel based on the television series
created by Joss Whedon & David Greenwalt

POCKET
BOOKS

New York London Toronto Sydney Singapore

Historian's note: This story takes place in the second half of *Angel's* second season.

First Pocket Books edition August 2002
™ and © 2002 Twentieth Century Fox Film Corporation.
All Rights Reserved.

POCKET BOOKS
An imprint of Simon & Schuster
Africa House
64–78 Kingsway
London WC2B 6AH

www.simonsays.co.uk

The text of this book was set in New Caledonia.

10 9 8 7 6 5 4 3 2 1

A CIP catalogue record for this book is available from the British Library
ISBN 0-7434-4980-0

Printed in Great Britain by
Cox & Wyman Ltd, Reading, Berkshire

To Denise,
my love, my heart, my partner in all things.
—S. C.

To Marie,
for far too many reasons to list here.
—D. J.

ACKNOWLEDGEMENTS

Scott Ciencin would like to thank Lisa Clancy and Micol Ostow at Simon & Schuster and Debbie Olshan at Fox for all their wonderful insights and incredible support; Jeff Mariotte, a stunningly talented author, for his friendship and assistance; Dan and Marie, natch; and the unbelievably talented cast and crew of Angel for their continued excellence and inspiration.

Dan Jolley would like to thank Scott and Denise Ciencin, for opening the door and showing me how to go through it; Lisa Clancy, Micol Ostow, and Debbie Olshan, for shepherding us along; Jeff Mariotte, for his invaluable input; Drew, Tony, Ray, Tom, & JD, for being there; and especially Marie, for putting up with me.

PROLOGUE

"You're looking at a murderer, Doctor," George Hampton whispered, his grip on Martin's wrist tight and unyielding as he looked up from his hospital bed with pale, frightened eyes. "Tomorrow morning, you're going to cut open a man who did the worst thing imaginable, and you're going to try to save his life, try to fix his heart. I've been trying to do that for eleven years, and the best I can tell you is . . . good luck."

Martin McCauley wondered briefly if his patient was exhibiting some bizarre and, until now, unsuspected form of dementia. He pried the pudgy man's fingers loose and took a step away.

"It's late," Martin said. "I think the medications may be—"

"I need to confess," George said, seized by a sudden fit of desperation. "Please, Doctor. You're the only one I trust."

Martin was startled, he couldn't deny it. George appeared lucid—his words heartfelt. But even if what he was saying were true, it didn't matter. Martin had sworn an oath: *Above all things, do no harm.* Even if he knew that the man before him had committed a dozen of the most heinous crimes in history, he was duty bound to do everything in his power to save the man's life. Judgment of any sort was not his to give.

"I don't know what it is you're talking about," Martin said softly, in his most reassuring voice, "and I think we should probably keep it that way. Patient-doctor confidentiality is not without limit, particularly with things like this. Let's just chalk it up to the meds . . . and maybe a bad dream you were having."

"No," George said, tears forming in his eyes as a cloud passed and moonlight fell upon him from the nearby window of his hospital room. The curtains rustled in the evening breeze.

"I can call a priest if you really need someone to talk to like that, but, honestly, George, we've been over the procedure a dozen times. A quadruple bypass is tricky, particularly for someone who's as overweight as you are, with such high cholesterol levels and overall lack of daily exercise, but I've seen worse; I've never lost a patient during one of these, and I don't intend to start tomorrow."

"Eleven years," George whispered, closing his eyes. "Eleven years tomorrow since I ran her down and left her for dead."

Martin drew a sharp breath. Somehow, he kept himself together and pulled up a chair. "Tell me what happened," he said.

• • •

Two hours later, Martin leaned against the driver's side door of his nice, safe, little Volvo, waiting for the woman he had called right after leaving his patient's room. From this steep, isolated hill overlooking Los Angeles, Martin smoked his first cigarette in twenty years. He'd quit the day his daughter, Amy, was born.

On the night of her ninth birthday she had crossed a street alone, somehow breaking from her small group of friends, and had been run down, her body crushed, by a drunk driver. It had happened as she was leaving a yogurt shop downtown where they'd held her party, since it was a weeknight and many of her friends from the ballet academy lived near the place.

She would have been nineteen right now, if she had lived. Twenty, tomorrow.

Eleven years since her death . . . and her killer was George Hampton.

The crush of tires on gravel alerted Martin to the approach of the sleek black Jaguar. Though he had never wanted to drive anything flashy himself—too much like wearing a target for car thieves—his oldest son, Robert, was into cars big-time. Robert had been floored at the sight of the 2002 S-Type V-8 sedan when it first pulled into their driveway, and had hardly stopped talking about it since.

The car pulled around and a driver got out, a huge man in a black designer suit. He nodded to Martin, then opened the passenger door and held out his hand to the most sought after woman in the world according to *Business Magazine*.

"Hello, Lily," Martin said to the ravishing, raven-haired woman who approached with deep sympathy in her eyes, the moonlight bathing her gray, double-breasted silk pantsuit. Martin had never seen a more beautiful woman than Lily Pierce . . . with the exception, of course, of his wife.

She held out her hands and he took them in his own, squeezing them gently. Lily's driver went for a walk, assuring their privacy.

"Thank you for coming," Martin said.

"You're one of the most decent men I've ever known," Lily said. "You're also a friend. I'm worried about you."

Martin released her hands. He reached into his pocket and took out a small silver locket adorned with an opal that sparkled in even the palest light. The moment the locket was in his hand, memories of his first-born, his baby girl, came rushing back to him. He thought of her first words, her laugh, the way she moved onstage, as graceful as an angel, her love of her craft giving her wings.

He had, by all accounts, the perfect life. He was a successful and highly respected heart surgeon, he was happily married, he had plenty of good friends, and he was raising four healthy, well-adjusted children with a woman he loved. He was a compassionate man who believed in the sanctity of life above all else.

And tonight, he was contemplating murder.

"You still have it," Lily said.

He nodded.

"I remember the night you first came to me," Lily said. "You told me you'd never met a motivational speaker who'd inspired you to do anything except pity the people who'd put money in their pockets. Then you asked for my help."

"Vienna," Martin said. "The first time I heard you talk. The conference that changed my life."

"Has it?"

Nodding, he clutched the locket to his chest. When Amy died, he'd been in no position to give in to the grief, despair, and rage that rose up inside him over the incident. He had to be strong for his family. He threw himself fully into his work, and life slowly returned to almost normal. Almost.

But since the day he'd buried his child, there had been a very small, but undeniable black hole of anger and loss inside Martin, a maelstrom he first tried to deny, then attempted to deal with through religion and therapy. Nothing had helped—until he met Lily Pierce. Though her New Life Foundation was already enormously popular overseas, Lily took a personal interest in Martin. She helped him find a measure of peace over the loss by acknowledging his darkest feelings over the incident and working through them to see that what he really needed was to fill the hole left in his heart.

To help him focus on that goal, Lily had given him a keepsake, a locket identical to the one buried with his daughter. As long as he kept it close, as he did now, he could feel the spirit of his lost little girl, he could draw on her strength and, he firmly believed, he could one day summon the strength needed to forgive his daughter's killer, whoever that person might be. What he'd wanted more than anything was to finally disperse that shred of darkness in what Lily had described as his otherwise "bright, shining, perfect soul," that waiting abyss that wanted vengeance and couldn't have cared less about compassion and mercy.

Be pure in purpose and perfect in execution. Lily's words.

"I looked into his eyes, and forgiveness was the last thing on my mind," Martin said. "It was one thing to forgive someone I thought I'd never meet . . . an abstract concept. Another to be face-to-face with the s.o.b. All the old demons came at me at once, torturing me with what Amy might look like today if she had lived, the life she might have had, all her dreams. . . ."

"I understand," Lily said, placing her hand on his arm, steadying him as they moved close to the edge of the hill and looked down at the sparkling lights of the city.

"I know what I should do," Martin said, trembling with anger. "I should call in another surgeon and later on try to launch legal proceedings, bring Amy's killer to justice. But it's not that easy, and I can't talk to my wife about this. I can't tell anyone what I'm feeling. . . ."

"You can tell me," Lily said, her deep, understanding voice filling him with comfort, with the strength he feared he lacked.

"I could do it," he said, whirling on her, tears streaming down his face. "I could kill him on the table tomorrow morning and no one would ever know I'd done it on purpose. I'm skilled enough to pull it off; I'm that good."

"I know," Lily said. "You're practically perfect."

"An eye for an eye, Old Testament retribution," Martin said. "Or I can forgive this man and finally let it go."

"But would you?" Lily asked. "And if you couldn't, do you really think there's any chance at all this man will repeat what he's told you to anyone else once his life is no longer in danger?"

He rubbed the locket over his heart. His handsome face was marred only by the dark emotions it revealed. He was forty-seven, but he knew he could have passed for ten years younger. Tall, broad-shouldered, with dark hair only lightly peppered with gray. Movie star good looks.

Amy would have been beautiful.

"I can't tell you what to do," Lily said. "All I can do is reassure you about one thing: No matter what choice you make—I will be there for you."

He collapsed into her arms, sobbing with rage and grief.

That night, he didn't sleep. He only stared at the ceiling.

And the next morning, on the operating room table, Dr. Martin McCauley lost a patient for the first time in eleven years.

Leaving the hospital, a part of him was sickened at what he had done—while another part was ebullient.

The feeling didn't last.

Soon he was back home. Martin's house was a beautiful brick colonial nestled high on eleven acres of prime California real estate, with woods out back, a pond where he fished with his children across the street, and a sparkling stream running along the property line separating his lot from his neighbors. There hadn't been one day in all the years he'd lived here that he hadn't marveled at owning a place like this, considering his own humble background.

No day before today, that is.

He pulled up to his space on the side of the house and entered through the backdoor, which opened into the spacious kitchen. The wooden table in the center of the room seated six: himself, his wife, Samantha, and their four children. He set his keys down on the counter and went through a passage to the family room, where pictures of his children lined the wall.

Martin always took pride in the photos of sixteen-year-old Robert indulging his twin passions, cars and astronomy, or fourteen-year-old Mary onstage with the latest school play. But looking at those photographs, and others of William and Sandy, his six- and eight-year-olds, Martin felt as if he might as well have been staring into the wide-eyed, smiling faces of total strangers. He knew who they were, but he felt nothing for them.

Walking through the rest of his house, his haven as he called it, he felt nothing at all. In the computer room he sat down and pulled up the latest chapter of the medical mystery he had been writing just for fun.

There was no joy in it now.

He looked outside to the in-ground swimming pool and thought of the many clandestine midnight rendezvous he'd had with his wife there when the kids were staying with friends; the memory, normally quite an exciting one, elicited no reaction in his heart.

Climbing the stairs, he went to the landing and looked in each of the kid's rooms, staring at their posters, their CDs, their toys and games and books. . . .

Nothing. He felt nothing at all.

The worst of it was Amy's locket. He didn't have to go anywhere at all to look at that. It had been in his pocket, where he'd always kept it. Normally, all he had to do was hold it in his hand and he would feel as if Amy were there with him. Even at the worst of times, its mere presence had always filled him with comfort, assurance, and warmth.

Now, there was nothing. He looked at the silver locket, staring into the depths of the beautiful opal in its setting. The sparkling streaks of blue, purple, and green were there, but the light no longer touched his soul.

"Opal is the gemstone of faithfulness," a voice called from the last room at the end of the hall. "Show your faith in me and come forward."

Martin found Lily standing in front of the full-sized mirror he had bought for his wife. Lily wore his wife's favorite dress, a black off-the-shoulder with a light Asian touch of red roses and emerald leaves. It shouldn't have fit her; Lily was close to six feet tall without heels and possessed a perfect hourglass figure, and his wife was a petite five feet one, slender, with almost no hips and a practically flat chest.

Yet the dress looked as if it were made for Lily. She looked perfect in it.

Martin couldn't have cared less.

"What have you done to me?" he asked, his voice low, dull. The mild surprise he felt at the sound of his emotionless voice was the first thing he'd actually felt since murdering a man earlier today. A part of him thought, *Of course you're not yourself. You're in shock, you feel guilty. . . .*

But that wasn't true. For the most part, he simply felt nothing at all.

"I offered you options," Lily said. "I allowed you the luxury of free will. That is the blessing of your kind, isn't it? The right to save yourselves, or damn yourselves, by virtue of your choices?"

"It wasn't a coincidence," Martin murmured.

"That the life of the man who killed your child simply fell into your hands that way? Of course not. My people put a great deal of research and legwork into this little enterprise. But it's paid off, I would say. Or . . . it soon will."

Martin stared at her, speechless.

Lily smiled. "Don't you like the new you? Don't you feel one step closer to perfection?"

He didn't answer. There was something about her now, something unearthly. A slight wind out of nowhere lifted her pure black hair as she approached him, and her eyes . . . they were *glowing*.

Turning away, he shrugged off his jacket and tie, loosening the top few buttons of his shirt.

"Don't think you can shun me," Lily said in a low, rumbling voice that made the floorboards shake.

He looked at her again. Her eyes flashed yellow, her beauty nearly blinding, otherworldly. She reached out her hand and drew him to her without a word.

He was powerless to resist.

When she held him in her sensuous embrace, she bit and licked his ear, then whispered, "I promised you, no matter what choice you made, I would be here. *For you*. And so I am. A deal's a deal, and a pact, once made, may never be broken. Not by either of us."

Martin was seized by a sudden, unreasoning terror, his first burst of powerful emotion since he'd arrived home. He had been faithful to his wife, faithful and true to her and all he believed in, yet today, he was ready to toss it all away—and for what? The vengeance he had sought was hollow and had robbed him of his connection to his darling Amy. And the release Lily promised, the joyous release of sensual abandon, the succulent ambrosia of forgetfulness, of no longer caring . . . it called to him and repelled him at the same time.

He tried to pull away from her, but Lily's grasp on his arms was like steel. The amber glow of her eyes intensified as she stared at him, lips parting and drawing near to him. He wanted to scream—and yet . . . he wanted this even more, wanted *her* even though he now instinctually understood what she offered, and it was not bliss, not abandon.

It was utter damnation.

She tore open his shirt and thrust her hand against his chest as their lips met. A stabbing, fiery agony lanced into his heart, followed by a terrible, numbing chill that quickly spread through every part of him and reached down *deeper*.

Martin had wondered many times what death might be like, if the cessation of life meant an eternal darkness, an end to memories pleasant and painful, or if an eternity truly beckoned, if the soul was real. Now he knew the answer, now he understood he had given up his most precious possession. His cry of horror was muffled against the fire and ice that was Lily Pierce, her lips, her hand, the press of her body.

Suddenly, it was over. Martin felt different, but he couldn't quite comprehend the changes in him, not yet. His bare chest itched, and he looked down to see a brand seared into his chest, a mark of a two-headed serpent.

The locket was still in his hand. He opened it, staring down at his daughter's photograph. His memories of the girl were unchanged, but his feelings were completely different. She'd been his spawn, she had died, such was the way of the flesh, fragile and weak. He was more than flesh now. He was purpose, and, as such, he was eternal. . . .

"Caring and compassion is for lesser beings," Lily said coldly. "The taint of such human feeling has been seared from you."

Martin nodded. "It is good."

12

"And your soul belongs to me. I have taken it from you to use as I see fit when the time comes."

He bowed. "I live to serve."

"Yes, you do. So let's begin. I have located a beautiful young widow with a soul nearly as perfect as yours, and a belief just as strong that she must violate of her own free will if she is to damn herself and make her soul available to be harvested. Can you be of service to me in this regard? Can you make her love you, lose herself in you, and be willing to sacrifice anything, even her soul, for want of you?"

Martin smiled, every vestige of his personality now subjugated by Lily Pierce's will. "Show me the way."

"That's my goal," Lily said with a throaty laugh. "First you and others like you . . . then the world."

They walked out into a bright, shining day that might as well have been as black and cold as midnight.

CHAPTER ONE

Angel stood in the alleyway behind the Forsythe Shelter for the Homeless, taking in the unearthly stillness surrounding him. Nothing moved here. No pedestrians, no cars. Not even the air. The strange calm would have been odd and unsettling no matter where it descended, but in Los Angeles on a summer night it approached the surreal. His companions, Cordelia, Wesley, and Gunn, also appeared aware of the phenomena, but none seemed as unnerved by it as the young woman Angel was questioning because of Cordelia's guiding vision.

"It's been like this for months," the homeless woman whispered, pulling her tattered jacket tighter around her shoulders. She looked around, shuddering in apparent terror of this place. "It's s'posed to be a place where you can heal, y'know?" the woman said. "But me and the others here—it's like—it's like it just sucks the light in. Like it just eats it. And the . . . and the hope, too."

Angel gave the woman some money and pointed her toward an all-night diner. Then he, Wesley, Gunn, and Cordelia crept into the Forsythe Shelter through its back entrance.

A digital clock outside the bank down the street read 12:42. If someone had been listening at that moment—standing outside the shelter, paying close attention—he or she would have heard the stillness tremble and begin to crack. From inside came a muffled crash, the sound of splintering wood, and something lower. Something almost recognizable as a *growl*. . . .

The backdoor abruptly burst off its hinges, propelled across the alley by the weight of a creature not found in any encyclopedia listing. More than seven feet long, it combined the least appealing characteristics of arachnid and reptilian life—and as its pursuers emerged from the building it turned to face them, rising up on four hind legs.

They stepped out one by one: Cordelia Chase, a stunning brunette in her early twenties; Wesley Wyndham-Pryce, in his thirties, slight with rumpled hair and eyeglasses; and Charles Gunn, a tall, lean young African-American man in his twenties.

Angel followed them, wrapped in shadows, little more than glimpses of pale skin above a billowing black coat. He raised his face to the harsh streetlight, revealing the demonic ridges, the yellow eyes, and the fangs of a vampire. As he stepped forward, armed with a gleaming broadsword, his three human companions fanned out behind him, brandishing their own weapons.

The spider-lizard—a Krinj demon, according to Wesley's earlier identification—gave a hissing shriek and feinted toward Angel. A blade flashed, and black ichor splattered onto the pavement.

"It's bleeding!" Wesley called out, a double-bladed light ax ready in his hands. "The vulnerability spell worked!"

Angel took a step forward, raising his broadsword. "I'll take the front legs," he said, his words slightly distorted by the fangs. Usually Angel looked as human as he had when he was alive—he had even once been called "the one with the angelic face," a description from which he'd taken his vampiric name—but in times of battle, he allowed his vampire nature to manifest itself in his features.

Angel watched as Cordelia and Gunn, each armed with scimitars, moved with Wesley to flank the creature and try to take out its back legs. He was confident that they understood his strategy: If it couldn't stand, it couldn't fight. Only Cordy didn't look too convinced of their chances.

"Don't worry," Gunn said to her. "We're 'bout to have one less demon round here."

"I'm glad *someone's* confident about this," Cordelia murmured.

Suddenly, the creature lunged forward, roaring, intent on ripping Angel apart.

Angel snarled and lunged with his sword.

Twenty minutes later, Angel's '67 Plymouth GTX convertible cruised down an L.A. boulevard. Angel drove, and in the front passenger seat next to him,

Cordelia allowed herself to finally relax. She glanced at her companions and smiled at the sight of Gunn clapping his hands in the back beside Wesley.

"Now *that's* what I call 'finesse,'" Gunn said. Each member of the group drank in the sights and sounds of the vital, living city.

"Yes indeed!" Wesley said as he and Gunn bumped fists, grinning. "'The vorpal blade went snicker-snack'!"

Gunn lost his grin and cocked an eyebrow at Wesley. Wesley noticed—and then further noticed—Cordelia watching over her shoulder from the front passenger seat.

"What?" Wesley said, suddenly at his most defensively British. "It's Lewis Carroll! As in *Through the Looking-Glass* and *Alice in Wonderland*? Hello?"

"Oh, I recognize the quote," Gunn said. "Read 'Jabberwocky' back in eighth grade. I just didn't ever expect to hear somebody quotin' it in real life."

Wesley crossed his arms. "I'm never going to master American humor."

Without turning from the wheel, Angel said, "I'm laughing on the inside, Wesley."

Cordelia closed her eyes and let the cool, ocean-scented breeze wash over her. It felt almost good enough to take away the lingering, throbbing pain of the vision she'd had a couple of hours earlier.

Languidly she turned to Angel. "So it fed on despair? All the hopelessness of the homeless?"

"Not anymore," Angel answered. Wearing his human face again, Angel actually seemed to be enjoying a rare moment of peace of mind. "We did good."

"Better than good, I'd say," Wesley said. "Not a single life lost. Location, containment, extermination. Rather embodies the whole game, doesn't it?"

"Yo, fire up the radio," Gunn said. "Find us some demon-slayin' music."

Angel voiced no objections, so Cordelia clicked the radio on and began surfing the stations. After a few moments Vernon Reid's raw guitar blasted from the speakers: Living Colour's "Cult of Personality."

"Sweet," Gunn said, settling back in his seat.

Cordelia glanced around at Wesley again. To her surprise, he was bobbing his head in time with the music. Even Angel, she noticed, started tapping his fingers on the steering wheel in accompaniment to the drums. She grinned, and relaxed even more.

For a few moments, maybe, Cordelia could pretend that they were simply four friends, cruising through Los Angeles on a Friday night like normal people. She could forget that Angel Investigations, the private detective agency Angel had founded, dealt almost exclusively with the vampiric and demonic underground flourishing in L.A. She could even gloss over her own connection to The Powers That Be—the mysterious otherworldly force responsible for her bursts of precognition, the visions that allowed Angel Investigations to pinpoint and neutralize the worst of L.A.'s demon-related threats in time to do some good, save some lives.

Tonight, after dispatching the spider-lizard monstrosity, she could melt back into what life *should* be.

Music's on. Top's down.

Life is good, she thought.

Cordelia's reverie lasted maybe forty-five seconds.

"Trouble ahead," Angel said, slowing the car and nodding at the flashing blue lights and chaos before them. His companions snapped to attention, and it was difficult at first to make sense of what they were seeing at the intersection ahead; what looked like a Jerry Bruckheimer action scene in mid-shoot had blocked both northbound lanes of the four-lane divided highway.

"Damn," Gunn said softly. "What a pileup. There's gotta be at least two dozen cars in that."

Angel was the first to hear the distinctive sound of a helicopter reach them from overhead. Then Wesley pointed up, and the Gunn and Cordy followed his lead just in time to see a police helicopter buzz over the intersection. "Air support," Wesley said. "Was this a high-speed chase, do you think?"

Cordy replied, "Dunno, but at least with the chopper already up there, you know the EMTs will be here soon."

"Maybe not soon enough." Angel pulled the big Plymouth onto the shoulder and opened his door. "Let's see if we can help."

A thick ring of bystanders surrounded what now appeared to be the aftermath of a police car chase and subsequent shoot-out.

"Five—no, six—patrol cars," Wesley murmured. "And that overturned SUV over there." He pointed. "They must have been traveling at terrible speed. . . ."

"Yeah, right into traffic." Cordelia shuddered as they got closer. "Oh my God, look at the *driver* . . ."

She gestured toward the SUV Wesley had mentioned, where it seemed a man had climbed up out of the passenger door, once the vehicle had flipped on its side, and opened fire with an automatic rifle. His body hung halfway out the passenger window, virtually torn apart by bullets, the rifle still dangling from one tattered hand. Through the shattered windshield she saw another body, also dead, its arms wrapped around the steering wheel, most of its head gone.

"Excuse me," Angel said forcefully, shouldering his way through the outer edge of the bystanders. Wesley, Gunn, and Cordelia followed close behind him, then almost bumped into him, he'd stopped so suddenly.

Cordelia moved up beside him. "Angel? What is it?"

He said nothing. He didn't have to. She *flinched* at the look of boiling outrage on his face.

The carnage was much worse than they had at first suspected; the damage caused by the multiple crashes and gunfire was so extensive, it looked as if a series of bombs had gone off. And while the criminals and the police were all dead, some of the innocents caught in the cross fire and the series of collisions still survived.

Gunshot victims moved feebly, some crawling slowly away from the wreckage, some clutching at their wounds. A flaxen-haired teenage girl, her hands clamped over her belly, rocked slowly back and forth as blood ran out between her fingers. A middle-aged Hispanic woman tried to get to her feet, but couldn't maintain her balance; her face and head glittered with embedded shards and slivers of broken glass. A young boy finally found his voice and began crying for help, tucking his bullet-mangled left hand under his right arm.

The boy's cries mingled with the screams and moans of the other victims, combining into a mass plea: *Help us, help us, someone please help us.*

Suddenly a loud voice barked in Angel's ear from behind. "Hey, buddy, get the hell out of my way, will ya? You're blocking my shot!"

Angel turned and found himself staring into the lens of a digital camera—then looked past the camera to the man holding it. The man with the eager grin and wide, excited eyes. "I said get outta my way!"

Snarling, Angel took the camera out of the man's hands and smashed it to the ground. The cameraman sputtered wordlessly—then backed away and disappeared into the crowd when he saw the cold fury in the vampire's eyes.

Scanning the crowd, Angel realized that the cameraman's attitude was far from the exception; everywhere he looked, people gawked, pointed, many of them chatting on their cell phones.

Not one of them made a single move to help.

Angel nodded toward the wreckage. "Get some first aid going."

They sprang forward, Gunn and Wesley already ripping up their shirts to form bandages and tourniquets. Cordelia began clearing debris away from a patch on the pavement so the victims could lie down.

One of the injured, a man who had apparently been clipped by one of the moving vehicles, staggered into view. Angel saw that the injured man was trying to get to the clear space on the pavement, but a woman with a digital phone blocked his way, standing between two of the wrecked vehicles. Though she seemed to be aware of the injured man, she also showed no inclination to let him through. Angel went to her and touched her arm, indicating that she should move so the man could pass by. "Miss, that man—"

Suddenly indignant, the woman jerked away: "Hands off, creep!" Then she turned her back to him and said into the phone, "Jeez, this guy just *grabbed* me! Can you believe that?"

But at least she did move enough so that Angel could help guide the injured man, who seemed to be going rapidly into shock, over to where Gunn and Wes could offer him some first aid.

Angel turned back, tried to look and listen for approaching emergency vehicles, and it struck him again: No one in the crowd was doing anything to aid the wounded. Not one of the two or three dozen people there was even lifting a finger. They were too busy gawking, taking in the horror show like it *was* some Hollywood movie, not real life.

He didn't want to believe that these people could actually be enjoying themselves, so Angel looked to another cell phone user and said, "These people need help."

The man, a slick-haired yuppie in a polo shirt, kept

talking and pretended not to hear him. Angel heard the man say, "No, never seen anything like it in real life. Wild stuff, man, really exciting!"

Angel spun, staring all around him. He yelled over the noise, "Are you all just going to stand there?"

But the only thing that accomplished was to make the crowd part and move away from him, ignoring him from a greater distance.

Turning back to the crash, he saw a middle-aged white man talking to Cordelia. The man suddenly turned and practically ran away from her; he jumped in a car at the edge of the turmoil and sped away, crossing the divider into the southbound lanes. As he went, Angel heard Cordelia shout after him, "But you're a doctor! No one's going to sue you! For God's sake, help these people!" But her words had no effect. The man's car disappeared into traffic.

Striving in his outrage to keep his face from changing, Angel joined the rest of the team in trying to help the victims of the horrible skirmish, ambulance sirens finally approaching from the distance. But as he bandaged wounds, carried people from wrecked cars, and carefully pulled a shard of glass from the corner of a young woman's eye, he couldn't help but think: *I can destroy a thousand supernatural threats. We can track down and kill a thousand demons, but it's not enough. It'll never be enough.*

Humans as a species seemed to be coded for self-destruction, for predation, for seeking out the basest, most animalistic impulses they could find and reveling in them. It had always been that way. Always. In the two hundred plus years of Angel's life, and for the countless millennia before that, humans had bitten and clawed and scraped the world and one another until blood covered the ground. He couldn't change the basic nature of humanity, no matter what he did.

But, oh, wouldn't he give anything . . .

Wouldn't he give anything at all if he *could*.

CHAPTER TWO

"Join us and you'll find life just *couldn't* be better," said the bright, confident, blue-eyed beauty on the TV. "The Lily Pierce Total Life Improvement System has been helping people of all ages in Europe for the past year—and now we're opening our first American New Life Center right here in Beverly Hills!"

"Oh, please," Cordelia said quietly. She sat in Angel Investigations' office behind what used to be the registration desk; their business operated out of the Hyperion, a refurbished Hollywood hotel that had seen its heyday in the 1950s. She eyed the television skeptically.

Gunn walked past her, leaned against a filing cabinet. "Since when did we get a TV in here?"

Cordelia didn't answer immediately. On the screen, the radiant, voluptuous woman in the ten thousand-dollar designer original continued: "Our mantra is simple: Erase doubt. Erase fear. Become pure of purpose. Perfect in execution." She paused a tiny moment for effect, then added, "Attain your dreams."

Cordelia snorted and hit the mute button. "I'm caught up on the paperwork, and you may have noticed the steady stream of *nothing* coming through our doors lately. I just thought a TV might pass the time. Besides, it was free. One of my neighbors moved out and couldn't fit it in her car."

"Not bad reception," Gunn said appreciatively, watching the gorgeous woman still on the screen.

Cordelia nodded, one eyebrow arched. "That's Lily Pierce—the woman whose hors d'oeuvres and champagne I will soon be eating and drinking."

"Didn't know you were into that self-help stuff."

"I'm not." She shrugged. "Just 'cause I'm going to a party she's throwing doesn't mean I have to buy any of her, y'know . . . hooey."

Coming through a door behind her, Wesley caught the name and saw the image on the screen. He set down a stack of books on the broad desktop. "Ah, yes, I've been hearing her commercials on the radio a lot lately. As well as seeing the billboards . . . and the ads in bookstores . . . and the stacks of coupons at the car wash. . . ."

"She's a real woman of the people, all right," Cordelia said. "I give it another six months before she's up on the shelf next to the Razor Scooters."

"Oh, I don't know, Cordy," Wesley said. "I'm somewhat intrigued by her philosophies, at least from an objective point of view. She seems simply to be saying that life doesn't have to be so hard. Know what you want and go for it. Sounds reasonable enough."

Cordelia yawned. "I don't buy it, but hey, it's her party. I'm just going for the agents and producers."

Gunn said, "Wait a sec—that the party David Nabbit invited you to the other day? That's Lily Pierce's deal?"

"The very one. I'll let you know if it improves my life."

Gunn raised both eyebrows, and Cordy could tell he was still thinking about Pierce's image on the TV. "Chance to meet a woman like that in person, I might put on a monkey suit myself." He paused, then said, "So you're only goin' for the professional contacts, huh?"

"It's a real gala event," Cordelia said. "The Lily Pierce thing is a total fad in Hollywood right now. I mean, she's like the love child of Deepak Chopra and Susan Powter. So you're definitely going to get your paparazzi, your mega producers, your bright shining superstars. . . ."

Carefully, Wesley asked, "Does David know that's the only reason you're going?"

She sighed.

Angel Investigations had helped David Nabbit out of a tight situation once, and he'd been their biggest fan ever since then. Nabbit was almost as rich as Bill Gates, but with a greater appreciation for fantasy role-playing games and even fewer social skills. The man made more money by taking a nap than most Americans earned in a year, and he was a good guy—his financial acumen had allowed Angel to acquire the hotel and maintain it—but his high school math-nerd demeanor made him a little hard to take at times. He'd been smitten with Cordelia virtually at first sight.

Cordelia liked him. He was . . . nice. And rich. But she wasn't exactly looking for a boyfriend right now.

"David . . . ," she began awkwardly. "Y'know, David understands. Besides, he can rescue me if any creep decides to, like, fasten his suckers onto me." When Wesley and Gunn didn't respond, Cordelia added, "Metaphorical suckers. I'm hoping tonight will be refreshingly demon-free."

"A demon-free night?" a voice said, making all three turn. "In Hollywood? You're dreaming."

Angel stood in the office area, dressed in his customary black. He spent a lot of time brooding, even in the best of circumstances, but even he had a sense that this afternoon the metaphorical storm clouds above his head seemed almost visible.

Gunn said, "Hey, man . . . how long you been standin' there?"

"I came in at 'Deepak Chopra.'" Angel absently gathered some files from a table and riffled through them, obviously not really seeing the words.

Cordelia, Wesley, and Gunn remained silent for a moment.

Finally Wesley said, "Well, that conversation died with nary a whimper."

Suddenly, across the lobby, the front door opened.

The sound was one that the team, Cordelia especially, had come to equate with incoming profits—or at least with incoming excitement. With the exception of Angel, who still stared blankly at the files in his hand, they all moved to see who or what had come to visit.

Cordelia lost her grin immediately, while Gunn and Wesley both moved closer to a nearby weapons cabinet. After a few seconds Angel's nose wrinkled and he spoke without looking up. "What are you doing here?"

Across the lobby stood a tall, slender woman in a sleek gray business suit, a slim briefcase held in one manicured hand. Lilah Morgan's chestnut-brown hair, long legs, and perfectly sculpted alabaster features would have made her a heartbreaking beauty, if her bearing and demeanor hadn't been so relentlessly ice-cold.

Without preamble she said, "We have a job for you."

Lilah was the VP in charge of Special Projects at Wolfram and Hart, an L.A. law firm run by a group of immensely powerful, mind-bogglingly evil, extradimensional entities known collectively as "the Senior Partners." The firm had built up a lot of history with Angel in a short period of time, repeatedly attempting either to corrupt or kill him. Their interest in Angel arose primarily because of his anomalous nature: Angel was a vampire with a soul.

After decade upon decade of vicious, bloodthirsty mayhem, Angel—then called "Angelus"—fell under a Gypsy curse that restored the essence of his humanity. Now he possessed all his vampiric abilities and weaknesses, along with a human conscience perpetually crushed and ravaged by guilt. It was that guilt, that longing for redemption—along with a message from The Powers That Be—that prompted him to start Angel Investigations, whose stated mission was to help the helpless.

Wolfram and Hart, aware of certain prophecies that foretold Angel's crucial role in the inevitable Apocalypse, had striven for months to control his behavior, trying to manipulate him to their advantage. They'd had very little success.

"Get out." Angel's voice hadn't raised at all, but Lilah almost flinched.

"You really want to hear what I have to say, Angel," Lilah said, sounding as close as she could get to pleasant. "This isn't something just for my employers' benefit. The entire human race is in mortal danger."

"Human race at stake?" Cordelia said. "Not that we haven't heard that one before."

Angel's gaze narrowed. "I said get out."

"Well . . . there *are* four of us, and only one of her," Wesley said. "If it came to it, I think we could take her."

Angel glowered at him.

"Seriously," Wesley said, "if there actually is such a danger . . . we could at least listen for a moment."

"If you do the job right, it'll be fast, easy . . ." Lilah went to a small table, set the briefcase down, and opened it. "And lucrative."

The briefcase held a thick dossier and a ton of cash. "Two hundred and fifty thousand dollars. You get a quarter of the fee up front, and all the information we have."

No one moved or spoke. Apparently taking that as encouragement, Lilah continued. "It's a retrieval job. There is an object of power that has just arrived in Los Angeles, in the possession of a vast supernatural evil recently taken root here. Get it, deliver it to us. You get the money, we get to keep humanity alive."

"No." Angel didn't even look at the briefcase as he moved toward her. Lilah swallowed, but stood her ground despite Angel's glare.

"Angel, we really should hear her out," Wesley said. "Not for the money. But if people are in danger . . ."

"Fine," Angel said. "Make it quick."

"The evil is Lilith," Lilah said dispassionately. "According to the demon underground information network, *the* Lilith, first wife of Adam—"

Gunn said, "Adam—you mean fig leaf Adam?"

Wesley nodded slowly. "According to some texts, Adam had a first wife, before Eve. She refused to be subservient to him, and left Eden. That's when God created Eve from Adam's own body."

Angel crossed his arms over his chest, finding patience difficult. He noticed Cordelia eye the money, then shake her head and look away.

"And you believe that?" Gunn asked. "You think she's really connected with the Garden of Eden and all that?"

Lilah shrugged. "Every myth has some grounding in reality. Lilith courts the reputation that she's the oldest and most powerful human on the planet. Could just be hype. What's indisputable is that Lilith is very dangerous. According to the story, which she perpetuates at every opportunity, after she left the 'garden,' she lay with demons, and gave birth to hundreds of half-human, half-demon children. In return, she became part demon herself. She despises not only humanity in general, but also her own in particular, and wants to burn the taint of it from this world. She wants to make herself and everyone else pure."

"Pure evil," Wesley said, barely above a whisper.

Lilah nodded.

"You're not making it quick," Angel said, not wanting to be in the same room as Lilah any longer than he had to be. She had personally overseen a dozen or more plots meant to destroy the lives of every one of them. He could never trust her.

The lawyer ignored him. "It's said that when Adam and Eve were expelled from Eden, they encountered other humans. Their children married, and the human race began. But according to Lilith, those other 'humans' were a group of her children more in touch with their human than their demon sides. Outcasts from her ranks. They are our ancestors. Therefore, there is a 'touch of the Lilith'—a little bit of her tainted demon blood—in every human."

Angel thought of the callous, even maliciously gleeful reactions of the spectators at the accident site. Despite himself, he wondered for an instant if there could be something to Lilith's claims. Humanity certainly had its share of inner demons. It would almost be comforting to believe that that part of human nature could be driven out.

Wesley came forward, picked up the dossier, and started flipping through it. He shook his head. "But do you believe all this, Lilah? Yourself?"

Lilah lowered her eyelids a fraction, the very picture of noncommittal. "What I believe doesn't matter. I'm representing the firm. But the facts are thus: Lilith *is* ancient, incredibly powerful, thoroughly evil, and has produced countless demon spawn, which somehow got crossed genetically with the human race." She folded her arms, addressing the whole group. "The stories match up—Garden of Eden, early humans, the whole nine yards—and she uses that to her advantage, to raise her profile in the supernatural community."

"Great, ultimate evil with a really good grasp of public relations," Cordelia said.

Lilah raised an eyebrow. "What matters is that she's here and she has the object she needs to accomplish her goal. The threat she poses is enormous."

Though he felt no less hostile, Angel was now giving Lilah his undivided attention. "What's the object of power?"

"Here," Wesley said, holding up a page from the dossier for Angel to see. Gunn and Cordelia moved in to look as well.

On the page Angel and the others studied was an illustration of a torque—a style of necklace—fashioned to look like a long, vaguely reptilian hand. When worn it would appear that the hand was encircling the wearer's throat, forefinger touching thumb.

"My word," Wesley whispered.

"Okay, you could get me to wear that thing never," Cordelia murmured.

"It's called the Serpent's Hand," Lilah said as the group stared at the image. "It seems to fit in with known beliefs—and Lilith's story—as well. The Serpent was considered the most beautiful of God's creatures, but after it tempted Eve, God struck off its limbs and cursed it to writhe on its belly in the filth for all time. According to Lilith, the object is, literally, the hand the Serpent used to aim Eve toward temptation, and with it—provided it has been fed enough power—it can re-shape reality in whatever image its owner desires. But to do something this sweeping, this immense in scale, there's only one time the Hand can be used, one time when it will become vulnerable and can be destroyed. And that time is fast approaching."

Angel shifted his gaze from the dossier back to Lilah and glared at her. *Like I'm gonna trust you,* he thought.

"You said the Hand had to be fed power," Wesley said, adjusting his glasses. "What sort of power does it need?"

"Like Lilith and her brood, it feeds on souls," Lilah said, her eyes fixed on Angel. "And it is the most corrupting power in existence."

"No wonder you guys want it so bad," Cordelia said, but Lilah ignored her.

"Lilith needs a thousand souls for the Hand, but she

has a problem, you see. Not just any souls will do. She has to find those who are clean, pure, virtually perfect—"

"A thousand perfect souls?" Angel interrupted, thinking again about the accident scene he'd witnessed. "Good luck with that."

Lilah continued without protest. "And then manipulate them, pervert those pure souls in some way, so that of their own free will they commit an act of utter corruption. Finding a thousand souls of that caliber and performing all the work involved takes time, and it's time she doesn't have. She had to create a mechanism." Lilah reached into a pocket of her suit and pulled out a paperback book, holding it up for the others to see. The title was *The Perfect Life and How to Get It*, by Lily Pierce. "And so Lily Pierce was born."

It took a moment to sink in. Cordelia said, "Lily Pierce? We were . . . we were just watching her on TV. . . ."

Lilah tossed the book on top of the briefcase. "You and practically everyone else in L.A. She's trawling the waters. Harvesting souls."

Cordelia bumped Wesley with an elbow. "Told you I didn't like her."

"So, Lily Pierce is . . . Lilith," Angel began, his distrust clear in his tone. "Her self-help program lets people achieve 'inner purity' . . . and then she corrupts them and harvests them."

"Oh, it gets better," Lilah said coolly. "Not only is she collecting souls to feed to the Serpent's Hand, but her program is also drawing all of her demonic descendants to her from all over the world, adding to the ranks of her demon army, which is already substantial. And those humans whose souls aren't potent enough to be among the thousand still serve a purpose: They feed the ranks of her middle- and upper-management teams."

"Which are demons," Gunn said, more to himself than to anyone else.

Angel slammed the briefcase closed on the money and the paperback book and shoved it back in her arms. "I won't be Wolfram and Hart's errand boy. Ever."

Lilah regarded him for a few heartbeats, then cocked her head to the side, ever so slightly. She had the look of a woman who knew something no one else knew. Her voice almost too low to hear, she said, "Such *pride.*" Then she turned and strode back to the front door.

"Keep the dossier," she said over her shoulder. "You'll be needing it soon enough."

Angel stared holes in her back until she was out the door and gone.

The sun had begun to drop toward the western horizon by the time Cordelia pushed back from the computer and said, "Okay, I think I've got something."

The three men gathered near her as she tapped a pencil on the computer screen. "Turns out Wolfram and Hart do have a good reason to farm this out instead of do something about it themselves. Three weeks ago, Lily Pierce, Inc., retained the services of Khan and Associates."

Angel frowned. "And they are . . . ?"

"Hold on," Wesley said, "I've seen that name before." Cordelia waited while Wesley snapped his fingers in the air a few times. Finally he said, "Yes! In one of the texts on . . . on—"

"On what?" Gunn asked.

Wesley sat down in the closest chair, suddenly deflated. He said, "Revenge demons."

"Khan and Associates is another demonic law firm, which means this might even be funny, if it was all happening on, say, another *planet,*" Cordelia continued. "Khan and the boys aren't nearly as high-profile as Wolfram and Hart, but they seem to have the legal muscle where it counts, 'cause briefs have been flying back and forth between the two firms like . . . I don't know, one of those biblical locust-thingies."

"Briefs about what?" Angel asked.

"Lawsuits and counter lawsuits," Cordelia said casually. "Y'know, Wolfram and Hart representing people who claim Lily's program didn't deliver on its promises, or that it hurt them somehow, and Khan coming back saying Lily never had anything to do with these people, alleging false suits, fraud, defamation of character. All that kinda stuff."

"Just splendid," Wesley groaned from his chair, his face in his hands. "I checked the police records, and in the last three weeks there've been seventeen disturbances around Wolfram and Hart facilities that no one seems to be able to explain."

Gunn said, "Anybody hurt? Dead?"

Cordelia shrugged. "Well, it doesn't say, but Wolfram and Hart have their own mystical healers. None of their people would've gone to a hospital if they'd been hurt."

Angel turned to Wesley. "Anything specific about this Khan and Associates' supernatural connections?"

Wesley looked up. "Not as much as I'd like, I'm afraid. They're only mentioned in a cautionary tone— roughly the same as 'Do Not Enter Upon Pain of Death.'"

Cordelia folded her arms across her chest. "So Khan and Associates is bad enough news to tie up just about all of Wolfram and Hart's resources. And Khan's working for Lily Pierce, who already has this Serpent's Hand thing and is just waiting for the right time to use it." She shook her head. "Never thought I'd be rooting for Lilah's crew."

For a few moments no one spoke, each lost in his or her own thoughts.

Then Angel made a decisive gesture with one hand, scowling. "I won't do this. Not for them."

Gunn and Wesley simply watched Angel, unsure of what to say—but Cordelia immediately stood up and faced him. "What you need to do, mister, is to quit posing and acting all, all, all *tough*. Of course we're going to do this." Angel started to protest, but Cordelia cut him off. "The world's at stake, Angel. *Again*. Look, if we don't do anything, then either Wolfram and Hart get the Serpent's Hand and do horrible things with it, or Lily Pierce keeps it and does horrible things with it. And damned if I'll let either one of them use it."

What seemed like an incredibly long silence fell as Cordelia and Angel kept their eyes locked. Finally— and very slowly—Angel nodded. "All right." Cordelia grinned as Angel turned to Gunn and Wesley. "Let's get to it."

CHAPTER THREE

Angel cruised along in his GTX, following David's limousine as it wound along a narrow, ever climbing, tree-lined road in Beverly Hills. Gunn sat beside him; Wesley in the backseat. The clothes they wore were, well . . . interesting. Everyone was in character, and their lives—and so much more—depended upon each giving a flawless performance.

"My uniform's too small," Wesley said, pulling at the collar of his British military outfit. "And I'm having quite a hard time believing we're going to blend in, dressed this way. I feel ridiculous. Just look at these sashes!"

Gunn shook his head. "Get over it. At least you don't have to dress like hired muscle. *You* get to be royalty."

"Play nice," Angel said.

David had made it clear to Angel that the vast majority of the people who came out for these functions didn't dress tamely. Their objective was to be noticed by the paparazzi, to draw attention with unusual outfits and hairstyles. If Angel and his crew showed up dressed the way they normally did, they would stand out like sore thumbs, and Lily's people would target them as potential threats—instead of simply more oddly attired party goers.

The limo took a sharp curve, then turned down a small access road, where men with glowing green or red batons stopped cars, checked invitations, and directed them to parking spaces.

David's limo was waved ahead, and Angel could vaguely see the outlines of a great mansion on a hill bathed in twisting spotlights. The low branches of great trees and their dense coverings of leaves made it difficult to see details. But he could hear music, laughter . . . and he could smell both humans and demons.

Angel had heard David tell the attendant that the people in the car following him were his guests, so Angel didn't have to worry about not having his own invitation. However, Angel expected some remark from the attendant as his turn arrived, perhaps asking if he was in town for the rodeo, considering his clothing . . . but the man was stone-faced. He directed Angel to a space in a vast lot off to the left, while David's limo continued on to the right, where the guests would be dropped off in front of the mansion and the driver would take care of parking.

The three men walked to the mansion, nodding at couples and other small groups strolling along the narrow pathway up to Lily's mansion. Several were foreign dignitaries in outfits that were almost as over-the-top as theirs. The intelligence Lilah had provided was holding up, so far.

There hadn't been a lot of time to pull this operation together, and that worried Angel. Even worse, he'd had to coordinate with Lilah, and her tone during their brief phone call, though perfectly even, had still somehow contained a nasty ring of triumph.

"Now listen," Angel had said, "just because we're co-operating on this, and your guy's given us this information, doesn't—let me be clear on that—*does not* mean we're working for you. Got it? This is a temporary truce. We finish with this Lily Pierce business, everything goes back to the way it was before."

"Whatever you say, Angel," Lilah had answered, her voice filling with smugness, before Angel slammed the phone down in disgust.

Soon they were closing on Lilith's—no, Lily's mansion, Angel reminded himself, determined not to swallow *everything* Lilah fed them—and although he had studied the schematics that a lackey at Wolfram and Hart had e-mailed over, the appearance of the place was still striking, and a little surprising.

"Not exactly Wayne Manor," Gunn said.

Angel couldn't have agreed more. The mansion had been built closer in the style of a Renaissance-style Villa Rotunda, a large, imposing, perfectly symmetrical blend of circles and squares, a mix of the temporal and the spiritual domains. Classical porticoes were nestled above huge columns, a raised plinth, and wide, stony steps over the entrance facing the road, and a spattering of small statues representing the perfect grace of humankind stood here and there. The central rotunda had an ocular window that was right out of classical Roman architecture, and the entire place felt as if it had been lifted from another time, another place, designed solely to call attention to the grand nature of not only this mansion, but also its resident. . . .

Outside the villa lay a vast and splendid garden, with a single, high, overarching apple tree.

"Look out for snakes," Wes muttered.

There will be plenty inside, Angel wagered.

They met David and Cordelia outside the main entrance. David wore a well-tailored tuxedo. Cordelia was stunning, of course. Her dress had been chosen to draw the maximum amount of attention, and therefore had revealed the maximum amount of leg and cleavage possible. Only a few flesh-colored tie lines kept it from bursting open—and Cordelia from bursting out. Strategically placed patterns raced along the short, sheer number, creating the illusion that the viewer was seeing more than he or she thought, though not by much.

Cordelia smiled broadly, too broadly, and shot Angel a look that made it clear he would owe her for this . . . big-time. She was here at the party, yes, but now it was a job, not a career-booster. And even though she was the one who had insisted they take this case, she had still let Angel, Gunn, and Wesley know what she thought of having to pass up the chance to schmooze with so many Hollywood influentials in favor of keeping an eye out for trouble. "A demon-free night," she'd grumbled. "I guess I was dreaming."

"This is so cool," David pronounced, as soon as the men walked up. "I've wanted to do this, like, forever. I feel like Tom Cruise in *Mission: Impossible.*"

"Liked the series better, myself," Angel said.

"There was a series?" David asked.

Angel sighed and headed within. There they were greeted by flashing lights and probing TV cameras. The media frenzy Lily Pierce had inspired was in full swing, with hundreds of visitors here for the gala. Angel's gaze immediately went to "Lily's" executives and security staff, all of whom were almost certainly demons in disguise, or so their scent indicated.

The rest of the crowd—dressed very differently from Lily's conservatively attired staff—sprawled out across the floor in a brilliant dissonance of color; taking a moment to look at the party goers, Angel felt as if he'd stepped into a David Lynch film. Total weirdness. Within ten feet of him stood a man in a brilliant red-and-blue tiger-striped suit, the stripes continuing into his brilliant red-and-blue hair; another man dressed as a Saudi sheik, despite his pale skin and blue eyes; and a lushly curvy woman was done up in full-on jumpsuit Elvis drag.

The clothes seemed to get weirder the farther into the ballroom Angel looked. Yet this wasn't a masquerade: Some of the outfits were designed to shock, to grab attention, true, but many others were quite appropriate, like the traditional garb worn by two members of African royalty Angel recognized from recent CNN interviews.

Angel nodded as Wesley stepped up to his side, and both men stared out at the variegated throng. Angel murmured, "Still feel out of place?"

The Englishman answered, "Words fail me."

The main ballroom was a wide, circular affair crammed with ice sculptures, priceless paintings and statues, and tons and tons of perfect people. Everything in this place spoke of perfection. The lighting was perfect, the ambiance, the music . . . a string quartet played in one corner, their dulcet sounds perfectly countered by the steady sparkling stream from a delicate fountain exactly opposite them. The drinks were each a perfect blend, the conversation never lagged, and the press actually behaved.

"Do you know who some of these folks are?" David whispered. "I'm spotting at least three kings. I'm . . . even with my bank account, I'm feeling inadequate."

"You're with me," Cordelia said, simply slipping her arm through his. "They're not."

David smiled, his nervousness instantly fading.

They were just inside the door when Angel hauled the group to a small waiting area near the coatracks.

"Okay," Angel said, "let's review our objectives here—"

"No, let's not," Gunn said.

Angel was startled. "Huh?"

"You don't watch nearly enough movies," Gunn said. "Whenever the heroes go over the plan just before they're about to get started, that means for sure everything that can go wrong will go wrong."

"Uh-huh," Angel muttered.

"I'm telling you, that's how these things work," Gunn said. "Proceed at your own risk."

"Cheese Whiz, and I thought *he* didn't have a life," Cordelia said, nodding toward David.

"Oh, I don't," David said happily.

Angel cleared his throat. He knew his friends were just psyching themselves up, preparing to go into a situation in which one or more of them might not make it out alive. A little humor to help deal with the fear.

"Lilah's spy came up with complete schematics of this place, including where to find the Hand. He's also a telepath, so he's working double-time to make sure any other thought-spies Lily has working for her don't pick up our intentions, or—"

"Or read our lips while we're spelling the whole thing out right in the grand ballroom of the beast?" Cordelia asked.

"From where we're positioned, no hidden cameras can pick that up, either. So this is a simple snatch, grab, and replace."

"And you have instructions on how to reach the Hand without setting off any security measures, mystical or mechanical," Wes said. "And once you've exchanged it with a low-powered look-alike, we leave."

Angel nodded.

Gunn grinned. "Lilith won't even know the real Hand is gone until she tries to use the fake at the appointed time and nothing happens."

"And by then it'll be too late for her to mount a campaign to find the real one, and her moment will have passed," Wesley added.

Angel glanced around. "Stick to the plan and we'll make it out without a scratch."

"Ninja action all the way," Gunn said.

"Yeah, except for the dress-up part," Cordelia said with a snort.

"Here we go," Angel said, nodding to David, who took the lead.

Lily had yet to make her grand appearance, so Angel stood by as David was met by one of her Ambassadors of Perfection, a stunning frosty blonde who introduced herself as Elaine McCarthy. She had short-cropped hair and a winning smile, and wore a simple but elegant silver-and-black business suit.

David introduced himself and his date, then motioned toward Angel.

"This is Billy Bob Johnson, a friend of mine from the old neighborhood," David said, wincing at the sight of his date's obvious disapproval.

Angel smiled inwardly at Cordelia's perfect performance. She really came across like she thought he was a complete loser.

At least . . . he hoped it was acting.

"Howdy, howdy, nice to meetcha," Angel said, pressing flesh and laying it on thick as an eager little puppy dog. His outfit was a cross between something a country music star might wear and a costume from a Vegas lounge act. "David and me grew up together. We rolled our first dice together and everything. I'll tell you what—"

"Oh, please don't," Cordelia said.

"You're a gamer?" Elaine asked politely. "I wouldn't have thought, with the Western wear. Don't you fellows normally go in for the chain-mail, battle-ax look?"

"I'm dressed for my brand-new game!" Angel exclaimed proudly. "Invented it myself, and David's helpin' me finance it. It's called 'Six-Guns and Silver Stars'—gonna be the next big hit! Role-play in the Old West!"

Elaine seemed at a loss for words.

David grinned happily while Cordelia rolled her eyes. "We've already test-played it a bunch of times."

"David is, like, the best game master ever!" Angel cried, reaching into his deep pockets. "Hey, you wanna see my eight-sided dice?"

"Another time, I'm sure," Elaine said, turning back to David. "And who are your other friends?"

Wesley and Gunn stepped forward. Their costumes had raised the bar for tackiness. Wes wore a black British military uniform, with gold buttons down the front, a gold sash around his waist, and a blue taffeta sash sailing diagonally across his chest. The gold braid on the right shoulder drooped downward, then rose to hook onto the second central button of his jacket. Over the sash on the left side, numerous medals and medallions showed what orders Wesley was supposed to be a member of, including the Order of the Garter. He'd topped off the whole deal with spotless white gloves. Angel had been surprised to learn the outfit was completely authentic.

Gunn posed as Wesley's bodyguard, sporting a stylish Secret Service/*Men in Black* look, complete with Ray•Bans and a small earpiece.

Wesley cleared his throat.

"Yes," Gunn said, stepping forward, absolutely deadpan, "it's my pleasure to introduce his grace, the Lord High Duke of Omnium, Augustus Hesfestiphis Wimple."

Wes faltered for a moment. Before Angel could really worry that Wes's clear surprise at Gunn's creative little ad-lib would cause a problem for them, Wes regained his composure and forced a smile into place. "And this is my security specialist, Snidely."

"*Snidely?*" Elaine asked, blowing the word into the drink that had just been handed to her so hard, she nearly spilled it. "Like Snidely Whiplash, from Dudley Do-Right?"

Gunn nodded gravely.

"He gets that all the time," Wesley said.

"Well, mingle, enjoy yourselves," Elaine said as she excused herself. "Lily will be here soon. I've heard she has something special planned for her entrance."

Everyone was all nods and smiles—then they quickly broke up into groups, Wes and Gunn heading off to meet the party guests, Angel following David and Cordy around like a lost puppy dog until he was finally dismissed and allowed to take his position for the start of the night's true festivities.

Lily isn't even here? Angel thought. *This is going to be easier than I thought. . . .*

And suddenly, considering Gunn's warning earlier, he wished that thought had never come to him.

Cordelia and David mixed with the rich and powerful, the beautiful and, quite possibly, the damned, and made certain everyone believed they were having a just fantabulous time. People mulled about wearing badges that showed what they looked like before joining the Lily Pierce movement.

"This is sad and frightening," Cordelia said.

"I *know*," David answered. "They had those at my high school reunion. Hey, look, see what a geek I used to be?"

Cordelia barely heard him, she was so busy scanning the party for familiar faces.

David studied his shoes. "Probably both looked the same in my case."

That one registered, bringing Cordelia back to the ground after her moment of floating among the many stars in the room. She turned to David. "Now we talked about this. There's only room for one pathetic loser in my life at any given time. This is an unwritten rule of the universe. I'm still working for Tall, Dark, and Clueless over there. Yet I'm here with you. Ergo . . ."

"I'm not a total loser?" David asked timidly.

"Duh. So stop acting like a dumbass."

David looked as if it was the sweetest thing anyone had said to him in a long, long time. His whole face lit up. "Okay."

• • •

"Lord *Wimple?*" Wesley demanded once he had Gunn alone.

"I thought it sounded cool. And I got Omnium from the Pallisers." Gunn hesitated. "Watched a lot of British TV when I was a kid."

"Then you should know a duke is above a lord. There is no such thing as a lord high duke."

"Oh—right."

Wesley stared at him, gaze narrow, for several long moments. "You named me *Wimple.*"

Gunn frowned and looked away. "Okay, okay, next time we play Aliens versus Predator, you get to be the marine, deal?"

"Deal," Wesley said aristocratically. He looked over to Cordelia and David, then scanned the room until he spotted Angel. The vampire nodded and looked away.

"Time to get to work," Gunn said.

"Indeed it is," Wesley agreed. "Indeed it is. . . ."

Angel mixed with the party goers as well as he ever did in these situations, which is to say, not well at all. He kept to himself as much as possible, drifting to the periphery of one large group or another when he thought one of Lily's people was beginning to take too much of an interest in him. He'd learned from watching others that standing alone for too long was a surefire method of attracting a member of the Lily Pierce Movement, who would, of course, be hell-bent on creating another convert.

Shouldn't be long now, he thought, keeping an eye on his friends.

Then it happened, the whole thing coming together with clockwork efficiency. David went off to get Cordelia a drink at the same moment Gunn allowed himself to be distracted from his sworn duty to guard "the duke" by an attractive female member of Lily's flock.

Wesley strode up to Cordelia, his arrogant manner as he "came on to her" at once completely over-the-top yet somehow, sadly, all too believable.

Then Wesley's hands were on Cordelia, he was pressing himself against her rudely, suggestively. Just as a crowd of potential knights in shining armor were about to come to Cordy's rescue, David came back and hurled the drink he had gone off to fetch right in Wesley's face.

Wes sputtered indignantly, and Gunn hurried over, but the "bodyguard" couldn't possibly make it there in time. David's roundhouse punch connected with such a loud crack that Angel worried for a moment that Wesley had been laid out for real.

Then Gunn was in David's face, and Lily's security people were all over the situation . . . and not guarding the private staircase Angel had targeted. He slipped behind the distracted crowd, stealing silently upstairs.

At the top of the stairs he encountered a sealed metal door, with a keypad beside it. Typing in a security code that had been programmed just this morning, Angel opened the door and slipped inside Lily Pierce's private office.

Angel surveyed his surroundings. Lily's office had a marble floor, and all the furniture was handmade, carved from expensive cherry wood. An enormous desk with a large swivel leather chair for Lily and two smaller leather chairs for visitors faced the main door. Behind the desk was an enormous tapestry that portrayed Eve giving Adam the Apple of Knowledge in the Garden of Eden, the colors all slightly muted except for the apple, which stood out as a brilliant blood red.

"Give me a break," Angel muttered, remembering what Lilah had told them about Lilith perpetuating the Garden of Eden story every chance she got. *Hit me over the head with it, why don't you.*

Bookcases filled with ancient tomes lined one wall. Angel caught a few of the titles and realized they were secret histories written by scholars and seers throughout the ages. The Dead Sea Scrolls were a joke compared to the knowledge waiting in those tomes. Wes would have a field day.

One wall was mostly glass that looked out over the extensive gardens of the estate, a potentially convenient avenue for a quick exit, but it was unbreakable glass, fortified by a host of spells. There was also an enormous display case made of cherry wood and glass holding dozens of art treasures that all had common themes of serpents and demons.

More subtle decorating, Angel thought.

He knew exactly where the Hand was hidden, and went to work exposing its secret lair.

• • •

"No, no, it's perfectly all right," David Nabbit said to the hulking security guard. "Lord Wimple has made his apologies, and we're willing to let bygones be bygones."

David, Cordy, Wes, and Gunn stood at one side of the massive ballroom, facing three of Lily's rather frightening security personnel. While the tux-wearing guards were impeccably polite, David had no doubt that any of the three overmuscled men could throw him and his friends out the front door without unduly taxing himself.

The guard glanced skeptically from David to Wes, then back again. Wes did his best to look embarrassed, and carried it off pretty well; even more convincing was Cordelia, playing the offended girlfriend who would no doubt give her man a piece of her mind as soon as they were in private.

"You sure about this?" the guard asked David.

David had actually anticipated this reaction from security; enough important and/or staggeringly wealthy people were here that it was improbable they'd get the bum's rush like common barroom brawlers. *Not impossible,* he thought, noting how the guards' muscles strained at their suit jackets, *just unlikely.* Tossing them out would cause even more of a scene after everything had finally quieted down, and it might set a nasty precedent and make certain wealthy and powerful but unruly types avoid future Lily shindigs.

David stepped forward and inclined his head conspiratorially toward the security man. "Neither of us realized who the other was," he said in a half-whisper. "Turns out, we're supposed to meet tomorrow for a mutually beneficial business lunch, you see? No need to mar that tonight with any official complaints, is there? Make the shareholders unhappy?"

The guard's eyebrows drew together a fraction of an inch, then smoothed out again. David figured the man had seen this kind of thing before.

"All right," he said. "But behave yourselves the rest of the evening, got it?"

They got it, and told him so. David and the others watched with relief as the guards went back to their assigned posts.

David couldn't believe the evening he was having. Cordelia had related to him a pretty good chunk of what was going on, and—really, the only word for it was "wow!" He knew Angel and Cordy and the guys were into some big-league stuff, but some demoness passing herself off for Lilith? *The* Lilith? And whether she was or not, all this stuff with the end of the world, demons taking possession of Earth? His heart raced every time he thought about it, which had been more or less constantly since they'd arrived. As far as ways to get some excitement, this beat parasailing all to pieces.

"Man, that performance was sweet," Gunn said quietly as soon as they were out of security's earshot.

"You bet your butt it was," Cordelia said proudly, linking her arm in David's. "And what a right hook! You really landed one on Wesley, didn't you, David?"

"Yes, very impressive," Wesley said, utterly without enthusiasm. He rubbed tenderly at his jaw. "I found myself utterly convinced of your sincerity."

David thought his grin would split his head open, it was so wide. *What a night!* he said to himself. *On the arm of a gorgeous, wonderful woman, defending her honor in front of hundreds of people. What could be better than this?*

As if in answer, his cell phone rang. Cordy said, "Is that you?" as he took it out of his pocket.

"Yeah . . . sorry. Should've left it at home."

David turned partly away from the others and took the call. It was one of his plant managers, phoning to report a massive snafu at their Barstow location.

"Can't you take care of this yourself?" David whispered urgently. "I'm busy!" He turned back around to make apologetic hand gestures at Cordelia—and, to his horror, saw her talking to a tall, dashing older man in an emerald-green tuxedo. By her ravishing smile he could tell the man must have some connection to Hollywood.

"Sorry, big guy," the manager said on the other end of the phone. "This needs your special touch. You can get to the helicopter, right? Be here soon?"

"Yeah, yeah . . ." David hung up the phone and looked around. Gunn and Wes had drifted off again, so he approached Cordelia timidly. "Uh . . . excuse me? Cordy?"

Cordelia waited a full three seconds before she turned to him, obviously distracted. The older man looked David up and down, coldly evaluating him while he and Cordy spoke.

"Cordy, listen, I've got to take off." David hated the words as they came out of his mouth.

"Huh? You're leaving?"

"Well . . . yeah, yeah, I have to. There's a, uh, it's an emergency. Business stuff."

Cordelia frowned a moment. Then she said, "Huh. Okay, I'll get a ride with the guys, then."

David started to say, "Call you later," but hadn't even gotten the second word out before Cordy had turned back to Green Tuxedo Man. He bit off the rest of what he'd started to say and turned to make his way to the front door.

So much for excitement and heroics, he thought, completely dejected. *So much for helping to save the world. Now I just get a boring car ride and a boring flight in a helicopter to a boring plant. I'm the prince of boring.*

Just then, as he was midway to the door, a nasal female voice called out, "David? David Nabbit?"

David stiffened, then turned, hoping against hope that the voice did not belong to the person he was afraid it belonged to.

It did.

Lorraine Grotsch, who actually *was* an old gaming buddy of his, and was now a major shareholder in his company, waltzed up to him in a tremendously expensive dress a size too small for her fire hydrant–shaped body.

"David, it's just been *ages* since I've seen you, how are you, how did that Cthulhu campaign turn out, how's that latest little venture we've got going, y'know, you're really looking good, Lily's made such a difference in my life, I'm just like a totally different person now, you know what I mean?"

David sighed. *I have claimed the crown,* he thought, his dejection sinking to new lows. He knew from experience that there was no way he could escape Lorraine Grotsch; since she owned such a big chunk of his company he couldn't just blow her off. That meant he'd either have to stand there and talk to her, or take her with him to the plant. *I am now the king of boring, and I have found my queen.*

"Hey," Gunn said. "Check that out."

Wesley looked up and saw a small group of "perfect" people being led away from the party by some of the very large and imposing security personnel. Several of those being led away looked excited, others nervous; but none of them seemed to like the way the security guys gave them no apparent choice about coming with them.

"I wonder what's up with that?" Gunn said.

"Let's go see."

They followed the group and saw them led into a large chamber, then had to duck away before they were spotted by Lily's people.

"I remember this room from the schematics," Wesley said. "That's part of their training area. Everything that's done there is taped through two-way mirrors in small adjoining rooms."

"So let's get to one of those rooms."

It took several minutes before they could reach their

destination without being spotted, but soon they stood before a large window, looking into a darkened room where four people stood before the woman who called herself Lily Pierce.

Lily wore a black cloak that covered every part of her except her stunning, luminous face. Undisguised demonic minions held two weeping humans while others forced another pair onto their knees before the party's host.

"Not the same room," Gunn said.

"That must have been a waiting area," Wes added, breathless with fear and uncertainty.

What they saw next went beyond words, beyond reason. It was some kind of branding ceremony, with Lilith speaking of a Faustian deal she had worked with each person to make their dreams a reality.

"It's all free," Gunn said.

"Until you get the check."

There was nothing they could do—only watch in horror as Lilith burned her mark into the bare flesh of the first two people, taking their souls and cleansing them of all compassion. Or so they understood from the words passing between the predator and her prey.

Lilith eyed the terrified pair, who'd been forced to witness the transformation of the first two, being shoved down onto their knees by demons. "You're all that's left," she said. "Then the one thousand is complete."

The two who'd been branded were led away, their faces disturbingly blank, their eyes empty.

"She's drinking in their terror," Wesley said.

"That's why she wanted one pair to endure her treatment while another watched what was about to happen to them."

"Gotta stop this," Gunn said.

"But Angel—and the Hand . . ."

"You heard her. Lilith needs a thousand perfect souls. She gets these two, she's got it all."

Suddenly, Lilith grinned and called to her demonic assistants to wait, she wanted a chance to "freshen up"—and give her other two followers time to consider their fate.

Wes and Gunn weighed their options.

In the branding room, Elaine McCarthy knelt on the cold tile floor, a handsome man in his mid-forties beside her. He reminded Elaine a little of Dylan McDermott, from the TV show *The Practice*.

"I'm Victor," he said, his entire body shaking. "Victor Grimaldi."

"I'm . . ."

"Not talking to you," he said.

She started, and then understood what he was doing. He was attempting to appeal to their guards, trying to connect with them on some level, to make them see him as an individual, not some nameless, faceless creature lined up for the slaughter.

"I made a mistake," Victor said quickly. "I violated everything I believed in. Family, first and foremost. Is that how she got her hooks in you fellows? By making you betray what you believed in the most? Corrupting the most perfect souls she could find?"

"We were born to this life," the demon said. "You chose your path."

The other demon told the first one to be quiet.

"What?" the first demon asked. "Like it hurts to listen? Could be fun . . ."

"I thought I was being held back in this world from being my best because I wasn't from a wealthy family," Victor said.

"Ah," replied the first demon. "The old boys' network kept you down. We get that, too."

The other demon tittered—and Elaine felt a chill that had nothing to do with the cool temperature of the room.

Victor went on. "Lily used her connections to create a new family history of wealth and privilege, beauty and adoration for me, and that fiction became fact pretty much overnight. People believe what you tell them, so long as you sell it well enough. I had what I thought I wanted, access to a world I always felt should have been mine for the taking. But it wasn't worth the price. Nothing could be."

"I feel for you," the second demon said, getting into the spirit now. He kicked Elaine. "Come on . . . what's your tale of woe?"

At first, she didn't want to speak. She felt strongly that the demons were simply having some fun with them. Yet . . . if there was a way of getting through to them, if Victor's plan had even the smallest chance for success, she had to try.

"I wanted perfect love," she said. "The only way to get it was to ruin my best friend's life. I testified that she killed a man when I was with her the whole time. It was an act of perfect hatred, it violated every principle I believed in all my life. Friendship, loyalty, above all else. But it got me what I wanted: her lover. The perfect man. He lived only for me; he was everything I'd ever dreamed of. He just wasn't real. He was made from magic, made to love me."

"Is that it?" the first demon asked evenly.

Elaine had been a publicist for ten years. She made her pitch as elegantly as she could, under the circumstances: "I never really considered that love that is created, not given of free will, may be perfect in its simplicity, but lacking in so many other ways. I see that now. I just want another chance."

"That's a sad, sad song," the demon said, laughing openly now.

Elaine looked into the first demon's cold eyes and knew that Victor's plan had no chance of succeeding. Her fear had made her grasp at this desperate chance to avoid the fate she had seen Lily's last victims endure . . . but now, confessing her crimes, listening to herself babble, she felt only contempt for herself, a desire to receive the punishment she knew she deserved.

"You know what?" Elaine asked coolly. "I just changed my mind. I *want* Lily to do this to me. It's what I deserve . . . and once I'm transformed, I won't care about any of it, about what I've done, what I might do in the future, anything, ever again."

"Good attitude," the first demon said. "You're in hell now. Anything else would have to be a release."

"Wrong," his buddy added. "But entertaining to watch!"

"It's not fair," Victor said, trembling with fear and rage. "I couldn't care less that 'a pact, once made, may never be broken.' I want to live. I want to enjoy what I've worked so hard to get. I don't want to give up my soul!"

Victor broke down, whispering that he hadn't known, he hadn't understood what he was getting himself into.

Elaine's eyes held compassion for him. At least—they did for the moment.

Angel crouched over the safe bearing the Serpent's Hand. It lay in the floor, perfectly concealed by mystical means, but the right combination of invocations and quick, physical acts, such as touching the apple on the tapestry at just the right time or invoking a sacred flame over the twin candles gripped by steel gargoyles, could make it surrender its secret face.

A single spot on the marble floor became a shimmering vortex, and the floor safe revealed itself.

Crouching over it, Angel used the codes and incantations Lilah's guy had given him, and soon the safe was open. But inside, Angel found not one, but several dozen serpentine torques.

Great. I can't replace them all with fakes, he thought. *Which one is the right one?*

Footsteps rang out behind him. Angel turned and found himself looking up at Lily Pierce. Angel supplicated himself immediately, going into the routine he had planned just in case he was caught.

"Oh, great one," he said, fully aware that she would be able to sense the demon taint of his vampiric nature. He gestured over at the safe. "Do you see what I can do? I am skilled and strong. I've come to offer myself, and my services, to you. To grovel at your feet, to worship you, the first woman, the eternal one, mother of all our kind."

"Well, you're down on your knees," she said, amused. "That's an appropriate start, anyway. But, you know? Somehow, I'm just not feeling the love."

Angel did everything he could not to look up at her, but he couldn't help himself. Her ravishing beauty was a distraction, even for him. Her dress, ironically, was similar to Cordelia's, only with a slight crimson cast.

Waving a hand over the air, she dropped the spell she used to keep her true beauty and power from overwhelming mortals. Her skin practically glowed, and suddenly she stood naked before him, smiling and without a modicum of shame.

Just being in her presence was intoxicating, as if she gave off supernaturally enhanced pheromones. He saw her now as she truly was, Lilith, the first woman, created to satisfy man's desire, the ultimate temptress. *Or so she wants everyone to believe,* he reminded himself, trying to keep a level head. But she was perfect—or she appeared so.

"Mistress," Angel said, playacting the role of a would-be acolyte this time, "Queen of Night, I beg you—"

"Oh, stow it, Angel."

He started.

"Of course I was expecting you," Lilith said.

Angel's entire body stiffened. Wolfram & Hart had betrayed him, their inside man had given him up. That must have been it. . . .

"Ooh," Lilith said with a great shudder. "Raw betrayal, the elixir of life. I can *feel* it coming off you . . . very yummy. But I'm afraid it's wasted. Wolfram and Hart had nothing to do with this."

"Then how?" Angel asked, hoping he could keep her talking long enough to come up with a plan.

Lilith circled her desk. "I've been playing these games for a very long time, and before coming to Los Angeles, I had my followers find out who in this city was likely to oppose me. With all of Wolfram and Hart's usual suspects occupied, who else would the firm turn to *but* you?"

Lilith's hands rose, and fields of crackling mystical energy appeared before her.

Angel was running out of time—and options. "It doesn't have to be like this."

"This is exactly how it has to be and you know it," Lilith said, amused. "You're an intriguing specimen, a vampire with a soul. I imagine you'd have quite the imposing presence, too"—she looked him up and down—"with different wardrobe choices, perhaps. Honestly, you should've stuck with that long black coat I've heard about instead of this 'Cowboy Bob on acid' ensemble."

Angel eyed the door, trying to judge the distance between it and himself.

Lilith continued: "Under other circumstances, I'd take a very long time learning just how to bring you to the heights of pleasure and the depths of agony and despair. But I'm in the middle of something, I have some special guests to take care of, and frankly, there simply isn't the time."

"My loss," Angel said.

Her smile vanishing, Lilith cast her spells, and loosed Hell upon him.

CHAPTER FOUR

Angel lunged forward, trying to connect a punch that he hoped would end the fight before it truly got started—and was immediately blasted back, crashing hard into Lilith's opulent desk.

The mystical energy shield—which Lilith had erected in the instant before Angel's fist would have touched her—hung shimmering in the air, linked to her fingers by tiny electrical arcs. She let it fade, and Angel tensed to spring again, but then he saw her *move* . . . truly move, in a way no other human on the planet could.

Lilith had had thousands upon thousands of years to learn her own body, and now that she had let go of the glamour disguising her as a mortal woman, her true nature revealed not only beauty but also a grace, a fluidity, that made her seem to *glide* rather than turn, *fade* rather than step. It was dazzling . . . so much so that Angel barely got out of the way as a shimmering mystical dagger sprouted from Lilith's fingertips and stabbed into the desk where his head had been a heart-beat before.

Angel rolled, came up to a crouch, glancing from Lilith to the floor safe where the Serpent's Hand rested somewhere among the fakes.

"You handle yourself well," Lilith said, her voice caressing his ears like the sweetest violin music. "It's rather a shame I have to do this."

The shimmering dagger, still lodged in the desk, sank into the wood—and the desk exploded with a sound like multiple gunshots, the wood splintering into a thousand razor-sharp stakes. They hung in the air a moment, pivoting until every one of them targeted Angel's heart, then launched as if fired from a thousand crossbows.

Already coiled to spring, Angel leaped as far and high as he could, straight at Lilith. She dodged out of the way, as he expected her to, but he managed to interpose her body between himself and the stakes; most of them impacted and shattered on another of her shields, and the few that didn't he was able to knock out of the air.

Rising to stand, however, he was not fast enough to avoid a vicious kick that caught him in the throat and flipped him head-over-feet. He gagged, and barely rolled out of the way as Lilith brought down a barrage of blade-like shields, each one slicing deep into the floor. He aimed a kick at her ankle, and although it didn't connect—she saw it coming and avoided it gracefully—it did seem to distract her enough so that the descending blades dissipated.

The two combatants pulled back for a moment, sizing each other up. Lilith laughed, mystical shields dancing around her, even as Angel suddenly realized that he wasn't simply tiring; he could actually *feel* his strength draining away. With each second that passed he grew a tiny bit weaker, and the eldritch energy surrounding Lilith seemed to pulse just a little brighter.

Lilith read the knowledge in Angel's eyes and seemed to find it amusing. "Don't stop now, little creature," she said lightly. "It's been a long time since anyone has challenged me."

Angel rose, nearly staggering—and suddenly felt something like a pull, a *tug,* deep inside him. His eyes cut briefly toward the floor safe; the tug . . . was it coming from inside?

He had no time to think about it. As if sensing something had changed, Lilith launched herself at him, her amused grin transforming into a terrifying glare.

Angel fought back as best he could, but Lilith blocked every punch and kick he threw with a shimmering barrier, and her weaving, barely visible hands darted out like striking cobras, slamming into him in staccato bursts.

He stumbled backward, away from her, and there it was again: the tug, down near his still, silent heart. Pulling him. Guiding him.

Just as Lilith raised both hands, a horrific double-bladed construct forming above her in scintillating waves, Angel threw himself full-length on the floor over the hidden safe and thrust his arm down into the collection of torques.

One of them seemed to reach up to him, rising to his fingertips. He closed his hand around it, pulled it from the safe, rolled over—

—and Lilith halted the downward sweep of the mystical blades, her eyes widening, then narrowing in rage. "That does not belong to you," she hissed, her voice echoing up as if out of a cave filled with nightmares.

Angel got to his feet, clutching the Serpent's Hand close to his chest. "Does now." He edged toward the door.

Lilith hissed again, this time a pure animal sound bearing no trace of humanity at all. She gestured at the door, which locked by itself, then flicked her eyes back to Angel. Blade after gleaming blade materialized around her, as if grown out of the very fabric of her anger, every one of them poised to stab, slice, or shear. Still, she held them back.

Angel slowly neared the door, still focused on Lilith. Suddenly he spun, lashing out with a kick that smashed open the door, splintering its frame. In a flash he was through the doorway and down the hall, Lilith right behind him in screaming pursuit. Her sheer dress rematerialized on her body as she ran.

He reached a balcony overlooking the grand ballroom, the throng of attendees and vigilant news crews spread out below, when Lilith caught up with him: A shield, warped and curled in on itself to form a sphere, bashed into the side of his head. Angel reeled, almost dropping the Hand, and before he could regain his balance, another sphere rammed into his midsection, doubling him over. He clutched the balcony's rail for support.

"I will not damage the Hand," Lilith growled, approaching him, "but I have *no* qualms about damaging you."

On the dance floor, someone noticed the activity on the balcony and pointed up toward it. Lilith stopped about ten feet away from Angel, her unearthly beautiful eyes glinting. "Give me the torque," she said calmly. "Or it will get much worse."

Gritting his teeth, blood filling his mouth, Angel tipped over the rail, the Serpent's Hand still held tight to his breastbone.

Partygoers screamed and skittered out of the way as Angel dropped to the floor among them, landing on his feet, but the screams quickly took on a hysterical note when Lilith followed Angel down, descending slowly through the air, supported by flickering, twisting columns of mystical flame erupting from the palms of her hands. "I said give me the torque, Angel!" Her voice was hugely amplified, booming around the walls of the ballroom.

Angel scrambled to his feet and rushed into the crowd, slipping the torque into his coat pocket, instantly putting dozens of screaming men and women between him and his pursuer.

• • •

Lilith lost sight of him, but swiftly noticed the media crews, whose cameramen—every one of them focused on her—were keeping calm annoyingly well. Raising her arms, she whispered a word in a language that died before the pyramids were built.

Every light in the mansion went out. The cameras and microphones went dead, and the screaming grew louder as the crowd dove headlong into panic.

One of Lilith's lieutenants reached her side. "Want us to kill the news guys?"

She shook her head; she knew he could see her, even in the absence of light. "I've already wiped clean their equipment, and I'll haze their minds when I have a moment. For now, just don't let anyone leave the premises."

Lilith thought of the torments she would inflict upon the thief as her lieutenant scuttled away.

In the branding room, Wesley and Gunn remained perfectly still and quiet, hidden, as the fracas erupted outside. Immediately several of the demon guards ran out to see what was going on, leaving only Victor Grimaldi, Elaine McCarthy, and two guards. Wesley turned to Gunn; they used a few brief hand signals to agree on what they were about to do, then Wesley counted down from three on his fingers.

Swinging a couple of chairs as hard as they could, he and Gunn burst through the two-way glass and into the room, slamming straight into the guards. Victor and

Elaine jumped out of the way, badly startled; Elaine screamed, but the scream was suddenly matched by other shrieks from the ballroom.

Through sheer momentum, Wesley overpowered the first of the guards, running him headfirst into a wall. Gunn snapped a low kick into the second guard's knee, breaking it, then slammed the heel of his hand into the demon's left temple. The creature crumpled to the floor.

"Come on!" Wesley said urgently to Victor and Elaine. "Come with us, we're getting you out of here!"

Elaine hadn't managed more than a "but" when the lights went out. Gunn and Wesley paused for a moment, but when nothing overtly apocalyptic happened in the wake of the blackout, they continued hustling Victor and Elaine toward the door.

"Who are you?" Victor demanded, though he had enough sense to demand it quietly. "Where are you trying to take us?"

"Out of here," Gunn said with finality. It seemed to be enough for them, so he and Wesley led the pair out into the panicked, shrieking throng in the darkened ballroom.

Wesley had to put his mouth right next to Gunn's ear just to be heard. "Do you remember where the door is? I've gotten completely turned around."

Gunn took the lead. "Yeah, come on, this way." They made their way through the chaotic tumult for a few dozen paces, then a hand grabbed Gunn's arm.

He almost swung an elbow into where the connected face should be, but then recognized the hand's owner: Cordelia.

"What happened to David?" Gunn asked, pulling Cordelia along with him.

"He had to leave," she shouted over the din. "He got a call about some business thingie."

"Oh, yeah? He split? Well, at least he's safe, so we won't have to go lookin' for him."

"Yeah," Cordy answered. "Speaking of which, we're getting out of here *now*, right?"

Angel suddenly materialized out of the crowd, said, "Right," and hauled the group straight toward the front doors.

"Angel!" Cordelia said, excited. "Did you get the thing?"

Angel kept glancing back over his shoulder, into the frantic crowd. Distractedly he patted his coat pocket and answered, "Yeah." He nodded to Wesley and Gunn—and the "couple" accompanying them. "New friends?"

From behind them, Lilith's voice suddenly boomed over the crowd, even louder now than before. "Angel! Give back what you've stolen!"

The mansion's main entrance was there, not twenty paces in front of them, and beyond it the street and freedom . . . but stationed right in front of the entrance, blocking the way shoulder to shoulder, stood five enormous demon guards. They still wore their tuxedos, but Angel thought he saw at least two of them beginning to slip into their natural demonic faces.

Then he noticed something else: Framing the five bruisers were two tall, decorative Corinthian columns, each with an enormous planter nestled in its top. Angel took about a tenth of a second to eyeball them, his mental wheels turning faster.

By this point Victor Grimaldi's right eye had begun to twitch. "What the hell is she talking about?" he wailed, grasping at Angel's sleeve. "What's happening? *What did you take?*"

Angel shrugged off Victor's hand easily and turned to the group. "Fade back," he said, his words fast and clipped amid the surrounding chaos. "Be ready."

He made sure Wesley, Gunn, and Cordelia understood, then ducked away into the panicked crowd.

Elaine McCarthy, just as agitated as Victor but handling it slightly better, whispered to Cordelia, "Who is that guy? What's he going to do?"

Cordelia just shook her head and led Elaine away.

The terror she'd begun worked against Lilith as screaming party goers scrambled this way and that in front of her. Gritting her teeth, she lifted her hands, incandescent arcs of power crackling between them, as if about to unleash the fires of Hell itself on the hysterical mob.

But she didn't. With an expression of mingled frustration and rage, Lilith settled for shoving people out of her path, moving them but leaving them physically unharmed.

Lilith caught sight of Angel at the exact moment the biggest of the door guards did. The vampire was simply standing there, waiting, the torque held casually in one hand. Lilith scowled and headed straight for him. She reached out with her power and influenced the behavior of the crowd.

Focusing on Angel, the mob suddenly developed that indefinable sense that large groups of people so unerringly develop: *Fight. There's going to be a fight!* It spread through them as though by telepathy, when, in truth, it was Lilith's magic guiding them; they slowed, parted, and backed away, leaving Angel alone in a ragged circle composed of Lilith on one side and the advancing demons on the other.

For perhaps three seconds no one moved.

"Now, you die," Lilith hissed.

Then the circle closed on Angel with a snarling rush.

Angel knew there was little chance of overcoming the group of demons under the circumstances, and virtually no chance of outfighting Lilith. But if what he had in mind was going to work, he wouldn't need to.

As the closest of the guards reached for him, Angel twisted out of the way, trying to envision his bones turning to rubber. The demon's hands closed on air.

It was an aikido technique that Angel was trying to use, one in which a single fighter could slip and slither through a large, hostile crowd without running or even striking anyone. He'd seen it done before . . . and since the one idea stuck in his mind that might get him and his friends out of this hinged on his taking Lilith and the demons where he wanted them to go, he prayed silently that he could do it now.

He saw Lilith step back from the edge of the fray, eyes flashing, and unleash another cannonball–like energy projectile. It was aimed at Angel's head, but he twisted, pivoted—and spun behind one of the demons, so that the spherical charge slammed straight into the creature's midsection.

Angel took much less than the beat of a heart to re-orient himself. Only a few feet to go, and he hoped no one had noticed.

Another of the guards produced two long, thin knives, one in each hand, and barreled in, determined to bury them both in Angel's chest. Instead, it only managed to slice a bloody path along one of its cohorts' arms as Angel danced his elusive dervish's dance.

Lilith shrieked, enraged at the delay in what seemed so simple a thing. "Just grab him, damn it! Hold him down!"

But they couldn't, not for five or six more seconds—until suddenly there he was, practically gift wrapped: caught right out in the open, flat-footed, with nowhere to go and no place to hide.

Lilith wasted no time. With a laugh like high, crackling thunder, she let the full force of her fury stream out of her hands, directly at Angel's chest.

For just a moment Lilith and the demons all paused, frowning, since Angel seemed to have suddenly vanished.

Then three things became obvious simultaneously: First, Angel had been standing at the base of one of the huge decorative columns when Lilith unleashed her blast. Second, before any of the sizzling fire even touched him, Angel had leaped straight up and grabbed hold of the column's top. Third, the base of the column was now all but destroyed—and Angel was about to ride the whole thing down as it fell.

Angel looked to his companions and shouted, "Run!" as he dug his fingers into the wall, trying his best to guide the column's descent as it slowly leaned and began to topple.

Wesley and the others acted perfectly on cue, dashing for the door. One of the demons was still close enough to try to stop them—Angel saw it reach out and sweep one arm in a long arc that brushed past Cordelia's face—but it missed, not even slowing her down. And just as Gunn and Elaine, the last two members of his group, made it out the doors, Angel catapulted himself off the top of the falling column.

He smashed through the doors and rolled outside the mansion, even as the column itself collapsed into the door frame and lodged there, wedged tight. Hollow booms immediately sounded out from the mansion as Lilith and her warriors tried to break through the blocked door. It wouldn't take them long, but then Angel's group didn't need much time to get to the car.

On his feet and running, Angel had almost caught up

with the group and was on the verge of cracking a smile of triumph when he noticed Cordelia begin to stumble.

Elaine let out a piercing scream and pointed. "Her face! Look at her face!"

Spinning Cordelia toward him, Angel was instantly assaulted by the sight, smell, and sheer *amount* of Cordelia's blood. In a flash he realized that what he thought he'd seen, back there in the ballroom, was far from the truth.

That demon hadn't missed Cordelia when it stretched out for her. And its reach hadn't ended with its fingers.

The blade's tip had touched Cordelia's right cheek just beside her mouth, sliced up through skin and muscle, skidded up along bone past her eye into her hair, and opened her scalp. Blood gushed from the wound, all over Angel's hands and clothing. He grabbed her, kept her suddenly nerveless body from pitching forward onto the pavement. "Take her!" he bellowed as everyone else piled into the Plymouth.

Wesley and Gunn held Cordelia across their laps in the backseat as Angel practically dove behind the wheel. He cranked the engine, at the same time shouting, "Compress the wound! *Hold it shut!*"

As the car's tires squealed, Lilith and her demons blasted the wrecked column out of their way and poured from the mansion's entrance into the street. Angel barely noticed.

His only thoughts were for Cordelia, who quietly passed out from the blood loss.

Back in the mansion, where the lights had slowly started to come back on, David Nabbit crouched in a corner next to Lorraine Grotsch, who hadn't stopped talking since she first saw him. He'd seen Cordelia and the others leaving, and tried to reach them, tried to help, though he had no idea what, if anything, he could have done. Lorraine had held his arm in a viselike grip and acted as an anchor. By the time he freed himself from her, Cordy and crew were long gone. Then Lorraine caught up and attached herself to him like a parasite all over again.

Security personnel did their best to restore order all around them, and seemed to be slowly succeeding.

"Oh good, the power's back up, I'm so glad we can see again, so what do you think that was, all that light show stuff, and the pillar falling over, huh, was that some kind of stunt show do you think, with that cowboy on top of it just like Slim Pickens, did you see *Dr. Strangelove*, like when he was riding that big missile down out of the airplane?"

She never takes a breath, David thought. *It's amazing. The woman hasn't inhaled in fifteen minutes.*

Just when Lorraine began talking about the last gaming convention she'd been to, David saw several of the burly security men herding guests away from the front door. Seconds later Lily Pierce walked in, fierce and regal and *wow* she was stunning, but kind of ticked-off looking, too. Lily moved to the middle of the ballroom floor, scanning the crowd—and David was fairly sure he saw her *sniff* once.

His stomach turned to ice as Lily Pierce pivoted in place and looked straight at him. In a sort of detached way he noticed that his arms and legs wouldn't work when he told them to.

This has got to be a mistake, he said to himself as Lily strode purposefully toward him. He would have looked behind him to see if she was heading toward someone else, but he was backed against a wall. *It's just got to be.*

Lily came to a halt right in front of David, and Lorraine Grotsch actually stopped talking when Lily transfixed her with an icy glare and said, "Excuse us a moment, would you." The words were polite, but the tone was unmistakably commanding, and Lorraine scurried away. Then to David she said, "Stand up."

David stood, a little shakily. *Guess my limbs work when she tells them to,* he thought, not quite in hysterics yet. Lily examined him for a few seconds, then said, "You'll do just fine for the second-to-last, won't you?"

Completely cowed, David said, "Whnuh?" and then Lily Pierce leaned forward and, yes, she *did* sniff. She sniffed *him.* David's knees almost buckled.

"I smell perfection in you," Lily said, winking as she turned away, casually grabbing one of David's lapels. "Come with me. We'll talk about the things you want most . . . and maybe you'll get them."

Lily led David into a small sunroom off the ballroom, a cozy but luxurious space with a door opening onto the garden outside the mansion. David had recovered use of his brain enough to say, "Um, I'm sorry, I uh, the, uh, the second-to-last what, exactly?"

She pressed him against a wall, moved in very close to him, but David became suddenly and acutely aware that her action was anything but sexual. Lily Pierce had gone from the most desirable woman he'd ever seen to the most blood-chillingly terrifying instantly; as she touched him, ran her hands over him, he understood clearly that she was sizing him up like a morsel of food.

"The second-to-last of my thousand, you silly man," Lily breathed, and where her breath touched him, painful goose bumps rose on his skin. "Yes . . . there is perfection in you . . . and your want, a particular woman, how simple . . . look at me. Look into my eyes."

By now, David wasn't even sure whether he could retain control of his bladder, but he managed to do what Lily said, slowly raising his head and meeting her stare. Her eyes flashed, literally *flashed*—

—and she pushed away from him in disgust, eyes narrowed, lips curled into a sneer.

"Perfect *trust*," Lily spat out. "Your whole heart is filled with it. You're useless to me."

David had no idea what to do, and was only able to make a few vague hand gestures by way of trying to say, "May I be excused?"

Lily either understood him perfectly, or was so utterly through with him that she didn't want to expend another thought on him. She waved dismissively at the garden door. "Go on. Go. Get out."

Needing no further prompting, David slipped out into the garden, then sprinted around the side of the house toward where the limousines were parked.

Minutes after letting the frightened little rabbit with the trusting soul run away, still recoiling with disgust from the font of compassion and other loving emotions radiating from him, Lilith sat in the sunroom, occasionally murmuring something aloud as she ran over the options available to her.

Victor Grimaldi and Elaine McCarthy would have been her last two. The 999th and the 1,000th. Now they were gone, who knew where, and even though she knew she could retrieve them, they'd already become vulnerable by now, open to other influences such as love and compassion, quite probably rendered useless to her, anyway. Useless to her plan . . . but still to be considered. After all, a pact, once made, could never be broken, and she had entered a pact with each of them. They were bound to her in a way . . . and that could make them dangerous.

All of the effort she'd put into those two, every bit of it wasted, and all because of that blasted vampire! Her plan had been rocketing along perfectly, and now Grimaldi and McCarthy represented potential threats rather than assets. No way around it: They'd have to be eliminated. Time to make use of the backups.

The carpet where Lilith had been staring for the last several minutes began to blacken and smolder . . . and might have caught fire, if one of her security guards hadn't knocked on the sunroom's door and then entered.

She looked up. "Yes? What?"

83

"We have reports of a fifth person in attendance tonight, associated with Angel."

Lilith stood. "Explain."

"Angel was seen fleeing with a dark-haired woman. That woman came here with a man—mid to late twenties, sandy hair. Soft, weak looking. We're still trying to find him."

The words took roughly half a second to sink in: mid to late twenties, *sandy hair, soft, weak looking* . . .

The trusting rabbit.

She'd had him. She'd had him *right here* and she'd let him go! Even worse, she'd been so sloppy about things that she hadn't even bothered to cloud his memories of their talk. He would go right to Angel and tell him everything, and that meant the vampire might be able to deduce her weakness . . . if he could put all the puzzle pieces together, that is.

Lilith wanted to give herself completely to the rage that boiled up inside her then; she wanted to smash through the walls of the house, bring it all down into an overpriced pile of rubble, set it on fire, and roast Angel over the flame on a spit.

But she needed to implement her contingency plan to complete her collection of a thousand perfect souls, and didn't have time for all that. If the trusting fool she had "interviewed" had possessed the qualities she needed, he would have saved her some time, but her cause was far from lost. She was confident she would get the Hand back soon, and thus, she had to be prepared to use it at the appointed time.

Still . . . letting that silly little man go like that . . . it was maddening.

So she satisfied her rage by snapping the security guard's neck, then ripping his body in half with her bare hands.

Then she ordered two other guards, who'd come running at the sound of rending flesh, to hunt the man she'd let go. Hunt him to the ground—and kill him.

CHAPTER FIVE

No matter how fast Angel drove, it couldn't have been fast enough. Because as he sailed through traffic, ran lights, ramped up over curbs, and drove over sidewalks and down back alleys to get Cordelia help, there was a strange and wholly unexpected horror happening within him that he could not outrun. The sight and *smell* of Cordelia's blood called to him, tempting him to pull over and satiate his hunger, to take release in her blood, her misery.

What the hell is wrong with me? he said furiously to himself. *I've had more control of myself than this for ages! Besides which, this is Cordelia! How am I even thinking these thoughts?*

Was Lilith responsible? Had she hit him with some kind of spell before they'd sped away? Was she somehow exerting her influence over him, channeling some outside force into his mind, creating temptation within him? *So she's trying to drive me over the edge. Make me do something horrible. Well, if there's one thing I know how to handle, it's temptation.* He clenched his jaw, determined to fight off whatever insidious magic Lilith had cast upon him.

But even as the thought crossed his mind, he rounded a corner, shifting the wind so that the cool night air blew directly across Cordelia's wounds and straight into Angel's face.

His hands clutched the wheel so tightly, it began to bend. . . .

"Angel, slow down!" Gunn hollered.

"You're gonna get us all killed!" the man they had saved from Lilith screamed.

Angel put them on a main drag that was thankfully empty, a welcome rarity. As the bloodlust moved through him, he floored the GTX. At that moment, despite every shred of self-discipline he could muster, Cordelia's blood smelled better, more delicious, more heady, than any other human's blood he'd ever encountered. Angel scowled, enraged that anything or anyone could make him entertain these thoughts, especially about one of those closest to him.

Whatever you're trying to do, Lilith, you can forget it, he thought tensely. *I'm not your puppet. I can resist this, damn you!*

As the speedometer continued to climb, though, he couldn't help but think, *Can't I?*

Wesley tried to reason with him. "Angel, if the police see us—"

"Then we'll have a police escort," Angel snapped. "I won't hurt her."

"Hurt her?" Wesley asked. "What are you talking about?"

"I won't let anything happen to her," Angel said, still fighting the sanguinary urges welling up inside him, struggling to keep his vampiric features from appearing. *You won't beat me. You won't!* There were other complaints from the passengers, but he tuned them out . . .

. . . because hammering at his mind, at his soul, was one thought, coming back again and again: He wanted to hurt Cordelia. He wanted the sweet nectar of her blood to slide down his throat and fill him completely, to allow him to surrender his fear and doubts once and for all. The hunger rose in him, stronger and stronger, and he had to fight to force back his inner demon, which was suddenly bold and empowered.

He was so distracted, he didn't even feel the snakelike torque, the Serpent's Hand, writhe in his coat. And as it writhed, visions of Cordelia's death, of her blood, became more real to him than the road ahead or the buildings whipping past in a blur.

No! he screamed in the confines of his thoughts. The thought of harming anyone like that again was repugnant to him, but to entertain visions of harming this woman whom he cared so deeply about made him want to let the others out and drive straight on until the dawn washed over him and ended his temptation forever.

But then, suddenly, the goading temptation began to pass, as if ghostly fingers that he hadn't noticed until now unexpectedly began sliding out and away from the grip they'd had around his soul. Angel's vision soon returned to normal, and he spotted a sign for a hospital.

"There," he said, nodding toward a tall building several blocks away, as inside his mind he shouted triumphantly, *Thought you could control me, did you? Make me hurt one of my friends? Not a chance!*

"Angel, listen to me," Wesley said urgently. "Lilith knows one of us was injured. This hospital may be the first place she thinks to look."

"Right," Gunn said. "Listen, I know this guy who knows a guy who can hook us up with a magical healer. Quality work, good rep, no questions asked."

"And if she dies first?" Angel asked. So soon after overcoming whatever sorceress temptation he'd been bombarded with, Angel wasn't about to gamble when mere seconds could make all the difference.

"We have options," Wesley said.

"No, we don't," Angel snarled. He couldn't explain—didn't know *how* to explain—the urgency behind his harsh rebuke. "Cordy's *life* is at *risk*."

The look in his eyes was apparently chilling enough to silence every other objection.

At the hospital, Angel screeched to a stop at the emergency room's unloading dock, where ambulances were lined up and one went off fast, its crimson lights reflecting off the ER's glass double doors. Small groups of people huddled outside, looking with concern toward the ER, several copping smokes.

Vaulting from the convertible, Angel took Cordelia into his arms—some small part of his mind exulting as he felt none of the bloodlust from minutes earlier—and

89

moved fast, Gunn following along and matching his brisk pace to keep pressure on her wound. The doors hissed open, and Angel hurried inside.

This time the urge came over him so powerfully, he nearly lost control of his own limbs. He was immediately assaulted by a plethora of smells that nearly kicked his vampiric nature into high gear from a mixture of desire and disgust: warm, rich blood, the stink of homeless people, the meat locker smell of feces mixed with blood from gastrointestinal bleeders, vomit, alcohol, perfume, cigarette smoke clinging to clothing, *more blood, everywhere, blood . . .*

Cordelia slipped a fraction of an inch in Angel's arms, and Gunn looked at him sharply, but didn't say anything.

"Set her down!" a man was yelling in Angel's face. He came back to himself, struggling to concentrate now on the sights and smells that had nothing to do with the living or the dead . . . the doctor trying to get a look at Cordelia's wound, the gurney right before him, the rows of computers and desks, the "cubicles" formed by curtains hiding the beds of the wounded or ill from sight, the clicks and beeps of electronic equipment, the glare of the overhead lights.

Shuddering, Angel set Cordelia down, and allowed Wesley to haul him away, toward doors leading to a waiting area and the reception desk encased by bulletproof glass.

"Get him out of here," Gunn was saying. "Wes, go, I'll handle things here."

Angel stumbled back, only dimly hearing a nurse

hovering over Cordy as she said, " . . . starting evaluation of airway, checking breathing and circulation . . ."

Someone else was grilling Gunn, asking if there were other victims, what exactly had happened to the woman, her blood type and allergies . . .

"She'll be okay," Angel said, more to himself than to anyone else.

Wes motioned for Elaine and Victor to follow them into the waiting room while Gunn stayed behind. Angel shuddered again, looking around the crowded waiting room, finally noticing all the people and their worried expressions, parents, friends, family members who had brought their loved ones here. Police were everywhere, taking statements, and youths in gang colors hovered in two separate packs at either side of the wide room. Several eyed the oddly dressed group more than once.

Angel closed his eyes, tried his best to center himself. He was still horribly ashamed of what he'd been tempted to do, and furious with Lilith for putting him through it, but he felt a tiny bit calmer now.

They took turns going out to the car, which Angel had to move so that it wasn't towed away, getting the street clothes they had packed in the trunk, then cleaning up and changing out of their odd costumes in the bathroom. Then they were back in the waiting room, the minutes crawling by.

He noticed Victor fidgeting and glancing toward the exit, so he approached the man, who stood next to Elaine. Both of them were pale, Elaine trembling slightly.

"How're you two doing?" Angel asked in a relatively

stable voice, his hand grazing the pocket of his long black coat where the Hand now resided—

—and suddenly Angel felt the bloodlust again, his vision arrested by the long, delicate curve of Elaine's exposed neck. . . .

He fought the urge down quickly, and turned away before Elaine or Victor could reply to his question. The realization hit him, slamming into his mind as if he'd just been struck between the eyes with a baseball bat. The bloodlust, the near-panic, the disorientation that had kept him from thinking clearly . . .

It's the Hand, he thought. *Has to be.* The object was rumored to be one of the most corrupting things that had ever come into existence, wasn't it? Its power was undeniable, and suddenly Angel wanted more than anything to chuck the wretched thing away. But he couldn't just do that. The Hand was too dangerous.

He simply had to control it, and control himself. He could do this, he was no stranger to temptation. Struggling for so many years with the dark call of his vampiric nature, even after his soul had been restored, he had fought more battles on that front than he could count. Still, this felt like something new.

All the more reason to make sure the Hand doesn't end up with someone like Lilith, he thought, *or anyone from Wolfram and Hart, for that matter.*

Composed once more, Angel regarded the newcomers.

Victor stared away, his eyes cold and hard. "How are we doing? You've got to be kidding, asking a question like that." Finally, the man made eye contact, and his gaze was withering. Staring into the man's eyes, Angel was suddenly struck with the notion that Victor was the kind of guy who didn't care about anyone or anything except himself. Angel had known plenty like him in the course of his very long life. He didn't like them much, either, but he wasn't about to start making judgment calls regarding whom he would protect and whom he wouldn't. Victor needed his help—and so did Elaine. Lilith would be after both of them.

"We can go now, right?" Victor asked, his words tinged with anger and fear. "There's no reason for us to stay here."

Angel paused for a moment, trying to collect his thoughts amid all his worrying over Cordelia's condition—and, for that reason, again didn't notice the Serpent's Hand quiver and writhe in his pocket for a few seconds. Abruptly a thought came to him as if from out of nowhere, a sudden cold calculation. *I need information about Lilith, and these two are a valuable resource. From what Wes and Gunn tell me, they were slated to join Lilith's thousand "perfect souls." I can't let them go.*

Angel shook his head, disturbed by that cold, calculating thought, as well as by his rapid suspicion that it had not, indeed, originated with him. He moved his hand over the pocket where the Hand lay, but didn't touch it.

If the Hand was really as powerful as Angel suspected, he would have to find a way to contain its power, to protect himself from its influence. Of course, it might be a little hard to find time to do all that with Lilith's demon army tracking him.

Instead of commenting on how useful Victor and Elaine could be to their endeavors, he said, "Lily's people will be looking for you. You've got a better chance of staying safe if we're around to protect you." *That's true enough,* he thought. Angel wasn't about to use these people, to put anyone at all at risk just to make his life easier. But they really didn't have much chance out there on their own.

Victor looked unconvinced, but Elaine spent a few moments considering Angel's words. She turned to Victor. "He's right. I could run, but, y'know, to where?"

Victor shook his head and seemed about to list his own options, but then visibly began checking them off his mental tally. It didn't take long for him to agree with Elaine. His shoulders slumped. "Yeah, okay. I'll hang around."

Angel nodded, then rejoined Wes for the truly difficult part—the waiting.

Angel went over and over in his head the events, beginning with his first sight of Cordelia's blood. It made sense, he quickly concluded, that it was the Serpent's Hand that had influenced him, rather than a spell of Lilith's; increased temptation certainly fit what little they knew about the Hand and its power.

"Little" is right, Angel thought glumly. Lilah Morgan had only said the Hand was what Lilith needed to

reshape the world as she saw fit, and not much beyond that as far as its specific capabilities.

Disasters had been caused by ignorance of magical artifacts plenty of times in the past, Angel knew. He remembered vividly an acquaintance of his in France, in the summer of 1912, who'd gotten hold of something called a "demon fighter ring." Too late the man had realized the ring was called that, because as soon as he put it on, it summoned several dozen fighter demons, who immediately killed him.

First chance I get, I'll have to try to find out more about this thing, Angel thought, staring at his feet, *before having only a little knowledge ends up getting me or someone else killed.*

After what seemed like an eternity, Gunn emerged. "Okay, she's gonna be all right," he said. "Blood loss was the biggest problem. The cuts on her face and scalp looked worse than they really were. They've got her stable, and they'll be moving her to a room in a little bit."

Angel nearly buckled with relief.

When his cell phone rang, he almost didn't answer it; he wanted to focus on Cordelia and nothing else right now.

"Angel? Is that you?"

David Nabbit. His voice came in with better reception than most land lines; he could afford the best in mobile phones. "What's up, David?"

"Well, um, I'm in the limo, and I'm good, a chat with Lily notwithstanding. How're you guys? Did you get away okay?"

Angel wasn't sure he'd heard correctly. "With Lilith?"

"Lilith, Lily, uh—well, yeah. But I guess I wasn't her type or something, 'cause she let me go."

"What did she say?"

"I, just, I don't know, it didn't make sense. She said I didn't measure up or something. Pretty much the story of my life having beautiful women telling me that."

"That was it?"

"It was plenty, believe me."

Angel took a deep breath. It didn't sound like David had been questioned about them. Lilith was probably searching for replacements for Victor and Elaine. Fortunately for David, he wasn't perfect enough for her.

"So is everybody okay?" David asked. "How's Cordelia?"

"Cordy was hurt. We're at the hospital now."

David's voice cracked. "Hurt? Is it bad? What happened? Which hospital? I'll be right there!"

"No. Don't come here."

"But if Cordelia—"

"David. Listen to me. You're in danger. Lilith is going to figure out that you were with us, sooner than later if she talked to you directly. Do not come here. Keep moving, change vehicles often, I know you can do that. Understand?"

"But—"

"Cordelia's going to be fine. Listen, what I'm telling you to do is for your good as well as hers. Will you do it?"

"I guess so."

"I'll be in touch." Angel broke the connection.

Wesley had been listening in. "David's all right?"

Angel nodded. "He got grabbed by Lilith, but she wasn't what he was looking for."

"She must not have realized he was with us."

"Not then."

Both men fell silent, the implication of the danger David faced clear.

Within an hour, Cordelia was in a room, and a doctor came to address the group.

"Head wounds are often bleeders, and pretty severe ones at that, but there appears to be no neurological damage, no major risk of her slipping into a coma. The right side of her face is lacerated badly, though, and will ultimately require plastic surgery to fix—and I can't guarantee that she'll ever look quite the same."

"What about moving her?" Angel asked.

"We've got her medicated to help with the pain, and we'd like to keep her here for twenty-four hours for observation."

"I'm sorry, but no," Angel said. He hadn't risked delaying her medical attention, but by the same token he wasn't about to let her remain in one place long enough to become a sitting duck. "If she's okay, then we've got to get moving."

"Also, the police want to talk with you folks," the doctor said. "So I'd suggest you sit tight."

"We will," Wes said, getting between Angel and the doctor before the vampire could say another word.

With a quick, sympathetic nod, the doctor briskly strode off.

"Listen," Gunn said, glancing at Victor and Elaine. "I'll stay here with Cordy and these two."

"Right," Wesley said. "Angel, come with me. We need to look at our options. . . ."

Though he hated to leave Cordelia for even a moment, Angel followed Wes from the room.

As they wandered the corridors, Angel barely heard a word Wes was saying. His bloodlust was under control, but he was distracted by the suffering all around him as people were rushed from place to place. He saw young people with knife and gunshot wounds, a man with the side of his head caved in from an encounter with a drunk driver, women who'd been slashed, beaten, raped . . .

There was so much pain, all of it caused by "regular" people, everyday mortals who had no idea there was any supernatural darkness threatening their lives.

And just being around them, feeling their anger, their desperation and loss, nearly overcame him. Another thought surfaced unbidden, merely a flash, there and gone, but just as cold and calculating as his urge to make use of Victor and Elaine—and this time much more disturbing. *I could end all of their suffering, and they would thank me. . . .*

He shook his head again, hard enough to rattle his brain, and thumped the heel of his hand against one temple. Yet he knew the thought hadn't been about killing these people to put them out of their misery; it was about saving them in some other way he didn't quite yet understand. . . .

Wesley, walking a pace ahead of him, didn't notice.

Something was coming in at Angel from the outside, something was feeling around his inner defenses, trying to influence him by making him have these thoughts, these urges. . . .

The Hand. What did it want?

Angel forced himself to focus on Wes, on the here and now. It wasn't easy.

"Going back to the hotel is no longer a viable option," Wesley said. "Though I would like to have a few of my books, I can tell you that. . . ."

Then, within Angel—there was something else. A voice manifesting in his mind, delivering its words in a cool, breathless whisper: *I know what you really want.*

Suddenly, he felt the power of the stolen magical object flare near his flesh—and knew the Serpent's Hand was talking to him.

Your desire is for an end to the suffering humans endure; a world of peace and tranquillity; a paradise in which all the dark demons driving humankind are excised forever.

Clutching his forehead with one hand, Angel used the other to brace himself against the wall. He was imagining the voice; he had to be . . . yet his senses and his instincts, finely honed over the centuries, screamed to him that it was real—and that there was danger in listening to anything the Hand told him.

This is what was tempting me! he wanted to scream. *This is what tried to corrupt me!* But even as he steeled himself, determined not to listen to a word the Hand said, the quiet, sibilant voice echoed in his mind.

Think of it, the Hand hissed, its power moving through him now, filling him with the slightest taste of the incredible strength it could give him. *A perfect world, one in which you and your beloved Buffy could be together because you would be a mortal and there would be no need for a Slayer.*

Go to hell, Angel thought, avoiding the temptation to reach into his pocket, draw out the Hand, and toss it as far away from him as he could.

He had accepted the responsibility of keeping this thing out of Lilith's hands, and besides . . .

Maybe . . . maybe he didn't actually have to be on guard quite so much. . . .

Because, what if there was something to what it was saying? What if what it described could be made to happen?

You can picture it, can't you? the Hand asked. *I know you can. I can see what's in your head and your heart.*

What the Hand proposed was a daydream. A fantasy. Angel knew that.

Despite himself, he wanted to hear more.

Wes turned to look at him quizzically. "Angel? Are you all right?"

"Fine," he muttered, refusing even to look at Wesley. "Just . . . a lot going on."

"I quite understand," Wesley said, resuming his talk

as they rounded a corner and went down another long corridor toward a nurse's station.

The Hand was far from done with Angel. *You think the perfect world I'm describing is a fantasy? A vision? Perhaps. But I can help you make that vision a reality.*

Stop it, Angel thought, trying desperately to focus on what Wesley was saying. But he could no longer hear his friend's words over the roaring cacophony in his mind. With its words, the Serpent's Hand was clawing its way into his thoughts, tempting him with his deepest unrealized desires, and there seemed to be nothing he could do to stop it.

How? Angel thought, hating himself for even asking. *How could it become a reality?*

Just as Lilith wants to use me to remove the "taint" of humanity from this world, you could do just the opposite and remove all traces of demon-kind from Earth. You could fulfill the prophecy and walk in the light. It could all be yours . . . redemption at last for all the wrongs you have committed.

No, Angel thought. *This is wrong . . .*

I have waited an eternity for a champion like you. None before this time have possessed the strength, the clarity of vision, the sense of destiny and purpose that is yours. Just slip the torque that binds me around your throat, and our journey together will truly begin—

With a thundering cry, Angel smashed his hand into a wall, the sudden pain refocusing his attention—and allowing him to shake off the Hand's influence. He turned to Wesley, who was no longer talking about their options and had stopped dead in his tracks, ignoring Angel's sudden outburst.

At the end of the hall, a dozen of Lilith's demonic warriors had appeared. Unlike the demons Angel had battled at Lilith's mansion, this group made no effort to conceal their true nature. Their faces were pale and covered in oozing black scabs, empty sockets radiating crimson light were all they had for eyes, and their jaws were long and misshapen, practically crocodilian. They wore leather and steel mesh armor that seemed to have been woven into their flesh, and they carried blades of every description.

"You know what we want," the warrior in the lead said. "Give us the Serpent's Hand. If you don't, these corridors and every room in this place will be covered with the blood of the innocent . . . and yours, as well."

Angel stared at the demons, the words of the Serpent's Hand echoing faintly in his memory. A world without demons, no more creatures like this, not even the inner demons that drove ordinary men and women to such horrible things as he had witnessed recently. No more pain and suffering, no more battles, only bliss.

"You heard me," the warrior said, slowly advancing. "I demand your answer now!"

CHAPTER SIX

"No," Angel said flatly, emotionlessly.

The demon in the lead frowned.

"Angel," Wesley murmured, "given the circumstances, perhaps we could reason with these gentlemen . . . ?"

I've faced a lot worse than this crowd, Angel thought, confidence and pride in his own fighting ability swelling within him . . . or was it really from within him at all? *I can take them.*

With a tiny hiss, the voice of the Serpent's Hand breathed, *Yesss, my champion . . .*

Angel opened his mouth to tell Wesley what he thought about the Englishman's suggestion, but didn't get a chance to voice the words. One of the demons drew a throwing dagger from a thigh sheath and unceremoniously hurled it at Wesley's head.

Moving fast, Angel shoved Wesley out of the way and snatched the knife out of the air.

"We've got to get them away from all these people," Angel shouted as the first of the demon warriors rushed at him.

The Hand spoke again. *I could give you the power to rid the world of vermin like this with barely any effort at all.*

Angel resisted the temptation. He knew such power *always* came at a price.

Someone I once knew said the only way to rid yourself of a temptation is to yield to it. Why deny your true nature?

I'm not a killer, Angel thought. *Not by nature.*

Of course, the Hand hissed enigmatically. *You're a hero. A champion. But killing is an art you've learned very well, isn't it? One that could be put to many uses for the greater good, perhaps. . . .*

Angel shuddered even as he engaged the first of the demons and tried to channel all of his confusion and revulsion into the fight. Mercifully, the Hand fell silent, though Angel continued to feel its presence in his mind.

Nurses and patients alike screamed and ran from the fracas, and the hospital's relatively narrow corridors worked in Angel's favor for the moment; they were only wide enough to let four or five of the twelve demons attack him at one time. The first one slashed at him with a broad-bladed knife, so Angel trapped the demon's arm, broke it at the elbow, and took the knife out of the suddenly useless hand. He drove a knee into the second demon's solar plexus, sending the creature backward into a wall, then swung the knife in a vicious arc, bisecting a third demon's face across the nose and burying the blade in the first one's throat. The fourth one almost got a grip on him, but was driven back when a gurney suddenly slammed into him. Angel glanced over his shoulder and saw Wesley beckoning to him frantically.

"Come on, come on, we've got to get them to the basement!" Wesley hollered.

Angel broke free of the attacking mob and joined Wesley as they sprinted down the corridor, away from the demons, and toward the stairs. The chaos of the skirmish was spreading outward as patients, nurses, and doctors alike panicked and ran.

"What's in the basement?" Angel asked as they slammed open the stairwell door, the demons' footsteps closing in.

"Probably an exit," Wesley panted, "but definitely fewer people."

Angel nodded. Getting the demons away from all the innocents as far and as fast as possible sounded like an excellent plan. A demonic battle cry made Angel start and turn just as the demon in the lead threw himself headlong onto Angel's shoulders.

Angel moved with the demon's momentum, twisting his torso around, so that when they bashed into the wall at the next landing it was the demon whose ribs caved in, Angel's shoulder planted squarely in his sternum. Wrestling him around, Angel shoved the gasping, bleeding warrior back at the rest of the pack and tore down the stairs after Wesley. Several of the demons right behind the first tripped and stumbled over the body, but it only gained Angel and Wesley a few seconds.

They reached the hospital's lowest level and burst through into a hallway lit with harsh fluorescent lights. A door ahead read MORGUE. They couldn't see an EXIT sign anywhere.

In Cordelia's room, Gunn stayed near the door, periodically glancing out into the hallway. He'd heard the screams, and though he couldn't see the dying, throat-stabbed demon gathering a small, tentative crowd down near the nurse's station, he had no doubt about what had happened. Lilith's crew had found them.

He glanced back at Cordelia, still lying motionless in the bed.

Victor said, "What now? You going out to join your friends?" There was anger in the man's tone, accusation in his intense glare. He was covering up his terror.

Trying to, anyway. Gunn clenched his jaw for a few seconds before he answered. "No. I'm staying here." He moved to Cordelia's side. "Won't surprise me if she needs some protection before the night's over."

Victor snorted. "Right. Protect your own. We trusted you people. Do you have any idea what Lily might do to us now?"

"No. And neither do you. It doesn't matter worth a damn because she's not getting any of us. Got it?"

"Whatever," Victor said, turning away.

A frightened sob filled in the gaping silence.

Gunn looked up and saw Elaine shivering and hugging herself. "Hey, relax. I'll protect you."

Elaine nodded, visibly trying to calm down. Gunn wondered how obvious it was that he was fighting to do the same thing himself.

With the demons only seconds behind them, Angel and Wesley burst through the door labeled MORGUE, into a short hallway with a door to their left and one at the far end. Neither bore a sign—

—but at that moment the door at the far end opened and a young woman in scrubs stepped through.

She paused for an instant, frowning in puzzlement at the two men, then shrieked as the first of the pursuing demons crashed through into the hallway behind them, roaring growls echoing around them in the confined space.

Angel shouted, "Run!" at the young woman, then grabbed Wesley and pulled him through the door to their left, hoping to lead the warriors away from her.

They found themselves in a large, mostly stainless steel room, one wall lined with cadaver drawers. A tray on a nearby rolling table held a number of forensic science implements, including knives and saws of varying shapes and sizes. Angel grabbed a couple of them up, handing a knife to Wesley.

The demons followed them into the room, moving slowly now, knowing their prey was trapped. Angel made ready to attack, but then stopped seconds later when the last demon warrior dragged the young morgue attendant into the room by her throat.

"Let her go," Angel said, "or you won't get the Hand."

The demon holding the young woman grinned as well as he was able to, considering his demonic countenance. "Oh, we're getting the Hand," he said. "This little bit of fluff doesn't even enter into it. Except as amusement."

Angel knew instinctively what was about to happen and rushed forward, trying to reach the girl, but there was too much distance to cover and too many of the warriors in the way. The demon picked the woman up off the floor and slashed her throat with a sweep of his claws.

The wound was explosive, spraying bright red arterial blood. The young woman died without a sound, and most of the blood from her wound splattered onto Angel's face.

Wesley shuddered as a low growl issued from Angel's throat. He watched his friend's vampiric ridges appear, his sharp fangs extend. The transformation was something Wesley had seen many times before . . . but what he had *not* seen before, what turned his own blood cold in his veins and made his breath lodge in his chest, was the obvious pleasure Angel took as he ran his tongue out over his fangs and licked the woman's blood from his lips.

United, shoulder to shoulder, the demons' hands seemed to grow long and sharp as they produced multiple knives and axes from hidden places on their bodies. They advanced farther into the room, cutting off any hope of escape.

"Is she waking up?"

Gunn glanced at Elaine, then back to Cordelia's extensively bandaged face. After a moment he said, "Nah. Just mumbling something in her sleep. I'll keep watching the door. You guys—"

Gunn didn't finish his statement because, as he turned, he felt the point of a long, slender blade come to rest against his Adam's apple. He refrained from swallowing as Victor and Elaine gasped and moved away from the demon warrior who had just crept into the room without a sound.

Gunn and the demon stared at each other for a few seconds. "Didn't hear you come in," Gunn finally said.

"I can move silently," the demon said, a little smugly. "Trick my older brother taught me. Don't move."

Gunn didn't. "Thought you and your boys were all hunting Angel."

"Lilith sent twelve. Your vampire friend killed one of us, and I felt another one die a few seconds later. But wherever they are right now, if they bother to do a head count, they'll only come up with nine."

The demon took a small glowing crystal out of one pocket and held it up in the palm of his hand. It pulsed a few times, then pivoted until it pointed straight at Victor and Elaine. The demon said, "Tracking spell's working like a charm. You two shouldn't've run off like that."

Elaine started, "But they—"

The demon cut her off. "Save it."

Unexpectedly, the demon withdrew the blade from Gunn's throat and clubbed him from behind with a massive fist. Gunn stumbled forward and groaned as he heard another sharp *thwack* and felt an explosive pain in his skull. He dropped to the floor, struggling to stay conscious.

"He might be a good bargaining chip," the demon said. "But you, too, have outlived your usefulness."

Gunn's head cleared and his hands formed fists. He glared at the demon advancing menacingly at Victor and Elaine and struggled to his feet, noting exactly how close the demon was to the nearby window.

"Now you've made me feel all neglected and stuff," Gunn said, springing at the demon as it whirled on him in surprise.

Two figures collided and glass shattered as, on the bed, Cordelia made another soft, indistinct sound.

Angel took a step backward, still growling, Wesley a few paces behind him.

Suddenly, shockingly, the Hand's voice hissed inside Angel's head, cold and persistent. *You could have saved that girl. With my power, you could have taken the knife from the demon's hand and buried it in his chest before he even saw you move. You wouldn't have had to be so . . . slow. . . .*

Angel didn't respond; the human blood he'd consumed had fogged his brain and he couldn't formulate a retort. Still, the Hand's words sank in, bringing with them waves of guilt over the young woman's death.

Split seconds mattered, he knew, his thoughts becoming coherent again, though he didn't know for sure if his mind was beginning to clear on its own . . . or if the Hand was again guiding him to the conclusions it wanted him to reach. *Split seconds save lives. If only I had been faster. . . .*

The demon who'd killed the morgue attendant seemed to be the speaker for the group. "You may have noticed our fondness for blades," he began. "And make no mistake, we're going to cut you. Thoroughly. Into many pieces. But we know what hurts worst for a vampire." With one hand he held up a beautiful silver cigarette lighter. "Even worse than staking, yes? And just as final."

The demons advanced another step . . . and Angel heard the Serpent's Hand again, rustling in his mind. *I can help you now.*

No way, Angel thought, certain now that he had again shrugged off his influence—but for how long?

With my power, you can kill them all. And I mean all, Angel. Every demon who walks the earth.

I don't have the right to play God.

You believe that by allowing me to help you, you'll be playing God?

Shut up, Angel commanded inwardly.

The Hand continued, small and private in Angel's ear as the demons circled, stabbing and feinting, laughing with their silver blades. *Maybe you will be playing God,*

111

but is it any different from what you've been doing already? Your decisions put so many people at risk . . . and got that young woman killed, let us not forget. At least be honest about that much.

Angel shook his head as if to dislodge the voice. His bloodlust was rising again, making it hard to think straight, the call of battle exploding in his skull, fired by the blood he'd consumed.

Be pure in purpose and perfect in execution. You supply the first, I'll take care of the second. Now use me— put me on—or your friends and everyone else here will die!

Angel trembled, his hand hovering and twitching near the pocket where the Hand rested—

—and then the floor suddenly rose up and slammed into his feet as the entire room convulsed, an explosive blast of some kind sounding out as a harsh, blinding green light filled his field of vision. The concussion threw Angel and Wesley painfully into the back wall, but Angel kept his eyes open, and as his vision quickly cleared, he saw what happened to the demons.

The light seemed to *corrode* them. In less time than it took Angel's brain to process what it was seeing, the light ate into the demons' flesh, sizzled it off of their bones, burned it away into vapor. As the light faded, skeletal remains, an abundance of knives, and the silver cigarette lighter clattered to the floor.

Angel staggered to his feet—the Serpent's Hand had fallen silent again—and stumbled to a nearby sink, washing the blood away, forcing himself to ignore the thundering sound of two human heartbeats in the room. *Two* . . . he looked up, his face smoothing back to human, and saw an unfamiliar man watching them from the doorway.

The stranger was tall, easily taller than Angel himself, and wore a long, black, hooded robe—but then Angel blinked, and realized he'd been mistaken; it wasn't a hooded robe the man wore, it was a black hooded sweatshirt, over black jeans and motorcycle boots. A timeworn brown leather bag rested against the man's left hip, its strap slung across his chest. He pushed back the hood as he came into the room, revealing a deeply tanned head shaved clean and a face with thick, powerful features. His eyes seemed to glitter for a moment, then settle into an impenetrable dark brown.

Angel helped Wesley up as the man approached them.

"Who are you?" Angel asked.

The man cocked one eyebrow, vaguely amused. "You're welcome." His voice was thick, too, a rough, rich, low rumble, like molasses with gravel in it. He stuck out a hand, which Angel slowly reached out to shake. "Name's Coronach. I'm on your side."

Wesley gingerly rubbed the back of his head, which had cracked sharply against the wall. "What was that— what did you—what just happened?"

Coronach said, "That was a Malaysian item. The closest translation you can get to it in modern American is 'acid bomb,' which isn't really accurate, but you get the idea. Too bad I only had the one." He looked around at the array of fallen bones. "I count nine bodies here, then there were the two you killed. Didn't they send twelve after you?"

Angel and Wesley looked at each other in dawning horror.

They found Cordelia still unconscious, lying in her bed, with Victor and Elaine huddled together in a far corner.

The room's window had been shattered outward.

"There was a demon here," Victor explained, trying to preserve his dignity as he stood back up. "It was going to kill us. Gunn fought it."

Tears welled up in Elaine's eyes as Victor helped her to her feet. "They hit the window . . . ," Elaine whispered, "and went through it."

Angel and Coronach both went to the window and looked out. Cordelia's room was on the sixth floor, but trees grew right outside; it wasn't unreasonable to think someone could have survived such a fall.

"Your friend's alive," Coronach said with confidence. "Lilith will try to use him."

"Now wait a moment," Wesley said, coming forward. "It isn't that we're not grateful to you for what you did downstairs, but how did you come into this? What is your involvement here, and how do you know what Lilith will do?"

"My employers gave me a dossier," he said evenly. "Plus, I'd been aware of her for some time. I'm a contract mage; last year a father hired me to reclaim his daughter from Lilith's influence. Look, I don't mean to sound bossy, but we really ought to get out of here. I assume you have transportation?"

Angel regarded him closely. "Exactly who do you work for?"

"You know them," Coronach didn't blink as he spoke the name. "Wolfram and Hart."

CHAPTER SEVEN

Angel drove, uncertain of his destination, and this time he was careful to keep just under the speed limit. The streets were filling with cars now, the night coming alive. Dangerously alive. They had to get away from prying eyes and they had to do it soon.

The Serpent's Hand hadn't spoken to him since Coronach's arrival. Good. That probably meant he'd gotten the better of it, just as he knew he would, given time. And yet . . .

. . . more than once Angel had unexpectedly flashed back to the young woman's death in the morgue—the sight and touch and delicious *taste* of her blood, all over him, on his lips, on his tongue. And each time the memory filled him with the blackest self-loathing. Angel worried that having human blood in him was also affecting his thoughts and behavior, making him even more vulnerable to the Hand. Or was the Hand causing him to dwell on the memory of the woman's death, the taste of her blood and how it made him feel, in order to sway him?

He had no answers . . . only suspicions. Yet he could cope with whatever the Hand sent at him. He was sure of it.

In the car, where the group was pressed shoulder to shoulder in the front and back, Angel heard Coronach whisper a few arcane phrases and caught a flash of emerald light. Victor and Elaine, the refugees from Lilith's camp, both shouted in surprise as magical energies washed over them.

"They're clean," Coronach said. "Their locations can no longer be traced. I suggest we get some distance, then stop to catch our breath."

"He's right," Wesley said. "We need a plan."

Coronach nodded. "I know a place. A safe house."

Angel only grunted. *Wesley certainly seems willing to accept this guy at face value . . . even though he admitted to working for Lilah Morgan and company. I know he saved our lives, but still . . . how am I supposed to get past him working for them?* "So, Coronach . . . give me some reason why I should believe you're not just trying to lead us into a trap. Maybe this place is safe for you because you've got a couple dozen of your buddies from good old Wolfram and Hart waiting for us there."

"I agreed to perform a job for Wolfram and Hart," Coronach said flatly. "That doesn't make me friends with any of them."

"And what job is that, exactly?"

"Keeping you and your friends alive."

"So—you're not in the ancient artifact retrieval biz?"

"I know about the Hand, if that's what you're asking me. But I'm not here to take it from you." They came up to a light and Coronach pointed to the right. "The house is down that way, only a few blocks from here. The woman can rest. She looks like she needs it."

Snorting, Angel floored the GTX, running the light and playing havoc with his tires. Again. *This guy actually expects me to trust him,* Angel thought. It was all he could do to keep himself from laughing in the joker's face.

"Angel, please," Wesley said. "This man saved our lives. We should at least consider—"

"Anyplace owned by Wolfram and Hart could be compromised," Angel said.

"We can't go back to the hotel, either," Wesley said. "Lilith will have it crawling with her soldiers."

"So we'll see what's behind door number three," Angel said, gesturing ahead. "Out there."

Angel heard a murmuring and craned his neck to see Cordelia shifting against Wesley in the backseat. The drugs were wearing off, at least a little. She'd be waking soon.

He ended up picking a spot at random, pulling off the road, and taking shelter in an abandoned industrial park. Getting out of the car, an earlier thought returned to Angel, and he nodded to Victor and Elaine, smiling compassionately.

"You two. Victor and Elaine, right? You were part of all this—part of Lilith's plot, or plan, or whatever she's calling it. Is there anything you can tell us about her? Anything we can use to stop her?"

Elaine didn't answer immediately; she seemed confused, and at first only said, "Uh . . ." Then, when she could manage actual words, she murmured, "It was, that, that thing was going to kill us. I can't believe Lily wants to kill us!"

Victor's hackles had already raised. "Look, buddy," he started, "you people are the ones who grabbed us, all right? And, and—Lily must think we've been traitors all along, and we weren't! You've just about gotten us killed. Why should we tell you anything? What's in it for us?"

"She was going to harvest your *souls!*" Wesley sputtered, but Angel waved him quiet.

"You just want to get your friend back," Elaine said, a distinct coldness in her eyes.

"This isn't only about saving Gunn," Angel stated flatly, attempting not to lose his patience with these two . . . though they really weren't making it easy on him. "Your lives are at risk here, too, remember? Unless you *wanted* to become soulless slaves for Lilith. Is that it?"

Victor looked away, pretended to study one wall of the closest building, not answering Angel's question one way or another. But Elaine's face had clouded over, and it looked to Angel as if she at least wanted to help.

"I don't know much about her, really," Elaine began. "I mean, I never missed a meeting, but that was just at the place in Beverly Hills. I . . . the only . . ."

Angel stepped closer. "What?"

119

"I heard her say there was a place she liked to go pretty often, a theater. The LaRousse."

"Where is that?" Wesley asked.

Angel nodded and said, "I know the place. Victor? Anything?"

Victor swiveled his head back around and met Angel's eyes, but Angel immediately got the feeling the man wasn't about to offer up anything useful. Never had Angel seen the expression "on the fence" personified so perfectly. *Just like so much of humanity*, he thought wearily. Sure, there were the bright shining exceptions to the rule, the genuine unselfish souls like Gunn, Wesley, Cordelia, and even Lorne, the Host, but finding others like them was pretty tough much of the time.

Victor surprised him, though: As Angel stood there, the man let out a long, slow exhalation, and Angel could practically see the two sides at war in the man's face. Victor took a moment or two to look at each of the people around him, and his shoulders relaxed somewhat.

"All I know is, she's got some guy," he said hesitantly. "A fellow named Balthezar, who does all her dirtiest work. I've never seen him, though, just heard him talked about. If it were me, I'd work on taking him out of the picture. Help cripple the operation."

And then, bang, it was over: Victor frowned and crossed his arms, growing sullen again. "Look, why do you want to know all this stuff? Why are you even interested in helping us?"

Coronach had gotten out of the car shortly after Angel did, but until now had been simply standing, silent, listening. He cleared his throat. "The answer should be obvious. You two have a certain tactical significance to our mission."

"Waitaminute," Angel said quickly. "Yeah, in a way that's true, but that's not why—"

The mage cut him off: "Victor, Elaine, you were both part of Lilith's perfect one thousand souls, yes? You still share a kind of 'open circuit' with her, a connection that could be valuable."

Angel sighed and looked away. *Perfect*, he thought sarcastically. *This guy really knows how to deal with people who are already completely wigged.*

Then the response Angel anticipated thundered in.

"*Valuable?*" Victor shouted, scrambling out of the car. "What the hell are you talking about? All you want to do is use us the same way she was going to!"

"Oh, no," Elaine whispered, suddenly looking panicked and cornered.

"We can use that open circuit to send mystical energies at Lilith, spells that might confuse or even damage her," the mage said evenly. "Naturally, there might be a cost to whichever of you served as the vessel in such a plan. A good deal of pain, perhaps even lasting damage. However, I'm sure you'll agree it's worth any price to retain ownership of your immortal soul."

"Coronach, shut up," Angel said decisively, and the mage fell silent. "That's not what we're all about."

121

"Oh, right," Victor said with a sneer. "You just want us to help you to help us, right? You're like Jerry Maguire with fangs." He shook his head. "Demons, vampires, magic . . . I can't believe I'm buying into all this."

Oh, great, now he's heading into denial, Angel thought. *Coronach really messed this one up. The man's got no people skills at all.*

"Yes. We need your help so we can protect you better."

"What about this circuit thing?" Elaine asked. "She can still get to us. She wants to kill us both!"

"There should be a spell of some kind to prevent her from using that open connection," Wesley said. "If I could get to my books, I'm sure I could find one."

Coronach pulled something out of his leather pouch.

"Hold on," Angel said cautiously.

"Don't worry," the mage said soothingly. "I got rid of the tracking spell that let them find you at the hospital, didn't I? Here—"

Before Angel could stop him, Coronach flung a double pinch of dust toward Victor and Elaine. The dust separated, swirled through the air, and came to rest on Victor's and Elaine's foreheads, settling on their skin in intricate patterns that glimmered once, then faded to invisibility. *"Tana renai,"* Coronach intoned.

Angel watched with deep concern as Victor's and Elaine's heads both wobbled a little, but then they looked up, seeming no worse for wear.

"What was that?" Elaine demanded.

"My question exactly," Angel said, feeling his anger rise. "Wesley?"

"I've seen this magic," Wesley said, sounding genuinely impressed. "Coronach cast a ward of protection. Lilith won't be able to take Victor's or Elaine's souls now—"

"Unless either of them want her to," the mage added with a shrug. "Only they can reverse the spell. Free will and all that. It's how these things are done."

"Leave myself open to her again?" Elaine said quickly. "Not a chance."

Victor nodded, his hand rising quickly, but not quite quickly enough to disguise a thin smile. It looked like ideas about how to use this new development to his advantage were already forming in his mind.

Wesley continued: "She'll have to find replacements. And she won't know the ward is in place until—and if— she tries to take either of their souls. Ingenious."

Coronach nodded. "That's correct."

Angel hated the way Coronach was acting, just doing things without checking with him first. Still, what was done was done.

He looked to Victor and Elaine. "Feel better?" Angel asked. Neither of them answered.

I suppose I can't blame them, Angel thought. *I'd be pretty shook up, too, if I'd been through what they've suffered tonight.*

"Wes, stay here, take care of Cordelia, and keep an eye out for trouble," Angel said as he walked away, motioning to Coronach to follow him. "I need to have a chat with the great wizard here. . . ."

Cordelia woke up slowly, incredibly fatigued and a little nauseated. The whole side of her face burned and ached, and was covered in some kind of bandage.

Suddenly, it all came back to her. The blade, the blood, the terror . . .

Looking up, her first sight was of Elaine. Beautiful. Perfect, by practically any standard. Elaine's eyes were filled with pity—and, perhaps, just a touch of superiority and contempt.

You're not one of us, anymore, honey, Elaine seemed to be saying with her look. *Your days of hanging with the beautiful people are officially in the past. . . .*

"Are you all right?" Elaine asked.

"I think so," Cordelia said, her voice rough, gritty. Her hand went to her face, gingerly. "What's—I'm bandaged?" She looked around, confused. "What, uh . . . what'd I miss?"

Wesley succinctly filled her in on their trip to the hospital, her treatment, then the encounter with the demon pack, Coronach's arrival, and Gunn's abduction.

"So now we're here, while Angel and Coronach discuss exactly how we'll be proceeding," Wes said softly.

"'S what I get for taking a nap," Cordy murmured, her thoughts still not completely clear. "My head's killing me."

"Another vision?" Wesley asked.

She shook her head, regretting the motion instantly.

Then, in an instant, her imagination made those words into a lie. She did have a vision, only not one delivered by The Powers That Be. This was a vision of a woman who'd lost it all except her beauty, then lost even that. A woman who couldn't even go to the grocery store without being looked at like a freak.

Cordelia hadn't even seen her face without the bandages, yet . . . she didn't want to. She tried telling herself it probably felt worse than it really was, but she could see in the look of that guy, Victor, the other one they had rescued from Lilith's party, exactly how bad it was. He glanced at her quickly, with disgust, and looked away.

"I'm fine," she lied. "Where's Angel?"

Angel found a dark, narrow alley between a pair of warehouses and led Coronach into it. Clutching a nasty, serrated blade in his coat pocket, Angel turned his back on the sorcerer, giving him every chance to cast a spell or launch some kind of attack.

Nothing.

"You can put me through whatever tests you like," Coronach said. "All you'll manage to do is lose time, and that's precious right now."

Angel turned to face him, his body tight and still ready for a battle. He did not release his hold on the knife.

"Give me the Serpent's Hand," Coronach said.

Smiling, Angel produced the blade. "I knew it would come to this. Wolfram and Hart—"

"Are you always this stupid?" Coronach roared.

Angel's smile faded.

"Give it to me so I can protect you from its influence," Coronach said, "so I can get it away from you and those you love."

"And that'll make us safe from Lilith," Angel said.

"Yes, it will, but it will also keep *you* safe from *it*. The Hand is bad enough on its own, but it can . . . well, it can bond with a person. Become a part of him."

"And?"

"And it corrupts that person, somehow or another . . ."

Angel put the blade away. "A real font of knowledge, aren't you?"

Coronach crossed his thick arms over his thicker chest. "I can tell you facts. I can tell you about the last known owner of the Hand, a fisherman on your northeast coast, a man who obtained the Serpent's Hand and went from being a petty con man to the most successful gambler on the planet overnight."

"Uh-huh . . ."

"He'd achieved his dream, his potential, but at a cost. A sore loser eviscerated him and set him afire on his old fishing boat. And there were others before him. Many others. Like a struggling actress in France who went from being a chorus girl to the most successful actress in the country in less than a month."

"Let me guess how that turned out," Angel said, still not buying any of this. Coronach worked for Wolfram & Hart. He couldn't be trusted. Period.

"A deranged admirer loved her face so much, he sliced it off of her skull and nailed it to his wall."

Angel shook his head, clearly unconvinced. "Doesn't sound like corruption to me, just people who didn't know how to handle themselves."

"Oh, and you know how to handle yourself? You know how to resist the power of one of the most horrific, oldest evils that has ever existed?"

Angel's hand strayed over the pocket where the Hand lay. "Yeah, ultimate evil, blah, blah, blah, to quote a friend of mine. . . ." Something close to the words Buffy had used on the being that had sprung Angel loose from Hell to use him for its own purposes. "You bet I do."

But as Coronach paused, obviously irritated, Angel couldn't help thinking, *Wait a minute. Is this me? Am I really this cocky . . . this full of pride? I wouldn't ordinarily say things like this, would I?* But then thoughts came to him, memories of the things he'd accomplished in his past. *No,* he realized, *this is not me being cocky. This is just me being realistic. Doyle said it himself, just weeks before he died: I'm a hero, a true hero. I can do this.*

Out of nowhere, like a cool breath of air, the Serpent's Hand rustled in his ear: *You are correct, Angel. You are a hero. You are the one with whom I was meant to be. Do not listen to the mage's nonsense.*

Then the voice of the Hand fell silent again.

Tendons stood out on the mage's neck for a couple of seconds. "The Serpent's Hand gets its hooks into you, I know that much. And they stay there. I've had years of training in dealing with dangerous mystical artifacts, and I know I can take care of it. You haven't, and you can't. Look, Lilith doesn't care about you. Once she knows I have the object, she'll leave you and your people alone."

Angel narrowed his eyes at Coronach. "You know what I think is really going on? I think Wolfram and Hart had this all planned out ahead of time. They knew they couldn't get the Hand without my help, just like they knew I'd never give the Hand to them once I got it away from Lilith. So they had to have a backup plan."

"A backup plan for what?"

"For getting the Hand away from me," Angel said, his body coiled, ready for a fight. Spoiling for it, actually, he suddenly realized with alarm. But he didn't go looking for fights; he wasn't like that at all.

Was this the Hand's influence?

In the deep shadows of the alley, Coronach's body crackled with blue-white energy, and Angel could feel his anger and frustration.

"The plan, as I see it," Angel said coldly, "was for you to act like our friend, show up at just the right time and win us over, then valiantly offer to take the Hand away to someplace it would be 'safe.' Really, taking it right back to Wolfram and Hart."

"I explained my association with them," Coronach said, the light show intensifying. "Why would I tell you I had any connection with them at all if my only reason for being here was to steal something you find so precious as the Hand? I could have told you any of a number of stories regarding where I was from, but I didn't. I told you the truth."

"You know what they say," Angel hissed. "The most convincing lies have a little truth in them."

Coronach sighed. The light show ended abruptly. "You're half-right. Wolfram and Hart told me to get the Hand from you and bring it to them, and I told them I would. I have never broken my word to an employer, so I felt confident they would believe me, and not send any others to ensure that I did my job."

Angel almost drew the blade then and there. But there was something more Coronach had to say, Angel could sense it, so he waited.

"I lied to them," Coronach said. "To fulfill my function as a protector, I told them I would do a thing that I had no intention of doing. I'm here to protect you, to offer my magic—my life, if necessary—to do that very thing. And if you did give me the Hand, even after all I've told you, I would also pledge my life to making sure the world was safe from it. But I don't know how I can convince you of that, at this point. So I leave it up to you. Tell me to leave and I'll go. If, however, you think my talents can help you in your quest, and you're willing to take a chance and trust me, then I will do whatever you say from this moment on."

Angel felt the Hand call to him. *It's a trick!*

Maybe, Angel thought. *On the other hand, I couldn't have gotten out of that hospital without Coronach's help. I need this guy right now . . . that doesn't mean I'm not going to watch my back when he's around.*

"You've got a deal," Angel said. "For now. So let's talk about Gunn."

Coronach sighed heavily. "She'll keep him to make sure you don't get back in the game," he said. "But you have my word I'll do everything I can to save him."

Angel frowned. "Where would they take him?"

"I would imagine that place Elaine knows about," Coronach said. "Lilith would guess that you would get whatever information Victor and Elaine had from them, and she would act on that assumption."

"She wants me to try to get Gunn back?"

"Of course. A rescue attempt is exactly what Lilith would expect, exactly what she would want. That way you'll walk right into her trap with the Hand on your person and she can take it off you once she's defeated you. Doing this thing would be suicide, Angel. And it wouldn't just be you who would pay the price. She wants to reshape the world."

"I can handle her."

"There's another way," Coronach said beseechingly. "Take the Hand, if you're determined not to let me have it, take your people, and get out of town. I'll pretend I have what Lilith wants and draw her fire to get you the opportunity to escape."

Angel hesitated. Was that really what Coronach would do if Angel let him out of his sight? Or would he just go running back to Wolfram & Hart to get reinforcements? Angel had to treat the mage as if the man was capable of anything, any act of heroism—or betrayal. It was the only way he could cover all of his bases.

"You're serious?" Angel asked. "You'd act as a decoy for us? When Lilith caught up with you, she'd kill you."

"Yes. If that's the only way to keep you and the others safe."

Angel combed his memories and worked out another plan quickly. "It's not."

Moments later, Angel and Coronach returned to the car. He wasn't entirely surprised to see that Cordelia was awake; he'd sensed that she was coming around before he left with Coronach. She met his gaze and held it firmly.

"I'm going after Gunn," Angel announced. "Coronach's coming with me."

The mage shook his head. "You're a proud man, Angel. That pride will be your downfall."

"This is not open to discussion."

"It should be," Wesley said, clearly distressed. "Angel, you have a responsibility *not* to do this. Gunn would be the first one to agree, if he were here."

"But he's not," Angel said in a cold, dark voice. "So I'm going to get him. Just like I would for any of you."

Cordelia stared at Angel. "What about us?"

"I've figured out a place where you'll be safe," Angel said as he got in the car and cranked the ignition. "We're going to Lo-town."

Gunn opened his eyes and immediately realized he couldn't move. Well, that wasn't quite true; he could turn his head, even tilt it forward a bit. But the rest of his body was held immobile by loop after loop of biting steel chains. He looked around, taking in the environment.

Lilith's demon stooge had brought him to a theater—not a movie theater, a *real* theater, an old one he didn't recognize—and chained him into a seat on the front row. The place was empty, and he couldn't figure out exactly where the flickering, purple-white light was coming from. The light gave the place an eerie, other-worldly quality.

Movement came from in front of him: A massive demon in a tuxedo walked through one of the stage doors, closely followed by Lilith herself. They came and stood about a dozen feet in front of Gunn, Lilith eyeing him speculatively; the demon didn't look at him at all, but Gunn couldn't shake the impression that the creature was taking him in on some other, preternatural level, that it had intense, incredible power, and senses far beyond his own.

In other words, it was going to be a bitch to try to escape with that thing around.

Lilith settled directly before Gunn, leaning down and lifting her long, flowing raven's hair from the sensuous, practically luminous arch of her magnificent neck.

Damn.

"I've seen you on TV," Gunn said. "Liked you better there."

Lilith smiled. Gunn had lied; in person she was twice as beautiful as on television. Three times. He found that he didn't want to look anywhere else in the room but at her face, despite himself.

132

"They'll come for you," she said. "You know that."

He shook his head "no"—but his eyes never left hers. "Ain't gonna happen. They're too smart." He was satisfied with the words, though his tongue was beginning to feel a bit thick.

Lilith smiled. "They're going to come for you, you *know* that."

"Please," Gunn said, with liberal sarcasm. "You never watched Austin Powers? This is the part where, if you knew *anything* about runnin' this kind of show, you'd pop a cap in my—"

Lilith silenced him with a single touch of her fiery fingers to his trembling lips. "Now it's my turn to say please. There's no cause for vulgarity. Not yet, anyway, and certainly not unless it's when we're both truly in the *mood* for it. . . ."

Gunn shuddered, straining not to let her seduction— or whatever it was supposed to be—have any effect on him. Unfortunately, he was failing miserably.

"But no," he said, his heart racing, "you got to tell me everything about what you're doin', and then I get out of here, and me and the rest of us gonna come and shut you down *hard.*"

She smiled languidly and caressed one side of his face with a long, perfect finger. "Coming down *hard?* Promises, promises. In any case, you're partly right," she said. "I *am* going to tell you some things. But not what you anticipate, and not for the reasons you expect." She leaned over even more, flashing him a generous view of her knee-weakening cleavage, and whispered in his ear. "What I'm going to tell you will sink into you. Right down into your bones. Right into your *soul*."

The last few words Lilith breathed in a freezing whisper, and any thoughts of lust Gunn had were chased away by tingling fear. He shuddered, squirmed, tried to get away from her—and then it snapped into his head what she was doing.

Magic. Of course. She was casting some sort of hex on him, working some kind of charm that would make him afraid of her. Him—afraid of *her*. Not bloody likely, as Wesley would say. He only had to think for a few seconds before he realized what she really wanted.

"All right, okay . . . I get it now. You wanna know about Angel. You expect me to talk."

Lilith laughed, a sound like wind chimes. "No, Mr. Bond, I expect you to die! At least a little."

Then Lilith grabbed Gunn's face in her hands and tilted it back, using a strength *much* greater than he expected—and she kissed him.

Gunn's lips and mouth suddenly flared with an icy, needling pain, his whole head and the rest of his body instantly following. His wide, horrified eyes could only scream silently as Lilith's arcane energies poured into him.

CHAPTER EIGHT

The whole group stood on the platform for the L.A. subway. Angel glanced around again to make sure no one was looking, then hopped down onto the tracks. He quickly got the group down below and out of sight of the few stragglers waiting for the next train. They walked about a block along the ledge of the darkened tunnel, then came to a fork where the tracks had never been laid.

"This way," Angel said. Behind them, the lights of a subway car approached. Soon the behemoth was roaring furiously, the ground beneath the group thundering with its passing.

The doorway to Lo-town was little more than an alcove with a handful of gleaming little rocks set into its seemingly impassable back wall. Angel touched the rocks in a specific order, and the stone wall eased back with an unearthly silence. A dim yellow glow could be seen in the empty room beyond.

"Hello?" Angel called.

There was no answer. Strange, considering the seers who lived here. Someone should have been sent to meet them.

"Come on," Angel said. He led them into the room and saw that the glow was coming off the walls. The floor beneath them was a rich, dusty earth, and it tilted downward as they made their way to the opposite door.

Slam!

The door leading back to the subway tunnels shut itself, and a sudden breeze kicked up.

"Wait, is this—" Wesley began.

Angel cut him off. "No, it's not normal." He tried the opposite door, but it was locked from the other side. He pounded on it. "Peregrine! It's Angel. Open up!"

The wind became brutal in seconds, whipping about violently, nipping at their faces, caressing and shoving at them as it whirled in every direction. Then the earth was in motion, trembling beneath them, and heavy, muscular figures made of earth and stone clawed their way out.

Golems.

"Peregrine!" Angel hollered. "What are you doing?"

The creatures of the earth surged forward, lumbering and clumsy, but incredibly powerful. They punched at walls as potential victims narrowly evaded them, or stomped so heavily, they tossed people off their feet. Angel tried to think of a way to fight them, but, in this place, there was nothing that could be turned into effective weapons against the creatures.

Elaine screamed as a golem approached her, Victor off in a corner, contending with another of the creatures. Wes darted ahead to set himself between Cordelia and yet another golem.

Then Angel saw Coronach conjuring, and some deep instinct told him that a counterspell of any kind would only make the situation worse.

"Don't do it!" Angel hollered. "Everyone, stand perfectly still!"

Something about his tone got through to the others. They stopped moving, and the instant it became clear they posed no possible threat, the golems sank back into the earth and the door leading to the second chamber opened.

"How did you know that would work?" Coronach asked, near breathless.

"Peregrine and all the others in Lo-town are refugees," Angel said. "They built this place to keep themselves safe. I figured as long as we didn't seem dangerous . . ."

Coronach nodded.

Angel turned and entered the second chamber. This one was lit by a crimson light emanating from the rapidly descending floor in oddly spaced patches. Above, stony stalactites were poised like daggers waiting to fall.

The moment they were all inside, the door behind them closed, and the first of the stalactites fell.

"Oh, man," Cordelia said, leaping out of the way. "Now why do I get the feeling we're trapped in a Tom and Jerry cartoon?"

Huge stone stakes began raining from the ceiling. There seemed to be no pattern to the attacks, no guiding force behind them, and for every stone stake that fell, another pressed out from the ceiling to take its place.

It was Wes who figured it out. "The light patches on the ground! The stalactites don't fall on them."

The patches of illumination dimmed and changed places, but when, at last, every member of the group stood upon one of them at the same moment, the danger from above ceased and the rocky wall split to reveal a passage to a third chamber.

"This *better* be it!" Angel shouted.

It wasn't. They were quickly sealed in the third chamber, whose walls slowly groaned and slid forward to crush them. Victor saw the hard wood slats and segments of pole lining the floor.

"It's a ladder," he said.

They worked together, assembling the ladder and climbing up to the pitch-black of the ceiling—where hands grasped them and hauled them out, one by one, the last making it just as the walls boomed together.

Angel found himself staring into a face that might have seemed more comfortable on the rooftop of a university or old public library. Peregrine, a golden-skinned gargoyle, greeted his old friend with what, for him, passed as a grin.

"Oh my God," Cordy whispered, covering her nose and mouth with one hand. The rest of the group—except for Coronach, who seemed not the least bit bothered—coughed and blinked back tears at the smell that assailed them as soon as they emerged: ancient, moldy earth, punishing body odor, other musky scents that clearly did not come from anything human.

"Relax," Angel said over his shoulder as he shook Peregrine's hand. "You'll get used to the smell."

"If I don't pass out first," Wesley muttered.

They were surrounded by half a dozen creatures out of myth—slavering lycanthropes, needle-teethed cave-trolls, other creatures from the fringes of humanity's consciousness—some of whom stood upright, gazing at them frankly with suspicious, blazing eyes, while others crouched along heavy roots that dangled from the high ceiling of Lo-town.

The underground village might have stretched for miles in every direction, but they couldn't tell; the thick, mossy roots formed curtains that cut off their visibility at roughly a dozen yards. Only the sounds that reached their ears—a constant grumble of voices, scurrying feet, and unearthly chirps and grunts—let them know that a substantial population surrounded them. Faint, murky green light that seemed to emanate directly from the ubiquitous plant life lit their way as Peregrine turned and led them through an opening in the root curtains.

In moments they found themselves on a trail of sorts, moving past huts constructed of mud, sticks, and the detritus of society that had found its way down beneath the city. One hovel had been fitted with a cracked but still functional door from a Los Angeles city bus; another's walls were decorated with hundreds and hundreds of bottle caps, clearly placed with pride and an artful eye. Lo-town was obviously a ragtag, patchwork place created out of desperation . . . and yet Angel couldn't help but appreciate the care that had obviously gone into its construction. Eyes peered out at them as they walked, showing plenty of wonder and curiosity, but no fear. Angel was amazed, as always, that this place actually existed here on Earth, below the streets of L.A. It felt more like a different dimension completely.

"What's up with the security?" Angel asked after a few moments.

Peregrine laughed. "You admit the traps were difficult and dangerous?"

"*Yeah,*" he said. "So why couldn't someone have just answered the door?"

"Our seers sensed that you were coming," Peregrine said excitedly. "So many of us owe you our lives. We wanted to show you how safe we had made Lo-town."

They emerged into a large, circular clearing; Peregrine led them toward the clearing's center, where a few discarded park benches had been placed in a rough circle on the hard-packed earth.

"You expect me to believe we're going to be safe here?" Victor growled, surveying the strange creatures gathering at the clearing's edge; as he watched, more and more shabby, ragged denizens of Lo-town appeared, all of them eager to see the visitors. "With all these freaks?"

"It could be," Wes said evenly, "that to them, you're the freakish one."

Victor quieted down.

Peregrine invited them to sit, and Angel succinctly updated him on their situation. "I need to leave a few of my people here with you," he finished up, the gargoyle listening to him serenely. "I need you to make sure they're kept safe."

"It would be an honor," Peregrine immediately replied. "Each and every one of us here owes you our lives. This is the least we could do."

The gargoyle and Angel shook hands again, then Peregrine left to prepare one of the huts for Angel's companions. The group was given a few moments to themselves—though they weren't exactly private moments, since the crowd of onlookers hadn't dispersed at all.

Angel sat back on one of the benches and tried unsuccessfully to relax, now that he had a few nonfrenzied moments. And yet, from out of nowhere, the young morgue attendant's face floated up before his mind's eye again, the taste of her blood filling his mouth. He grimaced, and tried not to push the thoughts away. He had to stay focused on his mission. Yet . . . what was his mission? Not the singular quest he was on tonight, but the overall course of his existence?

To help the helpless, of course. To make up for the evil he had done as Angelus. To one day find redemption.

Could he truly do it alone?

Angel shivered, his fists clenched and his eyes squeezed shut. But then, just as unexpectedly as the unwelcome memories of moments before, he heard the voice of the Hand: *This is suicide. Working together, we could do anything. . . . Just put me on. . . .*

Coronach approached Angel warily. "Something I need to go over with you."

Angel nodded, and accompanied Coronach to a huge, twisted root that had burst through the chamber's ceiling and dug its way into the floor. The two men moved around it, putting it between them and the rest of the group.

"The Hand has been tempting you," Coronach said.

"You just cut right to it, don't you?"

Holding out his hand, Coronach said, "Give it to me. There's nothing it can offer that I could possibly want."

"I don't know what you're talking about," Angel said. "Even if I did, why should I trust you?"

"All you need to know is that I'm a protector," Coronach said solemnly. "And I'm a man of honor."

"Who works for Wolfram and Hart."

"I only do certain types of jobs, the kind that need doing to maintain the balance, no matter who's asking." Coronach sighed and looked away. "If you're determined to attempt a rescue, I'll stay and protect those you care about. I'll protect them with my life."

"Yeah, *right,*" Angel said. "Buddy, you're coming with me."

Wesley approached. "If you're planning on going after Gunn, then I'm coming with you."

Angel shook his head. "One of us has to stay with Cordy and the others. It can't be me . . . and I'm not about to trust this guy with them."

"I see your point," Wesley said quietly. "Well, one of the residents here just told me Peregrine has squirreled away an impressive library of ancient texts down here, some of which may contain a bit of information we can put to use, some new way to get to Lilith."

"Sounds like a plan," Angel said. "Back soon." Without a backward glance, Angel and the mage departed.

Victor wandered off and soon found a pair of dirt-covered, blue-and-purple-skinned children with flickering bug-like eyes playing with a strange nebulous object. It took him a moment to realize they were playing hide-and-seek with several groups of other bizarre children . . . and using the object as a kind of radio, or walkie-talkie, to confer with others playing the game.

He watched them for a time, and waited until they had won the game. Then he confronted them. "You weren't supposed to be using that, were you?" he asked.

The boy and girl looked down, ashamed. His suspicion had been correct; they had been cheating by using the object.

He knelt before them, smiling kindly. "It's all right. We can keep it our little secret. Can I see?"

They put the quivering, cool bit of stone into his hand. He watched as it changed form a dozen times in as many seconds.

"How does it work?" he asked.

"You just think of someone you want to talk to, think

of them really hard, and then they can hear what you're saying."

Victor nodded. "I think I should hold on to this for right now. I might be a grown-up, but I still like to play, too."

He traded them his watch and electronic pocket planner for the object, amused at what shrewd little businesspeople these outcasts turned out to be.

Not shrewd enough, though.

Victor had been frightened at the thought of bearing Lilith's brand, and rightly so—his soul would have been consumed to power the Hand. But now he saw an opportunity for advancement, and he planned on making the most of it.

A soft shuffling came to him like a whisper of danger, and he looked over his shoulder to see a man made entirely out of straw and mud approach.

"Did you find something interesting?" the Lo-town resident asked.

Victor quickly pocketed the object he had bartered for, then turned to face the weird creature.

"I'm just admiring the setup," Victor said brightly. "I was trained as an engineer. I like learning about how things work. Those defenses of yours run like clockwork. What sets them off?"

"Well," the straw-man said, "not that I mean to brag, but I was instrumental in their design. . . ."

"Really?" Victor asked, slipping his hand into his pocket and clutching the magical call beacon. "Tell me more. . . ."

• • •

144

Ordinarily David Nabbit sort of enjoyed watching the motorists around him when riding in his limousine; no one could see him through the reflective-coated windows, but he could see them just fine, and he liked observing people. He thought of it as a way he could fit in, even if it was in a skewed sort of way; he was a part of the traffic flow, just as they were, and nobody thought twice about his presence there.

Tonight, however, he'd spent most of his time with just enough of his head poked up above the car door to see out the window, constantly watchful for the demons that Angel had told him would surely come looking for him. After all, humans couldn't see through the reflective glass, but who knew about demons?

Well, he was watchful for the first hour, anyway.

You can only ride around stewing in your own paranoia for so long, he thought, *before you need a change of scenery.*

Hitting the button for the limo's intercom, David spoke to the driver, a man named Judd. "Hey—seen anybody following us? Or any suspicious cars around us anywhere?"

"Not since you asked me ten minutes ago, sir," Judd replied.

"Thanks." What David truly wanted to do was go to wherever Cordelia was and try to help her. Angel had been maddeningly nonspecific about what exactly had happened to her, and David's concern for her raced neck and neck with how spooked he'd been by Angel's predicted demon attacks. But he knew Cordy was with

Angel, or at least was being taken care of by Angel, and that he'd get an update soon.

Maybe if I get more mobile . . . that way I could get to her faster, whenever I find out where she is.

That thought sounded reasonable to him—plus he was getting antsy like he'd never gotten before. Hitting the intercom again, he said, "Hey, Judd, let's head to the helipad."

"You got it, boss," the driver replied, and the limousine took the next entrance ramp onto the freeway.

David felt pretty good about his decision, even more so after an uneventful half-hour ride to where his closest company helicopter sat, ready for him to use it. He'd made a call to one of his pilots and had the man standing by.

When the limousine arrived, David looked around very carefully, then opened the moonroof, popped his head up out of it, and looked around some more.

"Everything okay, Mr. Nabbit?" the chopper pilot asked, watching his boss's strange behavior.

"Uh . . . I guess so," David answered, then dropped back into the limo and opened the door.

He cautiously put one foot out onto the pavement.

Nothing happened.

He stepped out, slapped the roof of the long car, and said, "Thanks, Judd." The driver nodded to him and pulled away.

David looked around one more time; still, he saw nothing, and finally went on to the helicopter.

"Something got you spooked, sir?" asked Harris, the

pilot. "Anything I should be on the lookout for?"

"Well . . . nah, I don't guess so. Let's get airborne."

The Bell 212 helicopter David climbed into ordinarily seated thirteen passengers; David had had it modified so that now it seated five passengers, a PlayStation 2, a GameCube, an Xbox, and a fifty-two-inch television. He settled in and flipped on the TV, hoping a few rounds of Virtua Fighter 4 would take his mind off everything happening around him.

Harris powered up the twin engines and lifted off—

—but hadn't gotten more than five feet off the ground when two of Lilith's demon warriors melted up out of the concrete, roared, and charged the chopper.

"What the hell are they?" Harris screamed, trying to get some altitude. He succeeded in evading the first of the demons, but the second one was faster, and with a sprinting leap it grabbed hold of the chopper's runner.

The Bell wavered and wobbled dangerously as David watched Harris struggle to control both the helicopter and the pilot's own apparent panic. David didn't know what to do, and continued not knowing what to do when the demon on the runner levered itself up and jerked open the side door.

Looking around for something to whack the demon with, David grabbed up a beverage tray—then dropped it when a nasty-looking dagger whickered past his head and into the cockpit. He heard Harris yelp, and saw him slump forward in his seat. The Bell immediately started to go out of control and began plummeting toward a field far below.

"Throw me that ladder!" the demon screamed, at

David, pointing at a rope ladder folded up on the cabin's floor and jammed into a crevasse so it didn't slide like so many other things when the chopper dipped down at a steep angle. "I can fly this thing; it's your only chance!"

Already freaked out, and afraid that he might upgrade to terminally freaked out, David did what the demon said, and threw one end of the ladder out the door. Grinning, the demon let go of the door and the runner and started climbing the ladder—

—but lost his smile as the ladder, which was not actually anchored to anything, slid freely across the floor. David watched with dinner plate–sized eyes as both demon and ladder slid out the door and disappeared, leaving a trail of enthusiastic curses behind them.

Watching the plummeting warrior, David thought, *Wow, that's one angry demon.*

He then heard a groan from the cockpit, and for a moment was afraid the second demon had somehow made it into the chopper. He racked his brain for what to do . . . then gasped as the Bell leveled out of its free fall and steadily rose once more. He could barely believe it when Harris stuck his head out and looked around at him, a big lump forming on the side of his head.

"Harris? I thought you were dead!"

"I almost was! That crazy maniac threw this huge freakin' knife at me, knocked me right upside the melon with the handle! I must've blacked out for a second." He held up the demon's dagger, waggling it by the blade. "Who were those guys? What'd they want?"

David collapsed backward into his seat, surprised his heart was still beating. He waved a hand vaguely and said, "I'll tell you later, just . . . just get us up, up, and away, okay?"

"No problem, boss," the pilot replied, and got them out of there.

Okay, lesson learned, David thought dazedly. *From now on, if Angel says jump, I'll say how high. Whatever Angel wants, Angel gets!*

Trying not to forget to breathe, David burrowed deeper into his seat, deciding to do nothing else but wait for Angel to call.

CHAPTER NINE

Angel and Coronach crouched behind a row of garbage cans across the street from the LaRousse Theater, or what was left of it. At one time the place had played host to major productions—touring Broadway shows, A-list stage magicians, even ballets and operas. But for years now it had sported plywood in place of beveled glass, and the only thing filling the seats was dust.

"He's in there?"

Coronach grunted, a sound like the lowest note on an electric bass. "Yeah. Once we got close enough, I used a simple locator spell similar to the one the warriors must have used to find those refugees in your friend's hospital room." He turned to Angel, frowning. "You understand what's happening here, don't you? Lilith's association with this place was common knowledge, or that woman Elaine wouldn't have known about it. Lilith made it simple because she wants us to find him. She *wants* us to walk in there."

Before the mage had even finished the last word, Angel was out from behind the trash cans and moving rapidly across the street, the blade of his broadsword flashing in the sick yellow glare of the streetlights. Coronach grunted again and followed him, his frown deepening.

At the theater, Angel carefully, silently pulled loose one of the plywood sheets covering a window, letting his vampiric features manifest as he did it. He was about to say something to Coronach about providing illumination, but the mage's eyes glittered briefly, just as Angel had seen them do when Coronach first appeared and saved his and Wesley's lives. Coronach made a gesture with his head—*come on*—and moved into the darkness, obviously able to see with no problem. Angel joined him.

They made their way down a hallway past what used to be dressing rooms and approached a stairway at the end leading up and to their right. Angel went first, his boots making no sound on the steps, and a few seconds later emerged into the wings of the grand stage.

A familiar shimmering radiance lit the scene, emanating from a floating globe of light about twenty feet above the stage.

"She's here," Coronach whispered near Angel's ear. "She's here right now, waiting for us."

"Maybe so," Angel answered, "but *there's* Gunn." He pointed with his chin at a figure at the far end of the stage, bound to a chair with chains, his back to them. The glare of ball lightning flickered over Gunn's bowed head.

Concentrating, Angel reached out with his sense of

smell, taking in everything around him: Gunn from across the stage; Coronach, behind him, a medley of leather and exotic herbals; traces of old grease paint, dust, and mold from the theater itself; and the sharp ozone smell of the lightning ball, the smell of Lilith. Coronach was right, she was there, with them in the theater—but not in their immediate presence. She was somewhere else. Hiding. Watching.

Angel knew this was a trap, and he understood that his actions might have seemed foolish, even suicidal, but he couldn't see any other way to save his friend. And besides . . . he'd faced worse than this before. He knew what he could accomplish. Some could say he suffered from foolish pride, but he liked to think of it as confidence.

He crept across the stage toward Gunn. Coronach stayed behind, doing something, Angel didn't know what. At this point, he didn't much care.

Nothing moved. Angel continued.

Halfway across the stage, and still nothing. Nothing but the sound of Gunn's breathing.

The lightning ball flickered and quivered as he passed under it, but did nothing else.

Almost there. The theater was still as a tomb. Step after step . . .

Reaching his friend, Angel whispered, "Gunn—can you hear me?" The young man didn't answer, so Angel stepped closer, put his hand on Gunn's shoulder—

—and would have gotten it bitten off if his reflexes had been a hair slower.

The creature that had been Charles Gunn rose from its chair, letting the chains draped around it fall to the floor. It still resembled Gunn in most respects, but now that Angel could smell its breath he knew that little to no trace of his friend remained.

The Gunn creature's face was gone; in its place, taking up the front of its slightly elongated skull, were three mouths, set one above another, each of them lined with serrated, triangular teeth like a shark's. Each of the mouths grinned at Angel. Gunn had been transformed into a demon.

"She was right," the Gunn-demon said in a chilling three-part voice. "Drop a couple of bread crumbs and you come running."

It lifted its hands, which were no longer hands, either; each of the creature's wrists stretched and expanded into a mouth nearly identical to that of a moray eel, spotted reptilian skin surrounding teeth like razor blades.

Angel was speechless, horrified by the transformation. The Gunn-demon launched itself at him.

Suddenly, something small and dark whisked past Angel's cheek and *thunked* into the Gunn-demon's sternum. The impact hurled the creature violently backward, so that he tore through a mildewed curtain and slammed into a wall.

Angel turned and found Coronach there beside him. "What the hell was that?"

The mage answered him in a distracted tone. "Shuriken. The whole time you were creeping across the stage I was adding kinetic energy to it. Glad I did."

But then, as the Gunn-demon rose and shook itself off, the lightning ball above them flared and expanded, filling the theater with intense eldritch light. From behind them Angel and Coronach heard Lilith's voice; they turned to keep both Lilith and Gunn in sight.

"You know, it's convenient to face someone this predictable," Lilith said. "But you're not much of a challenge after all." Angel saw a hulking presence just behind her, squinted, and made out an oversized demon in a tuxedo. Lilith's bodyguard? As if she needed one.

Coronach and Angel exchanged glances, and it only took an instant for an unspoken understanding to pass between them: Coronach would handle Gunn. Lilith was Angel's.

Picking up on the nonverbal communication, Lilith stepped forward, the air shimmering around her as she moved. Her bodyguard remained six paces behind her, vigilant and watchful, but mindful to keep his place and stay out of the action unless he was called upon.

"It's not complicated," she said lightly, unconcerned. "I'm going to take the Serpent's Hand back and I'm going to crush you while I do it."

Angel circled her, the broadsword comfortable in his hands. "Maybe."

Lilith curled her lip in answer, rolled her eyes as she shot a glance at her bodyguard, and pushed a hand toward Angel. A column of air between Lilith's hand and the vampire's face came alive with crackling electricity, and a blow that would have taken a normal human's head off smashed into him. The arcane force drove him completely off the stage and cracked his jaw for good measure; he landed in the fourth row, on top of the broadsword, which pierced a rotting seat cushion and nailed itself into the wooden floor.

On the stage, the Gunn-demon and Coronach struggled ferociously. Again and again Gunn tried to clamp one of his horrible sets of teeth into the mage's flesh, but each time Coronach's right hand flashed, producing a burst of silver light and a thunderous crack.

As he tried to get to his feet, Angel thought he saw what looked like a set of brass knuckles on the mage's hand, but he wasn't sure, and he didn't have time to pay close attention. Lilith was coming down the side steps toward him, grinning a nasty, carnivorous grin. The bodyguard strode casually behind her.

With a bestial roar, Angel wrenched the broadsword out of the planking, shattering the theater seat it had impaled. He picked up a piece of the broken seat and heaved it straight at Lilith, but didn't wait to see what effect it had because as soon as it left his hand he followed it, hoping that the chunk of wood might distract her long enough for him to land a solid blow with the sword.

Instead, Lilith batted aside the seat fragment with one hand, then nailed Angel with a full-body energy ram with the other. The impact sent him sprawling again, the sword flying from his grasp. He rolled as he landed, still moving away from her, but that was the only thing that kept him from getting skewered by a shimmering mystical spike that slammed down and punched a hole in the floor right in front of him.

Angel caught a glimpse of Gunn and Coronach; neither seemed to have gained significant ground on the other, though the mage had switched weapons. He now held Gunn at bay with a bloodred nunchaku that left faint trails in the air as he swung it.

Angel tried to get to his feet, tried to figure out what to do, what possible tack to take—and then the voice hissed in his mind again.

The voice of the Serpent's Hand.

The demon, Angel! The demon with her, he's her firstborn! Use him! Use him, don't be afraid!

There was no time for hesitation; no time even for thought. Angel dove, grabbed the sword where it had fallen, and sprinted past Lilith, who turned and didn't have time to stop him as he barreled full tilt at the tuxedo-clad demon, raising his sword. To Angel, the demon itself seemed even more taken aback than its mother, and barely got one hand raised to protect itself before Angel lopped its head off with one sweeping blow.

"*No!*"

That single word, spawned in Lilith's inhuman throat and released like a bomb into the air, would have shattered every window in the building if any had remained. It distracted Gunn long enough for Coronach to land a decisive blow and knock him on his back; it almost lifted Angel off his feet; and it revealed a side of Lilith that she herself had almost forgotten about.

From the look on Lilith's face, Angel figured that it was as if he, Coronach, and Gunn had all disappeared, and the only other being in the world that mattered at all lay dead on the moldy floor of the theater. Lilith went to him, dropped to her knees beside him. She didn't lift him up, though, didn't cradle his lifeless body. She simply stared in what looked like pure, unblemished disbelief.

Beyond her, its movements twitchy and spider-like, the Gunn-demon got to its feet, bleeding badly from two of its mouths—then, before either Angel or Coronach could react, it scrambled incredibly swiftly straight up a wall and into the rafters and dematerialized in a burst of red light.

Angel cursed under his breath, the whole point of the expedition having just vanished to who knew where. But then, taking advantage of Lilith's grief, he ran to Coronach, grabbed his arm, and quietly but forcefully said, "Let's go."

As they sprinted out of the building, Coronach muttered, "Hey, I didn't want to be here in the first place."

They made it to the end of the street, where Angel had parked the GTX, when an entire wall of the theater exploded outward in a cataclysmic burst of lightning and fire.

Lilith emerged from the wreckage and flames, levitating about two feet off the ground, and spotted them immediately. She let out a shriek of rage and fury, then began sliding toward them at incredible speed.

Digging in his pouch, Coronach said, "Get the car

started. I'll try to slow her down a bit." He pulled out what at first looked like a bundle of sticks—but as his hands moved over them they twitched, re-formed, and reshaped themselves until he held a lean, stripped-down crossbow and a handful of bolts.

Angel said, "No argument here," and pulled out his keys—just as the first of Lilith's demon warriors leaped from a nearby rooftop and crashed into him. Angel thought he counted six of them, maybe seven. In any case there were more than enough to eat up the few seconds it took Lilith to reach them.

Slashing and stabbing with the broadsword, Angel caught a glimpse of Lilith floating five or six feet off the pavement, her arms stretched out above her head, a blinding patch of electric brilliance growing between her hands. And he would have tried to do something about it if he hadn't been so busy keeping the pack of muscle-bound demons from hacking his head off with battle-axes.

"Look out," he shouted at Coronach, who now held two pairs of bloodred nunchaku, fending off three of the ax-wielding warriors. "She's about to try something—"

Angel didn't get to finish his sentence because, the same instant that Lilith fired an immense beam of mystic flame directly at him, Coronach slammed into him, knocking him out of the way.

The column of fire enveloped the mage, engulfing him. When he fell seconds later the fire was gone, but his body was ruined, charred and smoking. He hit the ground and didn't move.

"Hold the vampire," Lilith commanded, and the remaining demon warriors advanced on Angel.

Snarling, his face vamped and fanged, Angel slashed one demon's throat and severed another's arm at the elbow before they swarmed over him, took his sword, and pinned his arms and legs.

Lilith looked furious, close to losing control. Her eyes, still so ravishing, so unearthly beautiful, flared with blue-white sparks as her lips peeled back from her teeth in a savage snarl.

"You killed my child," she gritted out. "Back there in the theater, my firstborn. You made me . . . *feel*. Made my heart twist in pain." She drew closer, until her face was only inches from his. He could feel heat radiating from her. "I'm going to take back what's mine now, Angel. And then I'm going to kill you." Her snarl changed to a smile, though one no less nasty. "Appropriate, though, I think, that you would know precisely how I feel . . . were I to let you live."

She lifted a hand toward him, white flames crackling around it—but then snapped her head toward an unexpected sound: Coronach's voice. Angel couldn't believe it; the mage had lifted himself up onto one blackened elbow, and though smoke still wafted off parts of his body, he forced his blasted, damaged throat to work.

"Teru foram. Teru keiza."

Angel didn't recognize the words, but Lilith clearly did. Whirling toward him, away from Angel, she screamed, "Shut him up! Shut him *up!*"

Three of the demons sprang toward him, but not quite fast enough.

Coronach pronounced two more words: *"Teru baralis."*

Angel blinked, felt a chill snake through him as the world surrounding him abruptly changed. Lilith and the warriors were gone—and he found himself standing in a small, shabby studio apartment. Coronach lay on the floor nearby. Fighting off a strong sense of disorientation, Angel went to him immediately.

The mage was conscious, but just barely. His face was horrendously burned, and one of his eyes was gone, melted out of the socket.

"Should I get you to a hospital?" Angel asked.

"No." Coronach's voice was a faint, painful whisper. He closed his one eye, grimaced in pain.

Angel glanced around. "Where are we? That was a teleportation spell you did, right?"

"Right. . . . Hard enough . . . when I'm feeling . . . *good* . . ." He twitched a couple of fingers. "This place . . . my L.A. safe house. Go to . . . cabinet . . . bring me what's inside. . . ."

A small wooden cabinet occupied one corner of the apartment; inside, Angel found a variety of unmistakably magical items and an array of oils in small flasks. He scooped them all up in one armful and brought them to Coronach's side. "I, uh, I'm not sure what to do with these. . . ."

"Don't worry . . . I'll tell you. . . ."

Fifteen minutes later, after Angel had performed rituals with two of the items and liberally applied four of the oils, Coronach's pain level had subsided enough for Angel to help him up off the floor and onto the apartment's narrow twin bed. The mage sighed, his breathing a little easier.

"Sorry, but you still look like hell. Are you sure you'll recover from this?"

Coronach might have attempted a sardonic smile at that if his face hadn't been so ravaged. "Don't worry about me," he said, still barely audible. "It's your friends. You have to protect them."

Unbidden, again the morgue attendant's face filled his vision, the tang of her blood sharp on his tongue.

You couldn't protect her, the Hand whispered. *Not on your own. . . .*

Angel swallowed hard, feeling sick, but shook the apparitions off and stayed with the conversation.

"Huh? What do—"

And then it struck him. *You would know precisely how I feel . . . were I to let you live.*

He whispered, "Cordy, Wes," and then bolted out of the apartment.

CHAPTER TEN

Victor Grimaldi had never seen anything like the scene playing out before him now. At least fifty of Lilith's demon warriors were sacking Lo-town, killing practically anything that moved. Laughing maniacally, the demons tore the wings from hawk people, then sent them plunging into chasms to their deaths. They beheaded, dismembered, or disemboweled many victims; others were impaled and left to die, twitching and pleading for mercy on eight-foot-long pikes.

Several of the Lo-town defenders fought back, using magic and weapons new and old. Bolts of mystical energy and slugs from automatic weapons ripped into the ranks of Lilith's demonic fighters, but only a handful were even slowed. Most ignored the bold resistance, finding ways to turn the weapons, both arcane and mundane, upon their wielders.

The dusty floor was running slick with blood, much of it blue or a viscous green, some of it bright yellow or even iridescent. Mixing with the crimson lake of blood from the more human denizens of Lo-town, the colors ran with the brilliant effect of gasoline in a puddle.

It was all madness and carnage . . . and Victor delighted in every moment. He had never considered himself an evil man, never truly delighted in the suffering of others, but now that he had a taste of what hell on earth might actually be like, he found that he liked it.

A lot.

Soon, a red-skinned demon approached, his blood-drenched sword drawn. He looked the closest to a "traditional" demon of any of the monsters Victor had seen so far, his flesh scaly, his eyes blazing crimson, small black wings sprouting from his mid-back. He wore black leather pants and boots, a scabbard, and a spattering of sparkling jewels, many of which appeared to have been set directly into his flesh.

"You're Victor?" the demon asked calmly.

Victor nodded.

"I am Balthezar. You did an admirable job in lowering this place's defenses for us. And, as promised, you shall be rewarded."

Victor flinched. This was the demon he suggested Angel kill to help cripple Lilith's operations. Well . . . the demon didn't know anything about that, or the ward that would protect him if Lilith tried to take his soul, so Victor stood up straight and tall, raising his chin proudly.

Balthezar sniffed . . . and sighed sadly. Victor had no idea how to interpret that. Then something strange happened: Balthezar surged forward suddenly, moving so quickly, he was practically a blur, and a dull, aching pressure settled in Victor's chest, and he was somehow unable to catch a breath.

Looking down, he saw the sword hilt pressed against his shirt, and the demon's face swam up into his.

"Your reward, as promised," the demon hissed. "A quick, painless death."

Balthezar yanked the blade out of Victor, who sank to his knees and toppled onto his side, his own blood gushing and squirting to mix with that covering the floor.

Victor didn't understand; he had done what they asked. . . .

"Don't take it personally," Balthezar said as the screams of the dying rose up around him. "Once someone's been a betrayer they can never again be trusted. Company rules. Personally, I thought you were an okay guy."

"The . . . the thousand," Victor gasped. He could release the ward protecting him from Lilith, give her his soul, he didn't want to die. . . .

"Yeah, well, I did some sniffing around," he said with a smirk. "I got the sense you did something to undo all the good work Lilith had done with you. Y'know, her pushing you to reach your full potential, to be perfect . . . perfect for what she had in mind, anyway. Probably got a little bit of a conscience or something when you were with the vampire, right? Just for a second?

Long enough, it seems. She asked me to check, and to not bother bringing you back if you'd been tainted. This whole betrayal of Lo-town and the vampire's group was terrific, don't get me wrong, but I think we both know you were just compensating. Well, ciao!"

The demon walked away.

For a fleeting moment, Victor felt as if he were falling through a gaping hole in eternity.

Then all was darkness, and he felt nothing at all.

Angel passed through the subway entrance and all the other chambers leading to Lo-town without engaging a single death trap. Every door was open wide, and long before he saw the first body, he smelled the river of blood that awaited him.

Steeling himself for the worst, Angel entered Lo-town. He was far too late. Hundreds were dead, many others gutted, dying. Even those who were not wounded were suffering, drowning in loss. Victor was among the first he found, the man's eyes wide and unseeing. Angel shook his head. Victor had been . . . unpleasant. But he hadn't deserved this, so far as Angel knew.

The sight of the dead man filled him with dread for the fates of his friends. "Cordy! Wes!" Then, a moment later, almost an afterthought, "Elaine!"

He looked for Cordy and Wes, searching the dark corridors and main chambers, pushing through curtain after curtain of thick, dirt-clotted roots. . . . Crossing one rickety bridge after another, searching until he thought he might go mad, Angel found nothing but a charnel house, an abattoir.

So many people he had once saved, so many who had put their trust in him, believed in him . . . and now they were dead. All of them. Bodies heaped on bodies. The human and the inhuman alike. Only a few of Lilith's warriors had fallen, their corpses left behind in a blatant show of dishonor. To fall before rabble like this? They deserved to be left to rot. *That's how Lilith would see it*. Angel was certain.

"*Angel* . . . ," a voice called in a ragged gasp.

He whirled, one step from the entrance to the cave where all of Lo-town's ancient texts were stored.

Peregrine was there, on his knees, clutching at the ruin of his chest. His golden, gargoyle-like face was twisted up in agony, his breathing shallow.

"Damn fool demons," Peregrine said, spitting glowing, amber blood. "They just think everyone's heart is in their chest, or that no one has more than one . . ."

"Cordy, Wes," Angel said quickly, kneeling before his old friend.

A bitter laugh sounded from the dying creature. "Demons. Gotta love 'em, especially the warrior kind. Usually not even half a brain when you put 'em all together, and that's when you've got a legion."

Angel doubted that was the case. Demons knew full well that not every creature's heart was in its chest. It made more sense to Angel that they had left Peregrine to die a slow, lingering death on purpose, so that he could tell Angel all he witnessed. Lilith wanted Angel to suffer. But he wasn't about to go into all that with Peregrine. His friend was slipping fast. "What happened?"

Peregrine explained that the people of Lo-town convinced the enemy that only the "weakling," the one called Wesley, had been left behind to review their scrolls and ancient tomes; the others had gone. In reality, Cordelia and Elaine were hidden in a small, secret chamber off the library.

"And . . . Angel . . . it was your friend. Victor. He led them to us. I heard him speak with them and saw them kill him."

Angel nodded, his suspicions confirmed about Victor's betrayal. "I found his body. But if he was on their side . . ."

"He was a betrayer. And . . . no longer useful to them. The demon who killed him said you'd tainted him with a conscience, made him useless as one of the thousand, whatever that is . . ."

Angel understood. Victor had switched sides so often, he had proved that his only interest was in serving himself, and that would make him dangerous for Lilith to keep around, particularly if the tide turned against the demoness in the future . . . not that such an outcome looked terribly likely right about now. Victor had been one of the thousand Lilith needed to fulfill her grand plan, and she had sacrificed him.

Still . . . a conscience? How could any human with a conscience bring about all this death and destruction? It was a mystery. . . .

And Lilith—did she have other perfect souls in reserve, ready to be harvested? Or would she be scrambling now to find a replacement? And what did this mean for Elaine?

A human, not a demon, an ordinary human, responsible for all this. . . .

Or was Angel himself to blame? If he hadn't come here, Lilith wouldn't have sent her people. The thought was almost too much for him.

"What about Cordy and Elaine?" Angel asked breathlessly, worried that he would hear the worst.

With his dying breath, Peregrine told Angel how to find the two women. Then he sank to the ground, his eyes fixed on nothing as his body slowly turned to stone. Angel didn't know if Cordy and Elaine would be dead or alive.

Angel found them exactly where Peregrine had said. He was relieved to see that they had remained hidden and safe through the conflict. Elaine was in the corner, her eyes dry, her body trembling. Cordelia's steel calm and firm resolve had returned, though.

"They took Wes," Cordelia said urgently as he led her out of the library, Elaine hugging herself and staring at the ground as she followed.

"I know," Angel said.

Cordelia shuddered as she saw the bodies, the burning, and the blood. "I wanted to stop them, I wanted to do something, but—"

"I know," Angel said, holding her. A few paces away, Elaine stood staring, as immobile as a statue. Angel imagined that he could actually see her withdrawing from the reality around her. *Or is something else going on with her?* Angel wondered.

Cordelia moved away from Angel, watching the other woman. "Elaine? You okay?"

Elaine's head shook just a tiny bit, a tiny "no," side to side. "Victor and I were part of Lilith's one thousand. . . ." she whispered. "She needed us. Can she—is she going to, to come after us? Can she come after"— and her voice grew small—"after me?"

But then Elaine's features hardened, and her lips curled into something close to a sneer. "Of course I'm okay," she spat out. "Not like I knew any of these freaks."

Cordy's eye went wide at hearing such a brutal, callous remark. But Angel just hung his head. Elaine had skirted a single moment of humanity, compassion . . . and then sped right past it.

"She's in shock," Cordelia offered. Angel made a dismissive gesture with one hand, his eyes back on the scene of slaughter around them.

There was nothing anyone could have done. Even if he had been here with Coronach at his side, he couldn't have stood against the forces that had descended on this place.

You're wrong, the Hand hissed in his mind. *There is a way. You can avenge these deaths and balance the scales for all you have done and been responsible for.*

"The cost," Angel said softly, looking out at the carnage, the bodies, the flickering orange flames. "It's too high."

"Angel?" Cordelia asked, her eyes wide with concern. "You're talking to me, right? I mean, who else would you be talking to?" She hesitated, then cleared her throat. "That came out way too Travis Bickle."

Angel wasn't listening to her. The Hand was speaking again: *All great things come at a price. You stand at a crossroads in the history of your kind. No one but you can fulfill this destiny. Seize the power that is rightfully yours, Angel, embrace me, make your world a perfect place where a thing like this can never happen again. . . .*

"I can't win," Angel said. "I really can't do it."

"What are you talking about?" Cordelia asked. "You've faced down apocalypses. Notices the 's' at the end. That means more than one."

"This is different," Angel said. He couldn't help but consider the sheer inhumanity of Victor's traitorous act . . . which seemed to be reinforced by Elaine's lack of concern for the decimation of Lo-town, feigned or otherwise. He could defend the world from countless outside threats, avert catastrophe after catastrophe . . . but how could he save humankind from itself, when the species seemed so hell-bent on self-destruction? How could he save the human race, when it so clearly strove not to be saved?

The realization came to him: *I can't. Not without help.*

Angel reached into his pocket and took out the snake torque. "It's not an ending, it's a new beginning . . . one we won't be a part of, if Lilith gets her hands on this."

"Angel, don't do anything crazy," Cordy warned. "Tell me you're not thinking about putting that thing on!"

He didn't answer. Instead, as Cordy and Elaine watched, he slowly brought the Serpent's Hand to his neck.

CHAPTER ELEVEN

The Hand closed around Angel's throat, its fit snug and tight—and suddenly even tighter. Angel clawed at it, and though he hadn't taken a breath in more than two hundred years, he felt the torque choking him, squeezing out his life. . . .

Elaine took several steps backward, nonplussed, but Cordelia was frantic beside him. "Angel, what's wrong? What's it doing?"

The Hand came alive, writhed on his skin and, as Cordelia screamed, it burrowed in.

Down inside him it went, pushing, tunneling, winnowing, and he fell to his knees with pain so ferocious, it took away his sight. His eyes, his teeth, the contours of his face all changed and changed back, demon to human, and back again, as Cordelia stood nearby, tears running down her cheeks.

Next to Cordelia, Elaine stared now, openly fascinated.

Angel grunted and shrieked, his muscles spasmed and nerves long thought dead in his vampiric flesh burst to life with burning, blistering agony—

—and then it stopped.

Because the Serpent's Hand reached his heart.

Its long, supple fingers coiled around that long-dead organ in a tender caress, and all of his agony, all of the fires he felt raging within, suddenly transformed into a gentle, comforting warmth—as well as something else, something so bizarre and surprising, yet so incredible, that for several moments Angel was convinced he was hallucinating. As the Serpent's Hand tightened its grip ever so slightly . . .

. . . his heart began to *beat*.

Slowly, yes, but undeniably, and Angel gasped with the shock of it.

Only once before since becoming a vampire had Angel felt anything like this—once, when The Powers That Be had given him a single day as a human being. During that day, Angel had walked in the sun, enjoyed normal human food and, most importantly of all, made love with his soul mate, Buffy Summers. The one girl in his long existence who had completely won him over . . . and the one girl he could never be with.

Angel had given up his humanity at the end of that day of his own free will; he'd been human, yes, but because of that he was unable to protect Buffy from the dangers she so often faced. At the end of that day he'd relinquished his beating human heart, and the rest of the world remained unaware of his sacrifice, unaware that that day had ever taken place.

But this . . . this was different. This was as different from his single day as a human as it could possibly be. His heart was beating again, yes, but he still possessed his full vampiric might; in fact, as he got to his feet again, he felt his muscles fill near to bursting.

With *strength*.

With *power*.

Cordelia's tears still flowed, but she watched him now, gape-mouthed and as silent as Elaine, standing behind her, the woman's expression unreadable.

Angel pulled open his shirt and, looking down at his chest, where his heart had once pulsed with life, felt a new life taking shape. As he stared, red light burst forth from within, tracing that new life's image, inscribing its name upon him. After a few seconds the light died down, and a glowing red sigil remained, a burning tattoo just above his heart.

Just above the hand of the Serpent.

The sigil shone and glimmered on Angel's chest, displaying an image of two winged serpents facing each other within a circle, their wings folded forward, wingtips touching.

Now . . . The voice hissing in his head seemed so good, so natural. *Now you have the strength you'll need. And now you will know that I can do more than promise you salvation, redemption . . . your prophecy spoke of your walking as a living man once more. Living men have hearts that beat. So do you . . . now. Consider it a taste of what is to come when you have reached your full potential, when your destiny is fulfilled.*

"Angel?" Cordelia wiped tears from her face. "Are you all right?"

He shook his head, still growing acclimated to the new energy flowing through him. "I . . . Yeah, I . . . I think I am. I really think I am."

"Won't matter," a nonhuman voice said from behind him. The three of them spun toward it, to see the first of ten demon warriors approaching them. "The Lady thought you might come back here. Left us to wait and see." The demon doing the talking unharnessed a long, double-bladed war ax from his back, the bright, polished blades reflecting his grin. "Considerate of her."

Angel said, "Cordy, Elaine, run," but then two things happened: Elaine turned and bolted as fast as she could for the nearest cover, and Cordelia narrowed her one uncovered eye and picked up a fallen sword.

"Nowhere to run *to*," she said. "I'm tired of running, anyway."

The demon in the lead laughed, raised his ax, and charged. The first sweeping, killing blow missed entirely as the vampire nimbly stepped to one side, but the demon was obviously unconcerned, even as Angel balled up one fist and slammed it into the warrior's face.

What happened next stunned everyone there into silence, Angel included.

The ax-wielding warrior screamed, staggered backward, lost his footing, and fell flat on his back. By the time his head hit the ground, his body had already begun to wither, and less than a second later only a pile of slightly damp ash inhabited his clothing and armor. A stream of ruby-red eldritch light floated up from the remains, swirled in the air for a heartbeat, then soared straight into the glowing sigil on Angel's chest.

Cordelia almost dropped her sword.

After momentary confusion and uncertainty, the rest of the demons marshaled and attacked again, but this time Angel was more than prepared for them.

With greater speed and more punishing force than he'd ever used before, Angel whirled and kicked, dodged and punched, and smashed fists and knees and elbows into the contingent of demons. Each blow had the same swift and incredible effect as the first one, and for a few seconds the air around him grew hazy and red with sorceress incandescence.

The whole fight took less than seven seconds. When it was over, Cordelia went ahead and let her sword fall. It clattered sadly, its clanks and complaints rising up to fill the silent chamber until it finally settled and was still.

Triumphant, Angel towered among the ashen remains of the warriors, his body thrumming with energy and life, his miraculous heartbeat pounding slow and steady in his chest. His face was human as he turned to Cordelia, who simply stood there, surveying the carnage, the very picture of impressed.

"Damn," she said.

"I know!" Angel glanced around as Elaine timidly emerged from her hiding place, her eyes the size of saucers at what Angel had done. Then her gaze narrowed, and her cool facade, if that's what it really was—Angel had no way to be sure—returned.

He couldn't believe how good this felt; his emotions, filtered through the Hand, tasted sweeter than they ever had before—as if the best, brightest facets of his soul were amplified, shining, and brilliant. He felt empowered, filled with confidence and pride.

Enjoy this, the Hand murmured inside him. *Grow accustomed to the feeling . . . let the memories return of what it was like to live.*

Angel groped for a response, tried to formulate words, but nothing would come to him. The Hand continued. *This is but a taste, a whisper of the song I can sing, a fleeting glimpse of the beauty I can show you as a mortal man once more.*

Like in the prophecy, Angel thought.

Yesss . . . think on these things.

The voice fell silent then, but Angel's heart didn't. Its steady, wondrous, yet alien rhythm pounded through him, thrummed its way along his bones. Angel glanced at Cordelia, once again tried to communicate what he was feeling, but once again failed. He simply didn't have the words. Instead, he said, "Too bad there aren't more of them, huh?"

"More of what?" Cordelia asked hesitantly.

"Lilith's demons!"

"Oh, I uh . . . thought maybe you meant that mondo creepy thing you just stuck in your chest. Like, ewww, by the way."

177

No, Angel thought, *the power of the Hand is one of a kind. And it's all mine. Who else could handle something like this?*

"So now what do we do?" Cordelia asked. "Are you gonna take that thing out? It's not safe. It corrupts people. And I'm looking at you right now and I'm not sure I'm seeing good old-fashioned brood-boy at all. You look like you enjoyed all that a little too much for my comfort level."

"Oh, I wouldn't go that far," Elaine said, practically purring as she moved past Cordelia, giving Angel a very thorough—and not terribly subtle—once-over. "I thought your little display was pretty sexy."

Cordelia scowled at her. "That is wrong on so many levels."

Elaine shrugged. "He can protect us now. And with that thing inside him, there's no way Lilith can use it. No reason for her to come after me. This is a win-win for me, every way I look at it."

Angel wondered if Elaine was just behaving like this because she was still in shock, still taking all of this in . . . or because she really was this removed from her humanity.

Angel scowled at the bodies around him. The demons—and their victims. "They had it coming."

Cordelia nodded slowly. "No argument there. But that thing. You should get it out now, before—"

Angel fixed her with a look. "We've got work to do."

She followed him cautiously, throwing Elaine a foul look as she passed her, and he decided not to tell her of the rapture he felt inside.

• • •

Wes came back to consciousness slowly and painfully. The side of his head ached where he had been clubbed by a demon, but he couldn't move his hands to clutch his throbbing skull: They were manacled behind his back. His ankles were chained, too. The steady sounds of a vehicle on the open road came to him, accompanied by low vibrations. He was lying on his side on the vinyl backseat of some moving car, and he couldn't see much of the driver or the hulking brute in the passenger seat except for the backs of their heads, which grazed the car's ceiling. He could make out that their skulls were misshapen, with little spikes and points and long, sharply pointed ears.

Demons. Clearly he'd been taken from Lo-town during the gut-wrenching slaughter.

He had no idea if Cordy and Elaine had survived, and if so, if they had been captured, as well. The only safe bet right now was that the war between Angel and Lilith was still raging, or else there would be no reason to have kept him alive this long.

After a few minutes, the silence from the front seat was broken and the demons began to talk about their "glorious victory" and compare stories of sickening atrocities against the dwellers of Lo-town in horrifying detail. The demons referred to each other as "Panir" and "Taja." Focusing on details like that, trying to take in as much of his surroundings as he could, was the only thing keeping him focused beyond the pain in his head and his growing concerns for his friends.

The car made several turns, went over some bumpy, gravely roads, and lurched to a stop. The demon in the passenger seat got out, and soon Wes heard the sound of more chains rattling from somewhere outside, then metal gates screeching as they were pulled open. The car eased forward for another ten seconds or so, then stopped again. The crunch of heavy gravel-stomping footsteps came, and the passenger door near Wesley's feet opened up, thick hands closing over his legs. He was hauled out of the car by a demon who yanked him up onto his feet in a dizzying motion. The other one knelt and removed the manacles binding his ankles. He looked around, and was surprised to see what appeared to be a small abandoned zoo.

The two demons, who looked more or less human, if one discounted the bluish scales covering their skins, shoved Wes ahead, bringing him to the first of a long line of cages. They removed the shackles from his wrists, opened one of the cages, and unceremoniously threw him inside, locking the door after him.

"This is lousy," Panir said. "We can't question him at all?" He fixed Wesley with a contemptuous stare. "It's not like the guy's gonna break. Well, not much, anyway."

Taja, the taller and more muscular of the two, also seemed to be the more even-tempered. He made a noncommittal gesture with his hands and said, "Orders are orders." Then, "Hey, and that reminds me." Taja opened the door of the cage and reached one long arm in, grabbing hold of Wesley's jacket by one sleeve. "Off with the jacket."

For the first time Wesley spoke to the demons, even as he tried not to lose his balance and sprawl on the floor from Taja's tugging on him. He had hidden weapons that might prove useful in the jacket earlier. If they hadn't been taken while he was unconscious, they might provide him with a chance to get out of this mess. "My jacket? Why? I'm sure it wouldn't fit you. What could you possibly want it for?"

Instantly Taja's ham-sized hand let go of the jacket and clamped around Wesley's lower face. He pulled Wesley right up so they were nose to nose, and growled, "You're not here to ask questions, monkeyboy. Now take off the jacket before we break your arms."

He shoved Wes back into the cage, where the Englishman quietly did as he was commanded, trying to preserve a scrap or two of dignity. Taja took the jacket, and the two demons left without another word.

Alone now, Wesley tried to make himself as comfortable as he could, considering the only piece of furniture he had in the cage with him was an old hollow log. He sat down on the log, thinking.

Lilith must still be interrogating Gunn, he finally concluded. *He'll be a tough one to crack, I'm sure . . . and when she's done, she'll come for me.*

After a few more moments of consideration, he checked for some other items he had hidden in his clothing and was relieved to find them all where he'd left them. He stood up, having come to a decision. *Well, if they're going to be so sloppy that they don't even frisk me, it's their own fault.* Wesley produced a small lock-pick kit from inside one of his socks and set to work on the cage's door.

Getting the door open didn't take much time, or even much effort; the cage was designed to keep in animals, not humans, and the lock was very simply designed. Taking care not to make any unnecessary noise, Wesley swung the door open and sneaked out.

The cage was one of seven in a row that made up one wall of a low, cinder-block building. The nearest street was behind him, so Wesley crept to the building's closest corner and peered around it.

Panir and Taja both leaned against the wall, apparently unconcerned about any possible breakouts. Panir smoked a cigarette. Wesley made his way back down the length of the building to the other end, and found the way clear. *Splendid.*

He was just about to make his break for the highway when a strange, chilling noise sounded out behind him: something that mixed a ferocious beast's growl with his own name.

"Wesssleeeeey . . ."

Wes spun in his tracks and froze in horror.

Crouched not twenty feet away, ready to spring, was a creature so horrible that simply seeing it sent tremors up and down his spine. It wasn't the multiple mouths on the head, or the awful sets of teeth it had for hands that horrified him so; it was the undeniable certainty that the demon he now saw had at one time been his friend, Charles Gunn.

In a tiny voice, Wesley said, "Oh no," just as the Gunn-demon tensed to charge him.

Then Taja was there. He grabbed the Gunn-demon from behind, lifting it up off the ground in a fearsome bear hug. The Gunn-demon squirmed and struggled, but not too much. Wesley could tell Taja had done this to him before.

The big demon laughed at Wesley. "Thought you could sneak out, did you? Better not try that again." He turned and began carrying the Gunn-demon away, as if Gunn were now some kind of trained attack dog. Over his shoulder, Taja said, "We gave this critter your jacket, just so you know. He's got your scent. Leave your cage again, and I won't stop him."

"Gunn!" Wesley cried. "Gunn, it's me! Wesley! Gunn, say something!"

From Taja's arms the Gunn-demon only snarled and writhed, its hand-jaws snapping at the air. Taja took Gunn away.

A moment later Wes felt a blade poke him in the back. Panir had come around behind him, and began herding him with the broad knife in his left hand. "Go on, back to your cell," the demon said, and Wes complied, moving on legs that felt like rubber.

He couldn't help worrying about what Lilith would do to him, now that he had seen what she did to Gunn. And he couldn't help worrying even more for his friends.

• • •

As Wesley sat in the cage at the abandoned zoo, cooling his heels, an unremarkable late-model sedan crept down a side street thirty miles away. The reflection of a neon sign—TOMASI PALMS MOTEL—slid across the car's windows, the motel itself about half a block away.

"There it is," Lilith said to the car's driver, anxious to get this business over and done with.

The car came to a halt, and Lilith stepped out of the backseat, dressed in inconspicuous street clothes. She'd worked a potent glamour on herself, toning her beauty down so that she could pass for merely attractive among the mortal rabble, rather than blindingly exquisite. The sedan pulled away, leaving her on the sidewalk, and she strolled casually toward the Tomasi Palms. No one on the street gave her a second glance.

The man she was going to meet went by the name of Joey Packard. He was one of her "backup souls" . . . one of her ongoing projects, cultivated and shaped carefully to be what she needed, in case any of those slated to become one of the thousand was injured or failed to reach his or her potential before she could brand that person and swallow his or her very rare "perfect" soul.

Except now things weren't going so well for Joey Packard—or, by extension, for Lilith, either. Joey Packard was a man on the run, desperate to escape the mysterious commando-like assassins he'd been warned about, that he'd even glimpsed as he sped away from his office building earlier—or so he'd told Lilith when they spoke earlier. Now Joey had come to this motel, trusting her assurance that he'd be safe here. She could only hope that she'd been right, that her enemies at Wolfram and Hart knew nothing of this place.

It would've been nice if that trusting fool at the party had turned out to have what I needed, Lilith thought. *It would have saved some time . . . but I'm never without options.*

She reached the motel and began climbing the concrete stairs to the second level. She'd noticed a forest-green SUV in the parking lot and nodded. *Good, everything is in place.* Lilith walked to room 207 and knocked gently on the door.

After a moment, from inside: "Yeah?"

"It's me, Joey," Lilith said sweetly. "Open the door."

A chain rattled, and soon the door swung open. Lilith walked into the tiny, shabby room and eyed Joey Packard critically.

Packard stood about five feet six inches, considerably shorter than Lilith; he was forty-one years old, starting to go gray at the temples, but still a good-looking man, thin and with good muscle tone. A successful advertising executive, Lilith knew Packard had a reputation for keeping his cool under pressure. Not so tonight; huge patches of perspiration showed at his armpits as he shut and locked the motel room door.

"Lily, you've gotta help me!" he said, turning to her with desperate eyes. "I don't know what's going on! If you hadn't called and warned me, I think I'd be dead by now!"

Lilith didn't say anything right away. She knew exactly what was going on, had been given a full report by her intelligence officers: Wolfram & Hart was targeting her backups, taking them out one by one. Abducting them, sending them to some other dimension, maybe just killing them, she didn't know. What she did know was that this man, Joey Packard, was the last of her backups, and she had to act quickly and decisively.

Stepping forward, she put her hands on the sides of his face, and let her glamour drop by a notch. Suddenly much more radiant, much more beautiful, she could feel Packard's knees weaken at her touch. "Joey. Listen to me. I can protect you . . . but only if I know you're true to yourself. Only if you can prove that to me."

The man quivered like gelatin. "Anything, Lily, anything you say, just, just tell me! Tell me what you want!"

"Oh, it's not what *I* want, Joey," she said, releasing him and turning away. "It's what *you* want." She pierced him with a glance over her shoulder. "Your wife, Joey. Olivia."

Packard's face changed in an instant, hardening, his lips curling in a hateful sneer. "What about her?"

Lilith came back to him, whispered in his ear. "She's in the room right next door, waiting for one of her lovers."

Packard couldn't believe it. He ran to the front window and looked out. "I'll be damned," he muttered. "There's her SUV, right outside!"

And as Joey Packard's breathing suddenly quickened, Lilith reached into her handbag and pulled out two items.

One was a long, wickedly sharp knife.

The other was the key to room 208.

Lilith watched Joey Packard leave the room, knife and key in hand, with mingled relief and amusement. In a few moments his soul would be hers, and then she would only be one perfect specimen short of her goal.

Olivia Packard, Lilith knew, was a loving wife. Five years her husband's junior, she worked hard to support him in all of his endeavors, and last year had borne him a son. Never once had she entertained even a hint of infidelity, and she staunchly defended Joey if anyone dared say anything negative about him.

Yet Joey hated her. Hated her with a fiery passion, though he couldn't have told anyone why. She was young, she was pretty, intelligent and witty, she had no flaws that Joey or anyone else could identify . . . and he wanted her dead.

Lilith knew that Joey had been unfaithful countless times. He had slipped away and slept with another woman at their wedding while his wife was having her picture taken, and had rendezvoused with two others that night after she was fast asleep. He was a hypocrite of the highest—or lowest—order, depending on how you looked at it. More importantly, he knew it.

And that was such a factor in what she required: free will. Freedom of choice. And complete awareness of "good" and "evil" and the potential consequences of acting on one's own most terrible urges and desires.

To paraphrase a very wise woman Lilith once met, *we see the world not as it is, but as we are.*

Joey cheated. Joey lied. So, in his mind, it was inconceivable that his wife, or anyone else, really, didn't do the same. And that concept, that his wife was treating him with the same callousness, the same disrespect and contempt he secretly held for her . . . that was too much for him to live with. Or to even admit to himself.

Perfect *loathing* . . .

Well, as his *friend,* "Lily Pierce" could do no less than offer her assistance. It was a simple matter to arrange for Olivia to come to the motel tonight; the pretense of a spontaneous romantic tryst with her spouse was too intriguing for her to pass up, and faking Joey's voice was hardly a challenge.

Lilith stood in the center of the room, waiting.

Once the deed was done—indicated by a short, sharp scream, abruptly cut off—Lilith gave it two more minutes, then went next door.

Joey Packard sat on the edge of the bed, his shirt splattered with blood. Olivia, his wife, lay on the floor in front of him, her throat slashed, her chest ravaged from multiple stab wounds.

"How do you feel?" Lilith asked him.

The light in Packard's eyes could almost have been described as demonic. "I feel fantastic."

"Good. Then come to me."

Packard did as he was commanded; he came and stood in front of her; he opened his shirt obediently; and he received her brand, the sigil searing into his flesh with a tiny wisp of smoke as she consumed his soul. *That makes 999,* she thought. *Only one more to go. . . .*

And before that wisp had dissipated, the door to room 208 smashed down, the air suddenly filling with multiple voices—and then gunshots.

Lilith grabbed Joey Packard, now merely another drone, his true purpose achieved, and swung him around, using his body as a shield to absorb the initial volley of gunfire from the team of Wolfram & Hart commandos. She backed up farther into the room, allowing the men in black paramilitary uniforms to come flooding in—

—and then she seized every bullet lodged in Joey Packard's corpse, surrounded them with eldritch force, and sent them through the commandos' heads at twice the velocity at which they'd been fired.

Seven bodies fell to the floor, surrounding the late Olivia Packard. As Lilith let Joey slump down next to his wife, gazing at the bodies of the Wolfram & Hart commandos, an idea formed in her mind.

Perhaps I won't have to look very far for my thousandth perfect soul after all. Lawyers, and those who work for them, are usually only one step away from complete corruption, from a form of perfection I can use, and turning one of them to my cause would be . . . poetic.

Leaving the carnage behind, Lilith laughed inwardly as she strolled out into the night, away from the motel.

CHAPTER TWELVE

Angel smiled as he stared up at the night sky, taking in stars like diamond dust that shone down out of the cloudless sky. He sat patiently on the hood of the GTX convertible, which was parked out in the desert. Cordelia and Elaine stood close by.

Angel had his reasons for not telling either of the women what they were waiting for; and because of his decision to withhold that information, he'd been forced to endure Cordelia's progressively more heated demands concerning where they were going. Cordelia reminded Angel that they were partners, that they were all in this together, and that ever since he'd let that "Hand thingee" push its way into his body, he'd been acting like a "cocky butthead."

He'd smiled then, and the only thing he would say on the subject was, "It's a surprise."

Elaine had remained silent during the whole trip, but gave Angel a haughty sneer whenever he glanced at her in the rearview.

It was quiet and peaceful here, Angel noted, like it must have been long ago, before humans walked the planet . . . before they had fallen so far from grace and become their own worst enemies. But all that was going to change.

Angel had never before dared to imagine the things that now seemed within his grasp. With the power of the Hand aiding him, he would rid humanity of its own inner evils, stamp out the taint of demon-kind, and transform the Earth into a paradise. He had never felt so powerful, so filled with clarity and vision as he did right now. The night was practically perfect.

"Hello?" Cordelia said. Angel could tell she was about to erupt. *Here it comes*, he thought. He wasn't overly concerned about it; riding high on the power of the Hand, he felt confident and relaxed.

He glanced over to his companion, who was hugging herself against the desert breezes, and smiled dreamily. "What's up, Cordy?"

Her gaze narrowed as she stared at him in what he took as frank disbelief. "What's up? I'll tell you what's up! You're not acting anything like yourself, that's what's up, you doofus! How dare you drag us all the freakin' way out here with no clue why!"

He listened carefully, his expression unchanging as she unloaded the same litany of complaints she'd delivered for the last hour and a half as they'd driven from the city. When he didn't respond, or seem the least bit bothered by her distress, when, no matter how hard he tried, he couldn't quite hide his patronizing smirk, things really got bad, her voice sounding loud enough to split wide the endless starry sky.

It didn't bother him in the least when she went off delivering one of the more creative bursts of cursing he'd heard in at least twenty years, or that he was the object of her anger. He waited it out, watching her hands fly over her head, the sand kick up as her designer boots assaulted it. Only the look Elaine gave him as she sat a good dozen feet away on the hood of his car gave him the slightest cause for regret . . . and even then, all he had to do was concentrate on the deliberate pulsing of his heart to know that he was doing the right thing.

Still, he knew Cordelia needed this, and when she was done—or had, at least, run out of breath for a time—he touched her shoulder and said, "Don't worry. This is all for the best."

"*What's* all for the best?" Cordelia screamed. "What's going on? I thought we were taking the battle to that witch!"

"We are," Angel said. "Well, I am, anyway. You'll be there with me in spirit."

"Say what? Look, you'd better explain yourself, buster, and you'd better start—"

"Now," Angel said, turning away as he heard the low, steady rumble of an engine from the impenetrable darkness ahead.

"What is that?" Cordelia asked.

"Your ride." He glanced in Elaine's direction. "Flash the brights twice, will you?"

The GTX convertible's engine had been left running, the car's headlights sending two wide and quickly diffuse streams of light into the sandy blackness. Emboldened by the power of the Hand, Angel had returned to the theater, but the place had been deserted, his car left untouched.

Elaine hopped off the convertible's hood, reached over the driver's side door, and did what Angel said.

Suddenly, a blazing set of headlights appeared two dozen yards from their position, and far behind it, a soft glow lit the underside of something long, sleek, and aerodynamic.

The sand roared as the thick tires of a Land Rover described a half-circle around Angel and Cordelia— stopping as the headlights from Angel's car washed over the driver's side door. A friendly familiar face peered out.

"Took you long enough," Angel said as David Nabbit grinned at him.

"Well, it's not like you were asking for much," David said. "I, uh . . . y'know. Had to call in some favors from some of my gaming buddies."

More lights flickered on in the desert a good thousand yards beyond David's truck, runway lights revealing more clearly the shape of a small private airplane on a long strip in the desert.

Angel looked to Cordelia—and saw she was crestfallen.

"You're sending me away," Cordelia said in a low, disbelieving tone.

"You and Elaine," Angel said calmly. "Wish I could do the same with Wes and Gunn, but—"

"You're *sending* me *away*," Cordelia said, the heated passion returning to her usually melodious voice, giving it a shrill edge.

Angel nodded to David. "You might want to cover your ears."

Again, the tirade, this time even more inventive than before, complete with optional anatomical variations regarding exactly what Angel could shove where if he thought she was going along with this.

David got out of his Land Rover dressed all in black. He looked to Cordelia with growing concern, but Angel waved him off.

"Let her vent," Angel said. "It can't go on for much longer. Her throat's already dry, and she finished off the last Big Gulp an hour ago."

Angel waited patiently for Cordelia to finish, then she stood before the two men, her arms crossed over her chest. She stared at David's attire.

"What are you supposed to be?" she asked.

"Stealthy," David said. "You like?"

The muscles in her face twitched. "You look like a cross between Johnny Cash and a ninja raised by fashion-challenged wolves."

Angel nodded. "I'd say she likes."

Cordelia put her hand to the bandage covering the side of her face, her expression pained.

"I've got a nice Chardonnay on the plane," David said. "Angel said your throat might be dry. . . ."

"He's just hoping I'll shut up and follow orders." Cordelia grabbed Angel's arm. "You can't send me away. I can help."

"You can get killed," Angel said bluntly. "Or maybe Lilith will do to you what she did to Gunn. I can't risk that happening, and I won't be able to focus on taking this war back to its source unless I know you're safe."

"So that's the plan?" Cordelia said. "You're going after Lilith?"

Angel nodded. "Well . . . eventually. I'm gonna have to even up the odds a little, first."

"But you might need me!" Cordelia pleaded. "What if you need something looked up? I've gotten awfully good at that. And, you know, hey, when it comes to looking ahead, no one can beat what I've got."

Angel nodded. "I'll just have to get along without Vision Girl."

"Great," she said. "Now I'm a Marvel superhero."

"Cool, I love comics!" David said. "What kind do you . . ."

His words trailed off as Elaine slinked and sashayed her way over to them and stood before the Land Rover's rear passenger door. Angel only glanced her way as David mumbled and stumbled in his attempts to say anything intelligent and intelligible to the devastatingly beautiful Elaine, whom he had met briefly at Lily's party.

"The door?" she asked at last.

"Oh," he said. "Right."

He got the door for her. Cordelia huffed one final time,

punched Angel *hard* in the shoulder, then reached forward and hugged him close.

"You get yourself killed, I'll never forgive you," she said.

"I'm more worried about David," Angel said.

"Well, duh," she said as she walked around to the passenger side door and hopped in.

Angel led the wealthy entrepreneur far away enough from the vehicles so their little chat wouldn't be heard.

"Like I said on the phone, get them *away* from here," Angel said. "I don't want to know where you're heading, I don't want anyone else to know, either. Pick a destination at random. No e-mail, no cell phones, no flight plans. Do whatever you have to do."

"Got it covered," David said. "My pilot can keep it under the radar, and he knows all sorts of spots smugglers used to use as landing strips, like this place . . ."

"Safe, got it?" Angel asked. "Don't take her anywhere you could even imagine being dangerous."

"I'll guard her with my life."

Angel nodded, certain David meant it—and then nearly doubled over with the force of the Serpent's Hand shouting in his mind.

What are you doing? it clamored. *Have you lost your mind? These people are valuable. The man has vast financial resources, the injured woman is a seer, and the third is the most precious of all—she is directly connected to your enemy! That woman can be used against Lilith! You would be stupid to lose any of them, but the third you must keep! You must!*

Angel staggered at the force of the Hand's overpowering mental assault. He heard Cordelia call from the truck. "Angel? Are you all right?"

Managing to straighten up, Angel mumbled, "Fine, I'm fine," but the Hand's voice still raged in his head.

It would be sheerest folly to put the woman Elaine beyond your reach now!

I won't endanger her, Angel thought. *She's an innocent.*

The Hand's voice oozed sarcasm. *'Innocent'? You have heard her. You have seen her actions. She cares only about herself!*

Angel watched as Cordelia got back out, David and Elaine watching closely from inside. Approaching him, Cordelia said, "You don't look fine to me. You look the way *I* look after one of my head-splitters."

The voice of the Hand wouldn't stop. *Elaine can be utilized. Lilith's weakness can be exploited through her.*

No!

End this pointless denial, and get her out of that vehicle.

"No! I won't use Elaine as a weapon!" Angel barked out. Too late he realized he'd said the words aloud, rather than inside his mind.

Cordelia took a step backward.

In the Land Rover, Elaine's face drained of all its color. Tremulously, she said, "Use me as a weapon?"

You're a fool to throw your assets away, the Hand murmured disgustedly, fading out.

"Uh . . . ," Angel said, knowing there was little to no

chance of covering for this.

"Is that what you and Coronach decided to do?" Cordelia asked incredulously. "Use Elaine, what, as bait or something?"

Angel succeeded in recovering a portion of his composure. "No. I mean, we talked about that, yeah—and I could. I could use her. But I'm not."

A tremendous air of awkwardness descended on the scene; everyone stood for a few moments, silent, with no clue as to what to say. David seemed at a total loss for words, but eventually Elaine regained her poise and, with more than a little anger in her voice, asked, "Well, then, why not? If you could, then why don't you?"

Cordelia watched Angel's face, interested in his answer herself.

Finally Angel said, "Because you're not a weapon. You're not an object. You're a human being, and you deserve to be treated like one. You . . ." He stumbled over the words for a moment, the image of Elaine turning up her nose in disgust at the slaughter of Lo-town popping into his mind's eye. Still, though, Serpent's Hand or not, Lilith or not, he couldn't flatly deny his own nature, or denigrate hers. "You deserve . . . compassion."

The silence descended again, but Angel turned his back on the awkwardness and strode to the GTX. He looked back briefly—just in time to see the revelatory expression that flickered for an instant in Elaine's eyes—but he kept walking. Over his shoulder he called out, "Get that plane in the air."

• • •

Inside the plane, Cordelia took a seat near the front, Elaine hesitating in the aisle.

"He's quite a piece of work," Elaine said.

"David?" Cordelia asked. "He's a good guy. Stay away from him."

She laughed. "The other one. I've been around guys who don't need anyone all my life and it's nothing but pride talking, I swear. Seems to me, that's why they call them guys instead of men. A *man* can admit he needs other people."

Momentarily pushing aside her anger and frustration, Cordelia couldn't help but be amazed at Elaine's callousness. The woman had seemed shaken momentarily by Angel's inner conflict, but now she was right back to her old witchy self.

He did save your life, Cordy thought. *You could at least be grateful for that, instead of talking behind his back.* For the first time the realization really hit her that Elaine's cool exterior gave way to a cold that sank all the way to her soul. Maybe that had something to do with that pact she had made with Lilith, the way the demoness had her hooks in Elaine . . . or maybe it was why Lilith sought her out in the first place.

"Maybe, whatever," Cordelia finally said with a dismissive little wave.

From the cockpit came the voices of David and his pilot. Last-minute flight checks were almost done.

"I'm gonna find someplace I can stretch out, get some sleep," Elaine said. "Leave you two lovebirds alone. Wouldn't want to hurt your chances."

"Yeah, like you're competition," Cordelia whispered, feeling for just an instant like her old self. "Not that there even is a competition. I mean, me and David, we're just—"

She stopped the moment she looked into the perfect face of the woman who had nearly borne Lilith's brand, the truth crashing back on her. Right now, just about any woman would be competition for her.

"Ciao," Elaine said, strutting away with a satisfied little smile.

Cordelia *so* didn't like that woman. Elaine was so passive and pliant, such a girly-girl, just ready to do anything some big strong man told her to do . . . then complain about the guy later. Like being beautiful gave her the right to do or say anything that came into her head, despite all the drafts . . . and maybe it did. What did Cordelia know about it anymore?

She looked around, and when she was certain no one was watching, Cordelia reached into her bag with trembling hands and took out her compact, opening it to reveal a small mirror. Taking a long, deep breath, she peeled her bandages away and looked at the terrible scars she now bore.

She was hideous. What kind of life could she have now? What about all her dreams?

Suddenly, David was at her side. "Hey, gorgeous."

She raised her hands quickly to cover the scars, but he caught them tenderly, staring right at the ruined flesh as if it were no different than before. "No," he said. "It doesn't matter."

"Just don't call me that again," she said under her breath.

"What? Gorgeous? You are."

She nodded back toward Elaine. "I used to think I was perfect. Like her. Now . . ."

David shook his head. "Elaine's not perfect. Just pretty. And that's nothing."

Cordelia nodded silently as the plane jostled and bumped, wishing she could believe David's words. But she'd seen the way he'd looked at Elaine. . . .

Then the entire plane began vibrating like it was coming apart, and each of them were buckled up fast and grabbed hard at their handrests. The compact bounced out of Cordelia's lap, hitting the floor hard, its mirror shattering.

Good, Cordelia thought, closing her eyes as her stomach lurched and the little plane lifted off. She heard the tiny shards of glass skitter and slide down and away from her, like the hateful things they were. She could live with never again seeing what they had to show her.

Lilah Morgan let out a little yelp and barely managed to hold on to the files she was holding when she walked into her office and found Angel sitting behind her desk.

"What's the matter?" he asked pleasantly. "Did I scare you?"

"Just surprised me." Lilah set the files down on the front edge of the desk and crossed her arms. "What do you want?"

Angel swung his feet down off the desktop and stood, putting him eye-to-eye with her. "That's an awfully gruff greeting for someone who's helping you out."

"You didn't even want the job, as I recall."

"And I didn't take it, either. Our truce only exists because we have a common enemy. Once this is over, everything goes back to normal."

She cocked her head a little. "You've changed somehow. What's going on?"

Angel slowly circled her. She stayed where she was, rigid, back perfectly straight. "Don't worry about it. He reached up and toyed with a strand of her hair. "I want a list of every demon lair Lilith has."

"I can do that. Locations, head counts. All of it."

Angel smiled. "Never mind the head counts. Just tell me where they are."

Half an hour later, Angel stood outside a small, single-story office complex adjacent to a strip mall. The sign on the glass door in front of him read APPLETREE IMPORTS. The lighting inside was dim, but still bright enough for him to see shapes moving around.

Angel knocked on the door by throwing a blue United States Postal Service box through it. He stepped inside amid the spray of broken glass, his face turning vampiric, and saw roughly a dozen startled figures. They looked like regular office workers: young men and women in business-casual clothing. Until two seconds ago they appeared to have been engaged in regular clerical activities: filing, typing, et cetera. Now every one of them froze, staring at Angel in disbelief.

"You know what you people smell like?" he said into the silence, his yellow eyes flashing. "You smell like a bunch of demons. So let's not play coy."

Immediately the girl nearest him screamed, her skin transmuting into a thick, gray, rock-like hide as she leaped across her desk at him. Angel grinned and batted the girl's outstretched hands away, then pistoned a fist straight into the point of her chin.

The blow knocked her backward onto the desk she'd just jumped over, and by the time she hit it her body had already begun to deteriorate. Her spine snapped, the back of her head egg-shelled against a computer monitor, and even as she slithered to the floor not much of her was left aside from moist ash and a Gap skirt.

The other demons' shock grew deeper as the girl's essence flowed out of her remains and into Angel's chest, but seven of them sprang into action nonetheless, each reverting to demonic countenances. Angel waded into them, and every strike with a fist, every spinning kick, had the effect Angel had begun to expect—and to cherish.

He had always taken a certain amount of pleasure in ridding the world of danger, of evil; he'd always felt a gratifying sense of accomplishment. But now, with the Hand nestled so intimately around his heart, that pleasure had grown and intensified until destroying Lilith's demon servants filled him with an incredible rush of pure satisfaction.

Angel felt a sudden stab of guilt and fear over his actions, a prickling of his conscience. Only a monster would take delight in the act of killing, and he was no monster, he was a hero. No, the pleasure he felt came from knowing that these horrors would never hurt innocent people again, that he was removing predators from the planet, making the world safe.

That has to be it, he thought, wondering if he was telling himself . . . or asking himself. Because the feelings he was experiencing were so powerful they could overcome a lesser champion, the sensations so strong, he might come to crave them like blood if he wasn't careful.

I am careful. I'll always be careful.

The swirling red light grew more and more beautiful.

The rest of Lilith's minions tried to escape out the back of the office. Angel hunted them down.

One got as far as the rear parking lot. As Angel clamped his hand down on the back of the demon's neck, the creature twitched back to human form; grinding his teeth, he struggled in the vampire's grip.

"Get your hands *off* me!" the demon commanded.

Angel maintained the pressure—and a thought came to him unbidden, a faint hissing echo, accompanied by a momentary quickening of his heartbeat that nearly made Angel's knees weak with pleasure. *This is one of Lilith's lieutenants.*

One of her own children? Angel wondered.

Inside him, the Serpent's Hand whispered, *Yessss . . .*

Angel smiled cruelly. "So you're in the top echelon, huh? What—you're, like, a regional manager?"

The demon transformed again, its skin clicking and shifting into dark red chitin, like a beetle's shell. It clicked its mouthparts and spat into Angel's face.

Angel narrowed his eyes. "Hey, either way," he said, and drove the stiffened fingers of his other hand into the demon's chest, piercing its heart. The body crumbled out of his fingers as the glowing sigil on his chest sucked in its essence.

Angel strolled leisurely around the end of the building, back to where he'd parked the Plymouth. He felt something rattling loosely in a pocket, stuck his hand in, and pulled out bits and pieces of what used to be his cell phone, apparently smashed during the scuffle. He tossed the phone's remains away. *I didn't even notice the impact that did it,* he thought— then slowed down, wary, as a black Humvee rolled to a stop near his car.

All of the vehicle's doors opened simultaneously, and five huge, imposing figures stepped out of it. All males. Only two appeared to be human, but—he inhaled deeply—no, they were all inhumans, yet not demons; not the Hand's chosen prey.

The only thing they had in common seemed to be a taste for expensive suits. Some carried knives, some carried guns, and the biggest of them gripped an aluminum baseball bat in one hand. Angel smiled as he got closer to them.

"I've heard the term 'motley crew,'" he called out, "but I don't think I've ever seen one before. What're you guys supposed to be?"

One of the more blatantly inhuman types, a lean feline fellow with glowing orange eyes, bared impressive fangs as he spoke. "Don't get excited. We're supposed to help you."

Another one grinned and said, "Yeah. We're the backup."

A light breeze ruffled the tails of his coat as Angel stared at them. In the distance a car alarm went off. "Wolfram and Hart sent you? What, you guys are a *team?*"

Baseball bat laughed. "Not hardly. There's some of us as ain't too happy with this arrangement. . . ." He glanced significantly at one of the human-looking things, neither of whom seemed concerned in the least; Angel couldn't tell if that was out of supreme self-confidence or simple ignorance. "But hey, the price is right, we'll do the job. Together, even." He puffed his chest a little, tapped it with a thumb. "Name's Revodro." He pointed at the others in turn, who didn't acknowledge the introductions other than to continue watching Angel. "That's Sazh, Redbone, Montgomery, and Morris."

At the name "Morris," the cat-like fellow glared at Revodro and growled, low and menacingly. Revodro grinned. "Uh, beg yer pardon. My mistake. Kitty there's called Vorrl."

Angel said, "So you're Coronach's relief, huh?"

The bruisers exchanged glances. Sazh, who looked vaguely reptilian, said, "Who?"

"Never mind." Angel walked past them and opened his car door. He had a good idea of what was going on:

Lilah had found out—probably from someone else she had inside Lilith's organization—that Coronach was out of the game. That meant there was no chance he would be bringing her the Hand. These guys were her contingency plan.

Better to have them where I can see them, Angel decided.

"Look, if you want to tag along, fine. Just don't get in my way, all right? We've got a lot of ground to cover tonight."

The most human-looking one, Montgomery, approached him. "We see you made short work of this little venture." He jerked his chin toward what was left of Appletree Imports. "What's on the agenda for the rest of the evening?"

Angel said, "Killing Lilith's babies," and cranked the GTX's engine.

The second raid went much as the first one had, except that the bruisers tailed Angel in their Humvee. When they arrived at the second office building the hired guns followed him in, weapons in hand—and were quite clearly unprepared for the effects of Angel's attack on Lilith's demons.

They grumbled to themselves as the ghostly crimson soul-energy rose from the withered corpses and sank into Angel's body, and grumbled some more when Angel emerged from the building, stretching languidly and flashing a brilliant grin. The sigil on his chest glowed red through his shirt.

Revodro absently twirled his bat around him in an intricate pattern, frowning. "You ain't like what the file said, Angel. You're *enjoyin'* this." Angel walked right up to him, still grinning, and grabbed the bat in one hand. The other four bruisers moved nervously, hands jittering toward their weapons, but Angel made no further move except to speak.

"The night's young, boys, and we've got miles to go before we sleep." Then he laughed and vaulted in behind the Plymouth's wheel. "Try and keep up, all right?"

He revved the engine and peeled out of the parking lot as they rushed to follow him.

Over the next four hours Angel waged a small, private war on the streets of Los Angeles. Lair after lair fell to him—offices, clubs, even private residences, until the night became a montage of screaming, dying demons and the swirling bloodred vapor of their souls. Angel emerged each time, glowing and triumphant, exultant in his victory, reveling in the rush of blood pumping through his revitalized heart.

As he sauntered out of another building, the sigil on his chest pulsing, one of the demons—Redbone, who looked somewhat like a crustacean—stopped him to speak.

"Angel . . . you've obviously got a pattern to what you're doing, but damned if I can figure out what it is."

Angel smiled, and slapped the creature good-naturedly on the shoulder. "That's okay, buddy. You just keep jumping in and out of that great big truck and following me around like a pack of puppies, okay? You're really good at that."

Driving away, watching the Humvee fall in behind him, Angel fought down the urge to chuckle; in hours he'd accomplished what would ordinarily have taken him weeks, maybe months . . . *if* he'd been able to accomplish it at all. A single blow from Angel now meant death for demons, if he wanted it to. It was as if a gallon of adrenaline were being pumped into his veins every minute, and his body trembled with the sensation, his heartbeat sometimes so strong, he was surprised it didn't make the car tremble.

The Hand spoke to him without warning. *She knows.*

Angel half-expected to see sparks dancing between his fingers, he felt so electrified. "So it's working? Lilith can tell I've been targeting the lieutenants? Her children?"

She knows I have been allowing you to. A pause, then: *She is angry.*

Angel smiled. "Good." And he might have laughed out loud if a blinding blue-white spear of energy hadn't smashed down out of the sky into the pavement right in front of him, rending the air with a tremendous clap of thunder and setting the pavement on fire.

Angel yanked hard on the wheel, swerved the GTX so that it missed the blazing pillar by less than an inch— but couldn't quite regain control of the car before it ran up over the sidewalk and careened down a ramp into a private underground parking lot.

He jammed on the brakes and screeched the GTX to a halt, skidding it around so that the driver's side faced the lot's entrance; turning his head, he saw her coming down the ramp toward him.

Never had a woman more beautiful than Lilith existed, Angel was sure of that. Even as the electric radiance crackled out of her, bolts of mystical lightning springing from her hands and scorching random patterns onto the surrounding concrete, Angel couldn't help but appreciate her beauty. Only peripherally did he notice the curtain of sparks and white fire sealing off the lot's entrance, preventing the five thugs outside from coming in.

Lilith said, "Child-killer."

Angel stepped out of the car. "Well, I don't know that I'd call them children, exactly. I mean, the youngest one was, what, three thousand years old?"

"Only a few of them are left now. Only a *few* of the lives I delivered into this world myself. My forces still stand strong—but what you have taken cannot be replaced." She gritted her teeth. "Before I kill you, you will tell me how you found them."

Angel raised an eyebrow. Lilith didn't yet understand what had happened to him earlier that night.

His lips formed a slight smile. "Let's see if you can make me."

Lilith screeched, a horrible grating sound, and a hairline crack appeared in the convertible's windshield. Angel frowned. "Hey, now, there's no need to mess up my car."

Lilith sprang at him.

Even faster now than striking cobras, Lilith's hands shot forth, impacting on flesh and bone in a brutal machine-gun hammering. The force of it drove Angel back until his thighs pressed against the Plymouth's side panel.

Then he shot a hand out, two fingers stiffened into a stabbing weapon, and drove them into the base of Lilith's neck just above the notch of her collarbone.

She staggered, hands to her throat. Even more than the shocked disbelief on her face, Angel enjoyed the sudden, sliver-thin trace of *fear*.

"Not used to that, are you?" he said, pushing off from the car. Her blows had left no mark on him. "Not used to someone standing up to you, right? Up to now, no one could." Slowly, leisurely, he lifted his hands and pulled open his coat and shirt, exposing the bloodred sigil of the Serpent's Hand on his flesh. "But that's life, isn't it? Things change."

Angel laughed as every drop of color drained from Lilith's face, and kept laughing as he launched himself at her.

CHAPTER THIRTEEN

Angel snarled as Lilith gestured, causing a glowing mystical shield to spring into existence and separate him from his prey. He shattered the curved crimson and black barrier with a single blow and was on Lilith before she could erect another. One hand clamping over her mouth to prevent her from uttering an arcane ward or loosing a magical attack, Angel lifted her off her feet and slammed her against a nearby wall. The *crack* that sounded out as her body made a deep crevice in the wall—and her grunt of pain as her limbs slapped around like those of a rag doll—were the sweetest sounds he'd heard all night.

He smashed her against the wall again, then a third time. From the corner of his eye he saw her fingers twitch, and in the split second before he could react, Angel saw a large, round mirror rip itself free from the garage wall near the ceiling and rocket toward him, glowing with Lilith's magic. He tried to twist out of the way, but Lilith struggled so fiercely in his grasp that the best he could do was put his back to the mirror; it shattered into a hundred sharp, stinging shards, which stabbed him in the head and neck. Lilith gave him a nasty grin, shielded from the razor-sharp glass by Angel's body.

Lilith's feet rose in a blur, the heels of her boots stabbing into pressure points that made his arms go numb long enough that she forced him to loosen his grip on her. She dropped to the ground and kicked at him again, this time clearly intending to shatter his ankles, but Angel leaped back and away just in time.

Yanking shards of glass from his flesh, Angel heard Lilith utter a stream of mystical phrases. *Note to self,* he thought. *Next time, shut her damn mouth and break all her fingers.*

But Lilith was determined there would be no next time. A burst of raw, primal force struck Angel and lifted him up high, sending him flying a dozen feet and smashing him into the roof of a car, which collapsed under the sudden, brutal, powerful impact.

Looking up, he saw green fiery mystical energies racing along the ceiling. He calculated that he had just enough time to get out of the way as the fissures opened above him and a handful of cars and a truckload of debris rained down on him.

Instead, he only wobbled and dropped to the side of the car whose roof he'd caved in, risking being crushed to death, allowing himself to be buried alive in the deafening, concussive explosion.

For several moments, everything was still. He heard shifting among the rubble trapping him, and he waited until a large slab of concrete covering him was hauled away. Lilith stood above him, her eyes blazing, the slab held high over her head.

Knew you wouldn't be able to resist coming after the Hand, he thought.

"I'm touched," Angel said with a smirk.

Lilith's expression of ferocious triumph faltered. He launched himself at her, tackling her around the midsection and making her drop the slab. She hit the ground hard, the breath driven from her, a half-dozen feet past where the slab had fallen. Angel pinned her arms and legs, his fingers entwining with hers to keep her from calling up another spell with her arsenal of arcane gestures.

The waves of temptation he had felt before washed over him anew, but this time, he simply didn't care, because with those waves came *power.* Just touching her made him feel stronger.

Yessss . . . the Hand spoke low and softly, in counterpoint to the increasing rapidity of Angel's heartbeat. *You know the power that could be yours. The power of nearly a thousand perfect souls she's harvested. Take it from her!*

"No!" Lilith screamed.

"You're not gonna conjure again, are you?" Angel breathed into her ear. "If you are, I'll have to do something about it."

Her face twisted up in rage, Lilith indeed attempted

to cast another spell. Only one strange word leaped from her tongue before Angel brought his forehead down in a savage head-butt, the crack echoing loudly through the parking garage.

"Uhh," she moaned, her head lolling.

"What?" Angel asked. "I said I'd do something to shut your mouth. You didn't think I was gonna kiss you, did you?"

"Try it," she hissed.

"Yeah, said the succubus to the bishop." He head-butted her three more times, making sure she was dazed, then climbed off her. "The last girl I lost my soul to was a hell of a lot hotter than you, hon. No chance."

He let her get to her knees, then savagely kicked her stomach and ribs. She flew over onto her back again, and he kicked at her face.

Her hands flew up, grabbing his foot and twisting it sharply. If he hadn't detected her plan in time, she might have twisted it right off. Instead, he went with her motion, spinning in midair and dropping to the ground.

I got cocky, he thought. *That probably means I'm gonna pay for it. . . .*

He did. Lilith knew better than to allow any part of her flesh to come into contact with him now that he possessed the Hand, and so she conjured mystical energy constructs she could use as weapons against him.

A blazing crimson mace whirled through the air and caught him in the chest as he sprang upward. Its momentum captured him, yanked him off his feet again and smashed him, headfirst, through the passenger door of a late model Camry. He staggered back and this time saw Lilith flying toward him bearing a huge, blazing, crimson sword.

He jumped out of the way, and the sword came down, slicing the car in half.

The incredible effort had left Lilith expended, momentarily vulnerable. Angel sprang and delivered a series of powerful uppercuts to her midsection and chest, making her lurch backward, her hands and face flying back, the magical sword vanishing with a hiss as he broke her concentration.

Then it was pure payback time. He glanced contemptuously over at Revodro and the other hirelings, still pounding ineffectually at the mystical barrier keeping them out of the garage.

"This one's for Gunn," he said, hitting Lilith hard enough to shatter her jaw, which he heard go with a nasty little crackle.

"Cordy," he said, pounding her face with a blow that broke her nose and sent gleaming blood spraying everywhere, leaving her looking like a prizefighter. "Can't forget Wes," he said, hitting her so hard, he left her right eye blackened and closed.

She reeled back, somehow staying on her feet. "What's the matter, Lil?" Angel asked as he delivered another punishing blow. "I get the feeling you're not having *fun* anymore. And me, I'm a gentleman. I'm thinking it should be good for you, too."

His fists crackled with energy. Each time he touched her, he took a little of her power.

"You will pay," Lilith promised, the damage to her face already starting to heal.

"Yeah, yeah, yeah," Angel muttered, kicking her through the windshield of another car. He leaped onto the hood and looked down at her. "You know I'd kill you if I could, but that's just plain impossible. You've got that whole immortality deal going on, and the Hand can't take your essence. Well, not enough to *kill* you, anyway."

Grabbing her by the neck, he hauled her up high, staring into her dazed and darkened eyes. "But, hey! Just because you can't be killed doesn't mean you can't live, I dunno, without an arm. Two, maybe. Legs can go. How about the head?"

She gestured, and another mystical bolt flew from her fingers. He moved quickly to one side, easily avoiding the lightning-like streaks of magical energy.

He was about to ask if that was all she had left when he heard a woman scream. Risking a glance over his shoulder, Angel saw two women cowering near a car a hundred feet away, while above them, flares of Lilith's magic threatened to bring another section of the roof down upon their heads.

"Choose, hero," Lilith whispered. "Me or them."

He tossed her away and ran for the women. He reached them just as the roof collapsed, and got them to safety.

When he looked back, all he saw was a trail of sparkling light near the other hole in the ceiling, where Lilith had almost certainly levitated to freedom.

"Run, run, run away," Angel said with a laugh, his pulse racing, making him feel giddy, alive with an uncharacteristic cruelty and delight. "Live to get your ass kicked another day."

Then he stopped and thought of what he'd said and how he'd felt as the words were leaving his lips. Was he acting anything like himself anymore, or was the Hand changing him, corrupting him?

An image of Gunn transformed into a demon flickered in his memory, filling him with fury, washing away his reason. *Lilith deserves everything she's getting,* Angel thought. *All this and a hell of a lot more.*

He would give her that hell soon enough. The night was nearly over, and so much had happened, yet it felt early to him, as if the night were somehow still young. And with his heart beating once more, that was how Angel felt: Young. Fresh. Ready for anything.

He smiled and went to see the others.

Revodro confronted Angel by the van. "She got away. Did she get the, uh"—he tapped his chest—"the item away from you?"

"Still safe and sound," Angel said, stretching casually—and warily taking in the significant glances the rest of the crew briefly exchanged. These guys thought they were so subtle, but that couldn't have been further from the truth. Angel was confident that he knew exactly what they were really here to do: Get the Hand whenever the chance presented itself. "Don't worry about it."

Revodro continued. "She knows about you and the

Hand now—and she's gonna be out there, trying to figure out a way of getting to you. Doesn't that bother you?"

"Not really," Angel admitted.

Vorrl, the cat-man, hissed, "What about the hostage?"

Angel laughed. "Wes? She won't kill him. She'll need him to get to me."

Wesley didn't know how long he'd been sitting in the abandoned zoo's cage, but it felt like a very long time indeed.

Nothing had changed; still no Lilith to see him, nor any other interrogators. He'd simply sat and tried not to go insane with worry. He'd had plenty of time to think, though, and had come up with a conclusion: *Lilith must be holding me as some kind of ace in the hole. But why? Things are going her way, aren't they?*

His solitude was broken by the sound of many pairs of approaching feet, accompanied by low, growling voices. Within seconds, ten of Lilith's demons—his captors Panir and Taja included—rounded the small building's corner and came into sight. Wesley's breath caught in his throat when he saw the Gunn-demon on the end of a leash, the other end in Taja's meaty hand. The unfamiliar demons stared at him in hostile silence, an uncomfortable, nervous energy moving through them.

"On your feet," Panir barked, swinging the cage door wide. "Come on, we're relocating. Get a move on!"

Wes complied, and Panir immediately shackled his wrists together. The group then made its way through the zoo toward the parking area, where Wes could see the same car he'd arrived in sitting next to two others just like it. Again, he tried his best to pay attention to what was happening around him, and managed to glean a few interesting bits here and there as the demons' conversation picked up again. Foremost among these, and truly amazing to Wesley, was the feeling he got that the demons were scared.

"She's in a hell of a state," muttered one of the demons he didn't recognize. "The vampire did a real number on her. Drove her off . . . beat her to a pulp . . . she's all shaken up, body and soul alike."

"You shouldn't be talking like that," another demon said to the one that had just spoken.

"Why?" the first one countered. "You afraid I'll jump ship?"

"Not a bad idea," a third one said, almost too low to be audible.

A few quiet moments passed. Then, from the front of the group, Taja said, "Jumping ship. Betraying Lilith by abandoning her. Now there's a concept. One I'd like to see, actually . . . right before I kill the miserable coward who'd try it."

Silence fell on the whole group then; Taja's words seemed to carry a little extra weight. Still, the whole pack appeared to be jittery as hell, if Wesley read their body language correctly.

That gave him a little boost, tiny though it was. *Angel's managed to turn the tides somehow,* Wesley thought as Panir loaded him back into the car, a sleek, brand-new Lexus. *Good show!* Even as he was blindfolded, sealing him in darkness, Wesley grinned to himself and remembered a phrase of which Cordelia was fond.

These demons are totally wigged. I wonder if there's a way I can use that to my advantage. . . .

Then someone started the Lexus, and the vehicle pulled out.

CHAPTER·FOURTEEN

Revodro, Vorrl, and the others conferred quietly as Angel again climbed into the GTX. Vorrl approached him. "What are you going to do now?"

Angel paused before turning the key in the ignition, and glanced toward the eastern sky. "Well, since the sun's going to come up in about half an hour, and believe it or not, I'm a little tired, I think I'll head back to the hotel. Get some rest before we continue this."

Vorrl had something else to say, but Angel drowned out his words with the sound of the Plymouth's engine. Seconds later he was on the road, watching the hired guns clamber back into the Humvee in the rearview mirror.

Angel easily beat them back to the hotel. He'd gotten ahead of them by two or three minutes, so that when they walked in behind him all they saw of the seven demons who'd been there waiting for him was their sodden remains on the floor and a faint red shimmer in the air. The Hand's sigil glowed on Angel's chest like a small sun as he turned and spread his arms magnanimously.

"The hotel's yours, boys! Make yourselves at home." As he headed toward his room, he added, "I'm going to catch forty winks. Then we'll see about wrapping this up."

Angel disappeared up the stairs.

After a moment, Montgomery said, "So—what, then? We just wait?"

Sazh grumbled, "We didn't take this gig to just stand around and watch."

Vorrl shook his head and kept silent. "We have our assignment, we know what to do if he slips up." The catman took a small whetstone out of one pocket, extended the claws on his left hand, and absently began sharpening them. "The Serpent's Hand will go to Lilah Morgan, one way or another. We'll see to that."

Wesley sat waiting in a cinder-block storeroom. Taja and Panir had taken him from the zoo to this music store, which was "closed for renovations," shoving him back through darkened aisles packed with CDs and tapes and into the ill-lit storeroom. Nothing was stored there except the Gunn-demon, which snarled and slavered, tied to an iron loop protruding from the wall on the opposite side from where Wesley was deposited. The Gunn-demon had a little rope; he could move around a few feet, but that was all.

Again, Wes wasn't sure how long he'd been here, though it felt like less time than he'd spent in the cage at the zoo. From the way his stomach growled, he thought it must be nearing lunchtime. He'd tried to stretch out on the floor and get some rest, but Panir, apparently anxious to cause Wesley as much physical discomfort as was allowed, had decided that pose looked too relaxed and had forced Wesley to sit up again. So Wesley obediently sat, and carefully listened.

For the last good while it had only been Taja, Panir, the pitiful, horrible Gunn-demon, and himself in the storeroom. His jailers, who had at least seemed to be on friendly terms with one another back at the zoo, were now visibly getting on one another's nerves. Wes listened as closely as he could without making it obvious what he was doing.

"You're not hearing what I'm saying," Panir grumbled. "Lilith hasn't shown up yet, and do you know why?" Taja eyed him sourly. Panir continued: "Me either. That's the point. What's going on out there? Why're we in the dark like this?"

"Lilith is probably just regrouping after her encounter with the vampire. I have every confidence that her plan will proceed."

Panir snorted. "Her plan? Let's talk about that. Last I heard, she was missing a couple of key ingredients for her plan, like those last two perfect souls. What if the whole thing just falls apart?"

Taja got visibly upset at that. He faced Panir, and Wesley noticed Taja's hand straying close to the dagger in his belt. "I've said it before," the big demon intoned menacingly. "Anybody thinks about jumping ship, I'll put a knife through his head. And I mean anyone. Even you."

Just then Wesley heard the store's front door open and close; soon a new demon entered and greeted Panir and Taja—the former with noticeably more warmth than the latter. Wesley thought he recognized the newcomer as one of the disgruntled pack that had taken him from the petting zoo.

Only one? Wesley thought excitedly. *What's happened to all the rest of those chaps? Could their numbers be dwindling?*

"Gart," Panir said, shaking the new demon's hand. "You ready to move?"

"As long as one of you handles that thing." Gart indicated the Gunn-demon.

"Got it under control," Taja said, with an air of superiority. "No need for you to get your hands dirty." Wesley imagined he could see hackles rise whenever Taja and Gart looked at each other . . .

. . . and he decided to take a chance.

"I say, Gart," Wesley called out, causing all three demons to look at him in surprise. "Were you able to secure that transportation I heard you mention? Passage to Brazil, wasn't it?"

Panir barked, "Shut your hole, monkey-boy," while Gart simply stared in confusion, but Taja's inhuman eyes lit up with anger. He kept silent, but didn't take his stare from Gart's face.

Nervously, Gart said, "So, Lilith ought to turn things around now, huh? This thing—" and he indicated Gunn again—"ought to do the trick for the vampire, right? Won't take it long to find him and kill him, right?"

Ignoring that, Taja took a step toward Gart.

"What's this about Brazil? What's he talking about?"

Gart stammered. "Huh? I . . . I . . . I don't know! He's just making things up!"

For a moment, Wesley thought the tension would pass—but then Taja slipped his knife from its sheath and roared, "Liar! I've suspected your good-for-nothing hide from the beginning! You're a traitor!"

"There are traitors, yes," Wesley said wearily. "How do you think we knew so much about your operation if there weren't betrayers on the inside?"

"You're dead," Taja snarled at the accused demon.

Panir drew a blade of his own and said, "Hey, now, wait a minute," but already Taja was lunging past him, a vicious thrust aimed at Gart's midsection, and suddenly the three demons seemed to disappear in a whirlwind of flashing blades.

Or at least that's how they looked out of the corner of Wesley's eye; he wasn't paying attention to them so much as he was trying to get to the door, having jumped up and run for it as soon as Taja attacked Gart.

He actually had one hand on the doorknob when one of the demon's feet lashed out and struck him in the ankles. Wesley went down hard on one shoulder, and his head bounced off the poured concrete floor with enough force to make him see a few stars.

Wes twisted around, his hopes of getting out the door greatly diminished, and simply tried to move out of the way of the three combatants. Instead, he was right in the thick of it, barely avoiding knife thrusts—and the slavering attacks of the Gunn-demon, who was so crazed by the action that he went after anything that moved and was in his reach.

"Stop it!" Panir shouted, nodding at the raging Gunn-demon, who had already slashed him and another demon. "That thing'll rip us to pieces."

The trio of demon fighters pulled away from one another and the Gunn-demon, each nursing nasty-looking knife and claw wounds. Wesley was backed into a corner as Panir jabbed a finger at him.

"This is all his doing!" Panir hissed, and to Wesley's intense dismay, Taja now seemed to be in agreement. The big demon shifted his grip on his knife and approached Wesley, who hadn't made it back up off the floor yet.

"We were supposed to keep you alive," Taja said, his voice glacially cold. "But nobody makes a fool of me. Looks like you had a tragic accident here."

Taja raised the knife, and Wesley closed his eyes, and then the door to the storeroom exploded off its hinges and sailed across the room, slamming into the far wall right next to the Gunn-demon. A voice more menacing than even Taja's said, "You three are pathetic."

A huge, red-skinned, shirtless demon in black leather pants stood framed in the doorway, a wicked-looking sword in one hand. Wes recognized him from the Lo-town slaughter, had even heard one of Lilith's troops call him by name: Balthezar.

Panir said, "We were, uh, we were just—"

But Balthezar didn't seem interested in any of their explanations. With one long, graceful sweep of the sword, he lopped Panir's head from his body. Gart shrieked, but the shriek cut off as Balthezar skewered Gart's throat, briefly pinning him to the concrete block wall.

Pulling the sword free, Balthezar rounded on Taja, who said, "Hey, now, let's not be hasty here! I—"

"Oh, shut up," Balthezar said disgustedly, as behind him Gart's body slid slowly to the floor. "I was listening outside the door for ten minutes before I came in. You hotheads and traitors make me sick."

Taja tried to say "But," but he couldn't, as Balthezar had just sliced the big demon's torso almost completely in half in a move so fast, Wesley hadn't even seen it. Wesley swallowed hard when Balthezar turned to him.

"That was pretty clever," Balthezar said, helping Wesley to his feet. "Manipulating these low-level hairballs like that into fighting one another so you could try to escape." Several other demons trooped into the storeroom then, and began preparing to transport Gunn. Balthezar leaned down and lowered his voice: "Just don't try it with me, or you *will* have an unfortunate accident. Understand?"

Wesley gulped again, and nodded.

Balthezar said, "Good. Now come on, you've got a date with Lilith tonight, and I'm your personal escort."

In the tiniest of whispers, Wesley said, "I can't wait."

Laughing, Balthezar hauled Wesley away from the carnage.

What a gorgeous day, Cordelia thought bleakly as she stared out the huge picture window of David Nabbit's island estate, a place he'd purchased the year before, as he put it, "for tax purposes." Bright afternoon sunlight beat down pleasantly on the lovely beach below, and deep blue waves crashed in the vast Pacific Ocean beyond. *Wish I could appreciate it.*

Turning away, she surveyed the interior of David's luxurious house, aware of just how out of it she must be for this place not to send her into fits of excited giggles. How many times in her life was she going to get flown on a private jet to a private island in Hawaii and be lodged in a spectacular beach house? *Well, one thing's for sure, I could think of better circumstances for it.*

Outside, next to the gigantic swimming pool, Elaine McCarthy reclined in a deck chair, dressed in a tiny bikini, sunning herself. *Not a care in the world,* Cordelia decided, and would have frowned at the woman if she knew it wouldn't hurt. She gave David a mental scolding for keeping such revealing swimwear at the house for "unexpected guests." At least he hadn't suggested she try on one of the suits herself.

Elaine's nonchalant state of mind, Cordy figured, was the diametric opposite of hers; her stomach had been tied in knots since getting on David's plane, she hadn't been able to eat in something like nine hours and, despite the beauty of her surroundings, she was about to go completely stir-crazy.

From behind her, David said, "You, uh, you look about as tightly wound as I feel." Cordelia didn't move as David came into the living room, wearing fresh clothes, his hair still wet from the shower. By her count, it was the third shower he'd taken since their arrival; either he found comfort in bathing, or he sweated a lot when he was this nervous.

"I wonder what Angel's doing right now," Cordy murmured. "And what's happening with Wes, and Gunn." She looked over at David, who settled down onto a plush leather couch facing the window. "Hey . . . way out here, you think we'll know it if the world ends?"

David chuckled a nervous chuckle—everything about him seemed nervous, Cordy thought, even more so than usual—and he said, "Y'know, that reminds me. A funny thing happened to me on the way to the helipad . . . sort of a close encounter of the demon kind."

"Huh? What're you talking about?"

Embarrassed, and with his face growing slightly redder with each word, David related to Cordelia the close call he'd had late the night before with the two demons and his helicopter.

Cordy sat down in an oversized wicker chair near the sofa. "Well, thank goodness you and your pilot are okay, but, David, that doesn't make any sense! Why would Lilith send people after you?"

"Well, uh . . . Angel said it was because everybody saw me there with you, and then saw you with him. I'm sure it wasn't over anything I said to her when she cornered me after the party broke up."

Cordelia's jaw dropped open. "Excuse me? I thought you'd left before things went crazy!"

David explained how he'd been cornered, first by a shareholder, then by Lily Pierce.

"And you talked to Angel about all this?" Cordy asked.

He nodded.

Cordelia was dumbfounded. "But, but . . . why didn't you tell me about any of this earlier?"

His shoulders lifted, then dropped. "I didn't want to, y'know, worry you unnecessarily."

"Good grief, man, you had a conversation with, like, the Queen of All Bad Stuff! What'd she say?"

David bunched his eyebrows together. "Umm . . . she said she could smell perfection in me, and, uh, she got really close to me and looked into my eyes, but then she was, like, 'Perfect trust,' and jerked back away from me. She said I was useless to her, and I should just take off. So I did, believe me."

Cordelia sat back, amazed, as her mind whirled with the implications of this. *At least Angel knows about it,* she thought, remembering David mentioning that he and Angel had talked. *Perfect trust . . . and she couldn't use it, huh?* She glanced back out the window at Elaine, who had rolled over onto her back and untied the top of her bathing suit.

Cordy hooked one leg over one of the chair's arms and started thinking. According to what Wes had told her, the way Lilith had gotten to Elaine was through the woman's desire to find perfect love. She'd jumped through Lilith's hoops and wound up with the perfect man, the perfect relationship, the perfect romance, right? And she'd found it. She had perfect love inside her.

Cordelia couldn't help thinking, *Lilith didn't want David because of his perfect trust, but she was cool with Elaine and her perfect love.*

Weird. It just didn't add up. Adding to that, Cordelia vividly remembered the coldhearted things Elaine had said after the massacre in Lo-town, as well as all the rotten stuff that had come out of her ungrateful mouth about Angel after he'd done so much to save her sorry butt.

Perfect love, my eye . . .

"You look like your brain's going a mile a minute," David said. "What're you thinking?"

Cordelia exhaled slowly. "Just trying to figure some things out, that's all."

David squinted, and said, "Huh. Like what? Maybe I could—"

They were interrupted by the sound of a sliding-glass door opening and closing, and seconds later Elaine walked into the room, still in the bikini, a towel draped loosely around her neck. She was stunning, an absolute knockout, and Cordelia knew that Elaine knew it. The knowledge was conveyed in every move she made, every pose. Cordelia glanced at David, and saw from the color in his cheeks that Elaine's appearance was by no means lost on him, even though he seemed to be trying not to look anywhere below the woman's neck.

"How's, uh, how's the weather?" David asked, and Cordy could tell he instantly regretted the lame question.

Elaine just glared at him. "Don't you have any decent sunscreen?" she asked, as if it were the most normal question in the world. "That cheap American stuff leaves my skin feeling all oily."

"I'm, I'm, I'm sorry," David stuttered, taken aback. "I, uh, I'm sending my pilot to get some supplies soon, so he can try to find something else. . . ."

Cordelia watched the woman pace over to David's bar, which Cordy had already discovered was stocked with a wide variety of sodas and fruit juices—and nothing else. Elaine pushed a few bottles around, then cast a withering glance over her shoulder. "All I wanted was a scotch and water, and you've got nothing. Great."

David's head sank so far down, Cordelia thought it was going to disappear between his shoulders. She was up and across the room in an instant, eyes flashing. Elaine saw her coming and turned, one eyebrow cocked upward.

"Apologize to him right now!" Cordy demanded.

Elaine laughed softly. "Apologize? For what? For this lousy bar? He should be apologizing to me."

Cordelia almost balled up a fist and punched her. Instead, with every bit of contempt she could muster, she said, "You sold your soul for perfect love, huh? Is that what you think? Well, I've got news for you, you blond *tramp*. You've got no love in your heart at all, much less perfect love. What you got out of the deal is perfect *selfishness*."

Elaine looked poised to come back with a much more vicious retort—but then, as Cordelia watched, the words seemed to sink in. It was as if a mask had fallen away from Elaine's face, revealing a tiny, vulnerable, tragic young girl, exposing even more of her true soul to Cordy than had her brief moment of clarity at Lo-town.

Did that get to her? Cordelia wondered in surprise, watching Elaine's eyes. *Did that actually hit the mark?*

Perhaps. But after those few flickers of unshielded humanity, Elaine's mask returned, her features growing cold once more . . . though perhaps not quite to the same degree. She turned away from Cordy, withdrawn now and even more distant than before.

"I guess that one eye sees things pretty clearly, huh?" Elaine said, and then before Cordelia could respond, she glanced at David and offered, "Sorry." Then the tall, beautiful blonde turned and walked away, disappearing into one of the six bedrooms.

Cordelia tried to meet David's eyes, but he wouldn't look at her. A silence descended on the room, and Cordy sat back down, pondering Elaine's flash of vulnerability, and her subsequent reticence.

Maybe there's hope for her yet, she said to herself, but didn't know whether to believe it.

• • •

The sun crawled across the sky in Los Angeles, beating down on a city that continued in its routines even as corruption threatened to engulf it, like a cancer victim in fierce denial.

When Angel emerged from his room and headed down to the lobby, he found Montgomery, alone, performing a meditative kata, similar to t'ai chi but unlike any form he'd seen before—particularly considering the waves of lambent blue light Montgomery's hands left in the air as they moved. The hired thug stopped, the light fading as soon as he became aware of Angel's presence.

"Interesting technique you've got there," he said, descending the stairs. "Where's everybody else?"

"Raiding your icebox, I think." Montgomery paused, then said, "I could teach you, you know."

Angel gestured dismissively as he walked past. "Don't bother. I've got you beat hands down already. Gather the rest of the boys, would you? It's time to get back to it."

He missed the black look Montgomery shot him as he walked out the door.

As the sun's final rays faded out, Angel led them to another demon lair, this one a little more upscale than the last few; the floor of the office's lobby was inlaid marble, and security cameras tracked them as they came. Angel saw and ignored them. By now, Lilith's servants were well-alerted that he was coming, and had taken steps to arm themselves; the demons he faced in this suite of offices all carried wooden stakes, and two of them were actually outfitted with flame-throwers.

The flame-throwers might have worked, too—if Angel hadn't disabled one by throwing a demon into it so hard that the nozzle lodged inside the demon's ribcage, and taken out the other by knocking it and its operator through one of the office's windows. Angel took a moment to watch demon and flame-thrower disappear in a ball of fire as they impacted the concrete six floors below.

The rest of Lilith's minions were a simple matter. More of their essences flowed into him, sizzling, setting him alight inside.

Finally, there was only one demon left, a smallish male with yellow scales and fins. Angel found him cowering inside a broom closet and was about to drag him out when Revodro's baseball bat appeared in front of his face, blocking his path.

Angel's vampiric face grew even fiercer as he scowled and turned, raising one eyebrow at Revodro. "What is this?"

"You got to leave that one alone," Revodro said, and his colleagues drew their own weapons as Angel watched.

"Really. And why is that?"

"Because he works for us," came a woman's voice.

Angel recognized it immediately and said, "Lilah," even before Lilah Morgan stepped out of the shadows. "So your lapdogs called you, huh? Told you I was getting out of line?"

"You're doing your job very well. But that fellow in the closet is our employee. We don't want him hurt."

Angel opened his mouth as if to say something—but instead ducked below the bat, spun on the ball of one foot and drove his other straight into the cowering demon's chest. The Hand did its job, and the demon immediately withered as the sigil drank in his soul.

Angel straightened. "Hell do I care."

The sudden tension in the room crackled as the hirelings waited for their cue from Lilah. She gritted her teeth, livid. "So that's it? Hunting season on all demons? Your friend Doyle would have thought a lot of that plan."

Angel didn't respond, though Lilah's mention of Doyle caught him off-guard. Doyle, his former colleague, who'd given his life valiantly to save many others . . . Doyle, who was half demon himself.

This is different, the Hand whispered inside him. *There was no Lilith then, no chance to perform this heroic task. And who knows what hold Lilith might have been able to gain over your friend if this crisis had come when he was alive. Your path is straight and clear, Angel. Do not deviate from it.*

Heartened, Angel's resolve returned, and he squared his shoulders as he looked each of the bruisers in the eye, glaring, daring them to move.

Lilah pressed him. "What about the demon in you?"

He smiled, bravado solid. "I could ask you the same question."

"And Gunn?"

Angel's smiled quivered, then faded. *Sacrifices must be made*, the Hand hissed. *You're saving an entire world!* His features stayed vampiric, but he finally broke eye contact, his soul deeply and painfully conflicted. Finally he said, "It's a war."

Long moments passed . . . then Revodro lowered the aluminum bat. No one else moved as Angel walked out of the room.

CHAPTER FIFTEEN

Lilith stood in the basement of one of her lesser-known holdings in northern Los Angeles, an auto body repair business. Both of the bays above were littered with the bodies of some of her "stock," the prisoners she kept so that she could absorb their souls for sustenance whenever she needed to. These feedings, of course, had nothing to do with her quest for 1,000 perfect souls. She was part-demon, and immortal, but not all powerful. Not yet, anyway. And dipping into the wellspring of the 900 plus souls she'd consumed for this base purpose would have defeated her larger goal.

Now she was back to full strength, the injuries she had sustained from the vampire had completely healed, and the two people in the basement with her were about to make her night even better.

At a glance, this basement looked nothing like a torture chamber. Four cinder-block walls, a drain in the floor, presumably for oil spillage, a single cinder-block chair . . . and a round mirror floating in midair. Lilith walked slowly past the thin bald man shackled to the chair, running her finger along the edge of his trembling face. She didn't think he felt her touch; his teeth were gritted, his eyes squeezed shut, as he endured the latest horror to which Lilith's torturer was subjecting him. His designer suit was wrinkled and ruined, his body rank.

"Should've seen this guy as an opportunity to find a perfect soul from the beginning," she said.

The torturer shrugged. Or rather, he made the movements of his body that passed for a shrug. At nearly seven feet tall, with a tube-like body and two short, thick, powerful legs, writhing squid-like tentacles that could emit electric charges like an eel, and a head that held little more than a maw lined with sharp teeth, the torturer's true emotions remained largely his own.

I can tell what's on your mind, Lilith thought, looking down at the man on the table. *Because the torturer's mirror shows me.*

She glanced up at the round, smooth, reflective disk hovering a foot above the man's head; dark, murky images swam in the glass, nightmare shapes whose teeth and fangs snapped and tore. Those things only existed in his mind, but that was enough to do the trick, especially with this one.

Her victim's name was Anton Smythe, and he was the "inside man" Wolfram & Hart had planted within her organization: the telepath who'd fed Angel Investigations all of their information. The man who should, by all rights, have led Angel into a trap from which he could not escape. The very thought that Angel had invaded her property, taken the Serpent's Hand, and succeeded in fleeing with it still made her furious.

So much so that, since right after Angel's departure from her mansion, Anton Smythe had been here, having his life and his sanity slowly destroyed by the torturer. Or at least that was the plan; the torturer had been giving her status reports on the hour, every hour, all night long, and to both his and Lilith's surprise, Smythe wasn't breaking.

"What are you doing to him now?" Lilith asked the torturer. Rather than use conventional means, the torturer had settled on devices that would attack and damage the man's psyche. A telepath's mind was, after all, thousands of times more sensitive than his body.

The torturer answered her in a voice as dry as straw. "I have tapped into the violent ward of the nearest psychiatric hospital. All of the pain and anger and desperate rage of the patients there now inhabit Mr. Smythe's mind."

Lilith raised her eyebrows as Anton Smythe trembled in the chair. "And he still won't crack?"

The torturer's body swayed from side to side. "I have never seen such resolve, Mistress."

"Hmmm . . ." Any lingering doubts Lilith might have had slipped away. The psychic's incredible fortitude hadn't been apparent to Lilith until she'd confronted him with his current extreme circumstances, but she now saw that Anton Smythe clearly had some measure of dark perfection within him. She only had to identify its true nature . . . and exploit it. "Bring him out of it."

The torturer's body bobbed once. The mirrored disk flipped onto its back, then floated across the room and settled in a corner.

Immediately, Anton Smythe opened his eyes, aware of his surroundings, his breathing ragged, his eyes filled with pain. He focused on the torturer, then on Lilith, but remained silent.

Lilith went to his side and stroked his head. "Anton," she said softly, "I should've known you were something special. Telepaths are rare enough as it is, but for you to have resisted my specialist like this . . . well, it's just unheard of." She put her nose down next to his face, then his chest, inhaling deeply. Straightening, she said, "Oh, yes. You have what I need."

She turned to the torturer and said, "Get him out of these shackles. I want to have a talk with him, in a much more comfortable and private setting."

Minutes later, Lilith and Anton Smythe sat in her office upstairs. Each held a goblet of wine, which Lilith had poured herself. Smythe watched her like a trapped animal, his whole body tense, waiting for her to attack. Lilith noted that he hadn't brought the wine anywhere near his lips; he probably thought his glass was poisoned. Silly man.

"Anton," Lilith said, leaning forward sensuously, "let me ask you a question. What is it that you want most, in the whole world?"

Smythe stared at her as if she'd lost her mind. *Appropriate response,* she thought.

"You see," she continued, glossing over his silence, "I'm good at reading people. Very good, if I do say so myself. I think I know what kind of man you are. Now, when I combine that with what I've learned of telepaths in general, it leads me to hazard a guess. I think what you want most, in the whole wide world, is knowledge."

There, she saw it, the flicker in his eyes. *Knowledge it will be, then.*

She ticked items off a list in her mind. One, this man had such immense mental barriers built up around his psyche that it would be virtually impossible for anyone to break through them, as her torture master could attest; two, the objective of the "persuasion" to which he'd been subjected was information about Wolfram & Hart, which he was clearly prepared to defend to the death; three, he had the kind of training that takes a lifetime to master. Logically, that meant Anton Smythe had been *raised* by Wolfram & Hart.

She knew the law firm engaged in such activities—find a talented child, indoctrinate it with unshaking loyalty, cultivate its powers, then send it out to do the dirty work. It was practically a given that Anton Smythe's story was exactly that. Lilith decided to do some further digging.

"Anton . . . there is someone at Wolfram and Hart who trained you, isn't there? Someone who raised you, who's taken care of you since you were a little boy?"

Smythe's trembling grew more pronounced. She could tell he'd exhausted himself maintaining his mental shields, and was betting that simple requests for nonsensitive information wouldn't meet with much resistance. She was right.

Smythe nodded, reluctantly but unquestionably. Lilith kept on: "This man—is it a man? Or a woman? A man, then. This man is like a father to you, is he not? Someone you love, and respect? Someone you trust? Probably the *only* one you trust."

Her questions were dead on. Smythe actually spoke this time: "Y-yes."

"What is this honorable man's name?"

Tears formed in Smythe's eyes. "Nuh-Nathaniel."

"Nathaniel. I suppose Nathaniel performed all the duties of a teacher and a parent, did he not? Disciplined you when you failed, rewarded you when you succeeded?" Smythe nodded again, miserably. "And when he rewarded you . . . did he give you . . . knowledge?"

The strain of endless hours of torture finally broke through what little composure Smythe had left, and he collapsed forward, elbows on his knees, sobbing. "Yes, yes, he did, he did . . ."

Lilith adopted a much more businesslike demeanor. "Anton. Look at me." The telepath slowly raised his head, trying to get his tears under control. "The knowledge he fed to you, scrap by scrap, was it from texts? Ancient, forbidden writings, things such as that? Tell me."

Smythe swallowed. He didn't realize, Lilith could tell, that since they'd entered the office she'd been using persuasive powers other than the invasive psionic torture her specialist had employed. *I can still be subtle when I need to be,* she thought smugly to herself, gently manipulating Smythe's hormonal levels and neural responses. Easing him. Comforting him. Creating a more . . . suggestible atmosphere.

"Sometimes it was from books," Smythe finally said, wiping tears away with the back of his hand. "Sometimes Nathaniel showed me these, these glimpses. Glimpses of truth. You understand? Truths about, about *everything.*"

"Oh, I understand, Anton. And I know he gave you this knowledge bit by bit because he didn't want to overwhelm you. But I have something to tell you, if you'll listen to me."

Smythe's expression turned guarded, skeptical, and Lilith raised her palms, the image of guilelessness. "Don't worry, I'm not trying to deceive you. I only want you to know this one thing."

Obviously torn, Smythe still couldn't help himself. She had identified his dark perfection . . . *greed.* His hunger for knowledge, his desire to learn the secrets of the ages, was a form of greed he had wrestled with all his life, one he honestly believed only Wolfram and Hart could ever fully sate, thus his loyalty to them.

But her delicate persuasion, given time, was powerful indeed. He trembled. "One thing—what?"

"A look . . . a taste of what you want, Anton." She lowered one hand, but moved the other one so that it was directly in his line of sight. She spread her fingers wide, and there on her palm a kind of window opened up—a portal, a gateway for the mind. "I want to give you a slice of the truth . . . about *everything*."

Instantly Smythe was transfixed, his body rigid. Lilith knew the window she'd opened now seemed to be expanding, filling Smythe's entire field of vision, threatening to swallow him whole.

She hadn't lied. What she was showing him now was a vast ocean of knowledge, the sum of every bit of information ever recorded in human history; access to this pool of enlightenment was but one of the many hundreds of abilities Lilith had amassed over the millennia. She smiled as Smythe's wide eyes watered, and a thin, silvery line of saliva spilled from one corner of his mouth. The goblet of wine fell from his nerveless fingers.

And then she snapped the window shut.

Smythe shrieked, almost convulsed. "No!" he cried. "Bring it back, please, bring it back! That was . . . that was more than I'd ever seen before, so much more. I . . . I have to see it. I have to learn more, *please* . . . !"

Lilith relaxed in her chair, letting Smythe swing on the end of the line for a moment. Setting the hook nice and firmly.

"I can do better than let you look through a window, Anton," she finally purred. His body practically vibrated with desire. "I can let you *enter* that place, exist inside it." Smythe panted, his mouth hanging open, his eyes wild. " . . . for a price."

"Any price!" he nearly screamed. "Any price, anything, to go there, to *be* there, anything! Name it!"

Lilith leaned forward again. In a low, seductive whisper, she breathed, "Kill Nathaniel."

She enjoyed his reaction to that.

She further enjoyed the tears that spilled freely down his face as Anton Smythe's mind began formulating ways to kill off Nathaniel Reed. Easy ways.

"There," Smythe said, his voice shuddering. "There, there, I've got it! Now—now, give it to me, now, please?"

"Of course." Lilith smiled. Gesturing with one hand, she opened a doorway and let Smythe's mind slip through it. She could feel his joy, his exultation as his consciousness floated free in the ocean of knowledge, swam through currents of ideas, explored reefs built of history.

She smiled as hot, searing pain slammed Smythe's mind back into his body. Blinking, dazed, he stared down at Lilith's brand, newly burned into his chest— and gave out a high, desperate keening as he felt his soul rip loose from its moorings and disappear into her.

"I . . . ," he began, his eyes glazing over. "I don't understand . . . you said I could exist in that place. . . ."

"True," she answered, smiling sweetly. "But I don't believe I ever specified for how *long*."

Lilith stood, done with him, the sweet sensation of triumph flooding through her as the 1,000th soul joined the other 999. Now she had everything she needed . . .

. . . except, of course, to get the Serpent's Hand back from Angel, and to tie up the loose end called Elaine McCarthy. The McCarthy woman still posed a threat;

one so close to Lilith, connected on such a level—and yet tainted by improper influences and was indeed a danger. But, well, so long as she didn't get too close, it wouldn't really matter. Let her hide; let her witness the end of her world from afar.

Still irritated about the McCarthy woman, and still furious about Angel, but feeling somewhat better now that her acquisition of souls was complete, Lilith left the repair shop and headed back to her troops.

On her way out, she said to the torturer, "Dispose of Smythe for me, would you? Thanks."

Angel's raids on Lilith's holdings continued—though he was dismayed to learn that Wolfram & Hart had hired several teams of mercenaries, in addition to the group that was with him, to attack Lilith's holdings. His frustration was palpable as he went through the burned remains of offices and businesses that had belonged to Lilith, finding the bodies of demons he hadn't killed.

That feeling had troubled him deeply. The demons were dead, the overall problem that much closer to being solved, but Angel wasn't happy about it. Instead, he felt as if he'd been robbed of an opportunity. He wanted to fight this battle on his own, to stand victorious without the aid of those who were usually his enemies.

He wasn't working for Wolfram & Hart, and he didn't have any kind of agreement with them as to how this battle would be waged. He and the law firm were on the same side for the moment: Every human on the planet was at risk, and that gave Angel and the law firm a mutual interest. They had a kind of truce and it was temporary and that was all.

But he was the champion. He was on the side of right.

Why then did it feel like there was something very wrong about the way he was thinking and feeling about all of this?

Wolfram and Hart, the Hand whispered. *They only want to steal your glory.*

This isn't about glory, Angel thought, praying that he was right, that he wasn't deluding himself, or allowing himself to be led by the Hand. But he wasn't going to slip. He was in complete control. *It's about saving lives,* Angel insisted.

Of course, of course . . .

For a second, Angel thought he heard laughter deep in his mind, but the sound was coming from a couple of teenagers joyriding down the streets of the city just ahead of them.

As the war against Lilith's empire raged on, so did the normal reign of terror that faced L.A.

Pulling up before a supposedly abandoned power plant, Angel hopped out of the GTX, Revodro and his crew right behind him.

"What's the deal?" Revodro asked. "This place wasn't on the list of Lilith's hideouts."

"Just hang back and let me take care of it."

"Take care of what?"

Angel turned, furious at the very thought that *he* had

to explain himself to scum like this. But he didn't want them getting in the way, either, so . . .

"I checked messages after the last bloodbath," Angel explained coolly. "Turns out evil isn't napping just 'cause I've been busy. A couple of sorority girls got themselves kidnapped by Y'grath worshipers looking to do a little blood sacrifice to open a portal between this world and a pretty nasty one."

"You got all that on a message?" Revodro asked sarcastically. "My machine cuts off after the first thirty seconds."

"The source is reliable. This is just something I've got to take care of," Angel said. "Then we can get on with the really fun stuff."

Vorrl the cat-man shook out his fur. "This is bull! What do we care about some humans? We were hired to help you hunt down Lilith and her demons!"

"I wouldn't expect you to understand," Angel said as he walked up to the iron gate leading to the electrical plant. "So just deal another hand of cards or do whatever it is you losers do while I take care of all the heavy lifting. I never asked for any of you tagalongs, anyway."

Revodro and Vorrl sputtered and cursed, but went back to the van.

Angel entered the grounds of the plant, looking for signs of the victims.

The Hand decided it was time to make its displeasure known; Angel nearly stumbled as his heart skipped several beats.

Vorrl and Revodro were right. You have a mission, it

said, exerting a small, steady, painful pressure upon his heart. *Don't get distracted.*

He had a mission, all right. He had sworn to protect the innocent of this city, and those people were currently at a greater risk than ever because word was out that Angel was . . . preoccupied.

Suddenly, a small group of armored warriors blinked into existence on the power lines above, while others manifested atop the many small steel shacks surrounding Angel.

They weren't Y'grath worshipers at all; Angel could tell by their distinctive scent—and by the sudden excitement welling up inside him, delivered first class by the Hand.

Demons! it roared triumphantly as Angel's unnatural pulse accelerated.

"Not very smart, vampire," one of the demons growled. "You've come right to us, just as Mistress Lilith said you would."

"Come on," Angel said, practically laughing out loud. "This is the best Lilith can come up with for a trap? Two or three dozen of you and I'd say *maybe* you had a shot at taking me down. But this . . ."

Then the demons leaped down to face him, and Angel could see that they all wore matching armor and the exact same grinning death's head mask.

"We were told we're all the same to you," the closest of the demons hissed.

"Yes, the only good demon is a dead demon," another added with a snicker.

"So I suppose it wouldn't matter to you if one of us

was your friend Gunn, now would it?" a third taunted.

Angel realized Lilith's plan with a nasty shock: Since he couldn't see their faces, it was possible that any one of them might—or might not—have been Gunn. He couldn't use the power of the Hand to fight these warriors because it would kill indiscriminately; it wouldn't care if Gunn was among the slain. But Angel would.

The demons attacked, delivering crushing blows with bludgeons and staffs. Angel took their punishment, raising his arms only to defend himself, whirling and kicking only to try to gain some room to think.

Around them, the plant roared to life, the lines above crackling with blue-white energy. One of the demons sliced at the lines with a scythe, allowing several to fall directly at Angel. He moved just in time, the sparks striking the ground instead of him, but it was hopeless. He either had to use the Hand—or retreat.

"Come on, boys!" someone shouted. "Time to earn your pay!"

Angel saw Revodro and the others arrive, the aluminum baseball bat swinging and taking out one of the demons.

"Stay out of this," Angel yelled. "It isn't your fight!"

The mercs waded in, anyway, their pent-up fury and frustration clearly overriding any concern they might have had at their masters punishing them for disobeying Angel's direct commands.

"Don't kill them," Angel yelled. "One of them might be Gunn!"

A demon smashed Angel in the mouth, shutting him

up temporarily. Another landed a blow in his midsection, doubling him over, then a rain of blows fell upon his back and his skull. They wanted to take him alive, capture him and take him to Lilith so she could somehow extract the Hand. Angel was sure of it.

He couldn't let that happen, but he couldn't risk killing any of them, either.

With a bellow of rage, he rose upward, his arms jamming at the sky, and shook off his attackers. Grabbing a fallen staff, he used it to force the demons away. He fought as best he could without the Hand, but even as he saw the ranks of his enemies thinning because of Revodro and the others, he felt his own energy dropping fast.

Angel swept the legs out from under the closest demon and stumbled back, right into an attack from another of Lilith's warriors. A bludgeon struck the small of his back; another, his still-ringing skull. He faltered, the additional power he had drained from Lilith fading.

Take them, the Hand roared. *Don't be a coward, don't be a fool. We need their essences. The time will soon be upon us!*

"No!" Angel yelled.

The Hand punished him, wrapping its cold fingers around his heart and squeezing tight, and the pain was worse than anything he'd felt since his time in Hell. His pulse, so precious to him now, faltered and threatened to stop completely, and Angel teetered for a moment on the verge of genuine panic. But he wouldn't take the essences of his enemies, not when one of them might be his friend. . . .

"To hell with Angel," Revodro hollered. "I'm tired of sitting it out and letting him have all the fun!"

Angel gasped as he saw the mercs produce knives, a sword, a crossbow, and a semiautomatic.

"Don't!" Angel shouted as he saw Revodro stand over a fallen demon, his sword raised.

With a cry of triumph, Revodro sliced the demon's head clean off—and grinned as it rolled to Angel's feet.

"Grow up," Revodro said. "This is war. That means people die."

Angel knelt quickly and tore the mask from the severed head.

It wasn't Gunn.

Angel saw another of Revodro's crew about to kill one of Lilith's demons. He ran to intercede, delivering a flying kick that knocked the reptilian mercenary away from the demon warrior—then received a jarring blow from the demon's bludgeon for his trouble.

He couldn't fight them all; not the demons and Revodro's people. He couldn't win like this.

Grabbing the dancing live electrical line from the ground, he whipped it through the air, singeing as many of his opponents as he could—Lilith's demons and the Wolfram & Hart mercs alike.

"We're going," Angel said as he caught and held Revodro's gaze. "That or I'll kill you and every one of your people here and now."

Revodro hesitated for a moment, but he could see

Angel was deadly serious. He called for a retreat.

They fought the demons all the way back to Angel's car and the van, then took off, tires squealing in the night.

A few minutes later, Angel pulled the GTX into the parking lot of a strip mall, the van right on his tail. They all got out and met in a glaring pool of light cascading from a lamp set high above. Angel propped himself against the car with one hand, trying to make it look casual; his heart was still beating, but the rhythm had grown slow, the pulse feeble.

"What the hell's the matter with you?" Revodro raged. "Your friend's gone. She made him a demon, took his soul. There's no coming back from that."

Angel only glared at him.

It took Revodro a moment, then he understood. "Okay, fine. Except for you. But that was because of some Gypsy curse or something, right? That's what I read in your file, anyway. And you'd done a lot to get that kind of attention. This guy? He's nothing."

"Like that's for you to judge," Angel said with a snarl, slowly starting to feel stable again, his heart beating slowly, but regularly. "Understand something. I never wanted any of you people here. Coronach was one thing. He was a free agent, and he wasn't just in it for the money. But you guys are scum."

Vorrl hissed, the fur on his back standing up. Speaking in a low voice, but still deliberately loud enough for Angel to hear him, he said to his colleagues, "I've had my fill of this nonsense. I say we just take the Hand out of his chest right now and be done with it."

Before Angel could decide how to react to these guys finally coming right out and saying why they were here, he saw a slow-moving, preternaturally silent blue Dodge creeping up to them. The windows rolled down suddenly, and a collection of strange weapons jutted out.

"Look out!" Angel roared. But only he moved quickly enough to avoid the hailstorm of silver bullets, wooden stakes, and fiery mystical bolts that erupted from the old Dodge. From behind the van, Angel heard the mercenaries shriek in agony as they were shredded by the attack.

It wasn't until he heard the last of them fall, followed by the screech of the Dodge's tires as it sped off, that he emerged from cover to survey the horror that had been Revodro and his men.

Revodro's head had been sliced clean off. The others hadn't died so quickly or easily.

Floating in the lake of blood surrounding their bodies was a business card left by the attackers. Angel picked it up.

It read, simply, KHAN AND ASSOCIATES. The rival law firm Lilith had engaged to take on Wolfram & Hart.

Angel pocketed the card and didn't look back. He had work to do.

CHAPTER SIXTEEN

As Angel stood holding the Khan and Associates business card, the blood of five mercenaries seeping across the pavement near his boots, thousands of miles away Cordelia once again found herself staring out at the vast Pacific Ocean through the beach house's picture window. She was three time zones away from L.A., where it was already night. Here, the sun's rays had just begun to redden as Cordy watched it settle lower in the western sky.

Sitting on a huge plush couch, Cordelia gazed out at the waves washing up on the shore—a sight that had provided comfort for her since she was a tiny girl—and felt nothing. In the face of everything that had happened, the waves were just water, the beach merely sand. A shiver ran through her, and she crossed her arms, hugging herself, wishing she could feel a positive emotion, any positive emotion . . . anything besides the pain and fear and anxiety that gripped her.

David Nabbit sat beside her; every ten or fifteen minutes she heard him take in a breath as if to speak, but he hadn't said anything in the last hour. Across the room, Elaine McCarthy slept in a monstrously large recliner, her eyes covered by dark sunglasses. She'd come back into the living room, dressed in street clothes again, about an hour after her exit to the bedroom, but she hadn't said a word, just sat down in the chair and kicked back, acting as if she and Cordy hadn't spoken at all.

She looks so relaxed, Cordelia thought. She replayed in her mind the brief confrontation she'd had with Elaine, and wondered, *is it just an act?* Or was it just that she was so callous, so dead inside, so cut off from her emotions, that she actually didn't care about what was happening out there, and what might still happen to her, to all of them?

That was a scary thought, because if Elaine didn't care about herself, who knew what she might do and how it might affect all of them in the time to come if they were needed to return to action.

Cordy wondered if Angel had made a mistake, shipping Elaine off with them. Yet Elaine had been one of the thousand, a vital part of Lilith's plan, and keeping her here, Coronach's magic cutting off the connection they shared because of the deal they'd made, was important . . . it made Lilith's life more difficult, and hopefully lowered the woman's chances of making her dark dreams come true. . . .

Finally David broke the silence. "Cordy—would you

like something to drink? I've, uh, I've got all that stuff there in the bar. And I think I have some ginger ale, too, back in the kitchen."

"No thanks. I'm fine."

Another silence. "So, um, uh . . ." David tried again to start a conversation, "so that thing in Angel's chest, that's, uh, that's like the One Ring, huh? From, uh, from *The Lord of the Rings*?"

Cordy looked at him as if he had just grown two heads—and both of them were totally gross. At least, that's the look she was shooting for. " . . . I'm sorry, what?"

"The ring, like, in the book, and um, the movie, it tempts, corrupts, drives a person to evil."

"Angel's not evil," Cordy said curtly. "I've seen him when he's evil. This isn't it."

"But he's not himself. And, like, with the ring, it was gradual. Just little changes at first. Then—"

"He can handle it, whatever the stupid thing's supposed to be able to do," she said angrily. "And what you're talking about is some book, some movie . . . this is our lives. Catch the difference, the cool, refreshing flavor of non-geekcentric reality."

Cordy ran her hand through her hair, fighting back her frustration with David. "Sorry," she muttered, only catching his hurt expression out of the corner of her one unbandaged eye.

Can't he see that I'm worried enough about Angel as it is? Cordy thought. *But what am I supposed to do? He made up his mind about having us gone, and what he's doing is way out of my league in the sheer power to battle demonic hordes department.*

"David . . . ," she said quietly, "this One Ring comparison is helping exactly how?"

"Just saying—" David gulped nervously—"'Cause, y'know, the One Ring wanted to return to its master. Is that what this Serpent's Hand wants to do?"

She considered that for a moment. David had brought up a good point. What did the Hand want? But there was no way they could do anything to find the answers while they were stuck here.

"I really don't know what it wants. But . . . I don't think Lilith was its master, not from what we were told. She was just the latest person to get her hands on it."

"And now it's got its . . . y'know . . . Hand . . . on Angel. In him." David gulped. "The whole thing's kinda creepy."

Cordelia narrowed her eyes at him, the pain bringing out some irritability. "Why don't we go back to something you actually know stuff about, 'kay? Like dungeons and dumbasses or whatever your stupid game is called. . . ."

With a conciliatory expression on his face, David said, "Look, I know I was voicing some concerns about Angel, and I am worried about him, just like you, but in the end I'm confident he'll come through. Do what's right. Y'know, save the world again."

Cordelia looked back out at the waves on the beach, and didn't respond. Then she heard a low snoring from the recliner and realized Elaine was out cold. She looked back and shook her head at the woman. "Lucky her," Cordy said. "Maybe she can sleep through the end of the world, too."

David nodded.

"Y'know, I was thinking about what we were talking about before," Cordy whispered, not wanting to wake Elaine. Not that she worried about interrupting the woman's beauty sleep, or anything like that. She just didn't want her hearing this. "When you were with Lilith."

"Yeah, that was different."

"I mean . . . we've known Lilith was all about perfection, y'know, perfect souls and all that, but if she found perfect trust in you, and couldn't use it . . . and her, perfect love? I'm not buying it. I'm just thinking, that sounds like she can only use perfect, uh, badness, don't you think? Like she can't make use of positive perfection?"

David smiled enthusiastically. "Wow, that's great. I bet Angel wouldn't have been able to come up with a theory like that."

Cordelia skewered him with a look of alarm. "Why not? He saw how witchy Elaine was acting. And he knows what Lilith said to you, right? You told me you talked to him about this."

"I was trying to . . . y'know, pay you a compliment, I didn't mean—"

Cordy sprang up from the couch and whirled on him. "You told him Lilith talked to you, but you didn't tell him what she said?" she cried, and David flinched away from her.

"I . . . I . . . I'm sorry. It just, it didn't come up!"

Cordelia sat back down on the edge of the couch, her mind whirling with the implications of this. She bowed her head, slowly shaking it for a couple of seconds. *He's completely clueless,* she couldn't help thinking. "This could be important. You should have told him everything."

"But—"

And then, without warning, Cordelia's world came apart. She gasped and doubled over as what felt like a thermonuclear bomb detonated in her head.

"Cordelia!" David yelped, but she had to ignore him as the vision filled her mind, image after image, explosion upon explosion hammering at her skull. Her teeth ground together, and she pressed her palms against her temples, tried to endure, tried to ride it out—but the pain and the intensity increased. She'd had enough visions to know roughly how long they should last, but this one never seemed to end, and the mounting agony reached out and clamped down on her mind, forced her to look, to *see.*

To see the end of the world.

The violent, merciless beheading of the entire human race, the death of the entire species, etched into her brain like a tattoo done with ice picks. And as the torment reached inside her, wrapping itself around the core of her soul and tightening like razor wire, Cordelia saw the author of humanity's destruction, saw the eyes, saw the frigid, power-hungry grin.

She came out of the vision as if drowning, burst back

into reality with great gulps of air, her body spasming as David tried to help her calm down. The exertion caused her wound to open back up a tiny bit, so that a single rivulet of blood trickled down past her mouth. Without a moment's hesitation, David dabbed the blood away with a handkerchief, then produced another clean one for Cordelia's sudden tears. Her spasms degenerated into sobs.

Through all of this Elaine McCarthy hadn't moved, her eyes still hidden behind the dark glasses.

"That . . . that was one of your *visions*, wasn't it?" David asked, trying his best to be tender. Cordelia nodded mutely, blotted her eyes. "Are you, what do you, uh, can I, are you gonna be okay?"

At first Cordelia stuttered so badly that he couldn't understand her. Finally he made out her words: "I've got to call Angel."

He blinked and sat back slightly. "I'm sorry, we can't."

She surged toward him, resolve untouched by the residual muscle tremors. "This isn't the time to prove your loyalties, David! We have to call him! He has to know about what I just saw, and what you found out from Lilith before. It's probably why she was trying to kill you."

"I'm sorry, I'm sorry, but I really mean we *can't!* Angel was very specific about not being able to contact him—so I had all the phones and radios removed from the house!"

"*What?* Well then we have to get to someplace that does have a phone! Right now!"

"Cordelia—there aren't any phones on the island. At all. My, uh, my pilot's coming back, uh, sometime soon, though . . . I think. . . ."

"Sometime soon? David, you don't understand. 'Soon' isn't good enough! I can't even begin to tell you how serious this is!"

Shame bordering on what Cordelia thought was self-hatred flooded across David's face as he slowly, reluctantly spread his hands. "The whole point of bringing you here was to be, y'know, incommunicado. Not just to keep you and me safe, but to keep Lilith from tracing Elaine through electronic means. And that's what we are. Cut off. I'm *really* sorry . . . but we won't be able to call anyone until he gets back. Then we can go back down to the plane and call from there."

Cordy scowled. "How long is 'soon'?"

"I . . . uh . . . I'm not sure. Could be twenty minutes . . . could be more like four hours. I sent him to the next island over to get some more supplies."

"And there's no way we can contact him?"

David shook his head sheepishly.

Cordy stared at him for long moments, emotion after emotion playing over her face as she absorbed what he'd said. Then her shoulders slumped, and she sat back on the couch, holding her throbbing skull. "If I were in less pain I'd scream at you for a while."

"I'm sorry . . ."

She waved a hand vaguely in the air. "Not *at* you, David, just, y'know, at you. 'Cause you're convenient to scream at. 'Cause I really feel like screaming." She slowly looked up, met his eyes. "This is bad. I'm not kidding. This is very, very bad, and we need to contact Angel as soon as we can."

"I understand. And I'm really sorry. But we're going to have to sit tight for a while."

Cordelia had no response, except that fresh tears pooled in her eyes and spilled over onto her cheeks. Again, David attended to them with one of his ever-present handkerchiefs, but Cordelia couldn't help but feel that with each tear a little more energy and . . . she couldn't deny it, a little more *hope* drained out of her.

Suddenly, past all of the pain and fear, Cordelia felt very tired. She scooted closer to David and slowly settled herself against him, the unscarred side of her face resting against his chest. She heard his heartbeat flutter and accelerate as his arms hesitantly, carefully settled around her.

"Cordelia, I'm—"

"Shhh, David. You were right. We have to sit tight. So just, just be quiet and hold me, okay?"

"Okay."

She didn't add, *Because there may not be much time left.*

Elaine tried to imagine that. Tried to imagine what would happen if she herself were in, say, a car wreck, a bad one, one that sliced up her face, took away what she knew was the haunting beauty of her eyes and lips and cheekbones. Would anyone hold her the way Nabbit held the dark-haired girl across the room? Would anyone share the warmth of his body with her, and whisper in her ear that it didn't matter, that everything was all right?

The answer whispered out of the darkness.

No.

Elaine couldn't feel Cordelia's comfort, couldn't identify with the simple openness of David Nabbit's heart. And she knew with a cold, terrible certainty that no, she didn't have anyone like that.

Not anyone true.

Not anyone real.

The girl was right. She'd sold her soul to live a life of perfect selfishness.

Elaine closed her eyes behind the sunglasses, alone with her thoughts.

In Los Angeles, Angel entered Caritas, noting the place was packed, the crowd bebopping along as a sloth demon sat with his scaly blubber hung over the sides of a stool, lazily warbling at the stage's open karaoke mike.

"L . . . is for . . . the way . . . you . . . *look* . . . at . . . me. O . . . is for . . ."

Nat King Cole's swingin' rhythms never sounded . . . well, weirder.

"Love . . . was made . . . for me . . . and . . ."

Angel looked for Lorne and spotted him between a pair of attractive, ivory-skinned women with long curling tails and matching long curling horns. The women were dressed—barely—in matching gold lamé halter tops, skirts, and go-go boots. The Host tugged at the collar of his expensive pistachio-colored suit as one of the women breathed something undoubtedly seductive into his ear, then took his handkerchief from his pocket and dabbed at his suddenly sweaty forehead, careful to avoid his own short horns.

Demons. Demons, all, a pair of succubi and the Host himself, green-faced and scaly. . . . All around him, Angel took in the sight of demon revelry. Leathery wings flapped, blue-and-gold-scaled hands raised glasses and made toasts, scarlet eyes blazed.

A sudden anger filled him at the sight of these creatures enjoying themselves. He had come here countless times in the past and never before had felt so repulsed at the presence of demons and other creatures laughing and delighting in this haven of good cheer. But this time, things were different. Now he was on a mission. *I will cleanse the earth of scum like this. First, though, I have to get them out of this mystically protected place.*

Leaping on the stage, Angel snatched the microphone from the sloth demon's scaly hand and kicked over the karaoke machine, making it fall in a hail of sparks as the frightened sloth demon oozed and slithered away. His features morphed, and he went into full vampire mode as he raised the mike. "Pleased to meet you," Angel said. "Can you guess my name?"

Screams exploded, and a panic erupted. Demons fled, the place clearing out in seconds. Grinning, Angel began to count.

One Mississippi, two . . . oh, why wait?

He jumped down from the stage and strutted toward the door, ignoring the one demon who had remained behind.

Then a green hand clamped on his shoulder. "Hey, hey, what's with the ruckus?" the Host asked.

Angel pulled away from him, snarling like a wild beast. The power of the Hand rose up in him as his heartbeat quickened.

Take him. I can defeat the mystical barriers that prevent violence in this place. Together, our power is absolute!

"Whoa!" the Host hollered. "That's some major-league hunger I'm sensing there, buddy, and it's not for a hero sandwich. Or even a nice O-negative cocktail."

"I'm not . . . what I was," Angel said, struggling to keep his urges under control. This wasn't why he came here. He could kill demons any time. Yet—he wanted those who had run from the club, and he wanted the essence of the one standing before him now.

"Sorry, fella," the Host said. "Party's over. Now you just cool off and leave my patrons alone."

"I gave them a fighting chance. A full two-second lead. A lot longer now." Angel grimaced, his fangs glistening. "Maybe I don't need them, so long as I have you."

The Host stumbled back as Angel slowly advanced on him, the joy of the hunt, the thrill of watching the fearful prey see their end in his eyes overwhelming him.

No! This wasn't his purpose, this wasn't why he wanted to see the Host. He hadn't come here to kill.

Killing demons is not your purpose? the Hand whispered in the depths of Angel's soul. *It is your whole purpose now. . . .*

Shrill screams sounded from outside, in the far distance. His prey was getting away.

"News travels fast, and they're traveling faster," the Host said nervously. "Don't forget about the wards. No violence in my place!"

Angel cocked his head to one side. "I was thinking it'd be too fast to be violent." He shuddered. "I'm . . . not here to hurt you."

"Tell that thing inside you."

Forcing his vampiric features to rescind, Angel stared down at the floor, clenching and unclenching his hands. "Trying to."

"I don't have to hear you sing to know you've been a naughty boy," the Host said. "You've been playing with things that, well . . . like to play with things. Things like you. Not good."

His chest heaving, Angel said, "You've got to go. It's not safe for you here."

The Host took a few steps back, putting a table between Angel and himself. "As much as I always appreciate the concern of a dear friend, I think you might want to give me a little more to go on. Do you honestly expect me to believe you came here just to chat? You need help, doll-face, and you need it bad."

"I'm fine," Angel hissed. He hesitated, gripping the back of a chair, turning his gaze away from the Host. It was hot in here. Hadn't felt that way before, but now it was like an inferno.

He yearned to consume the essence of the demon before him. He wanted nothing more in the world than to be filled with the utter peace he felt when the power of a Hell-born creature flooded into him. Suddenly, the wood backing of the chair exploded in a cloud of splinters, jolting Angel from his thoughts and making the Host stumble back and nearly fall over another table.

"Sure, you're fine," the Host said with a nervous laugh. "And for my next number, I'll be singing a medley of Limp Bizkit's greatest hits."

"There's nothing you can do." Angel shuddered. The Hand was calling to him.

This one's no different from any other, it said. *Take him!*

Angel drew back, putting even more distance between himself and the Host. He forced himself to look at his friend.

The Host *knew* what he wanted to do. He could sense there was a part of Angel who wanted nothing more than to reach inside him and feast on his essence.

"You wouldn't," the Host said, a tremor of concern in his voice.

"It would," Angel answered coldly. A tremor passed through him as he fought his inner battle.

The Host shook his head. "So you're not in charge, huh, poopsie? Gee, who would have seen that coming?"

"Don't have time for this," Angel mumbled.

"You have time to brood, you have time for this." The Host hugged himself. "I mean, Angel, what were you thinking? The primal serpent's yacking in your ear, and it's, like, 'Here, come on, dude, just take one little bite, it's a California red apple, yum, yum, nothing at all like that forbidden one from the Tree of Knowledge.' 'Really?' 'Oh, sure.' 'Well, then, don't mind if I do.' Chomp. 'Hoo-boy, now I'm being tempted. Color me so surprised!'"

"I can control it," Angel said slowly. "I can use it . . . to make things . . . better. I can make a perfect world."

"Pride," the Host said. "It always comes downto that with your species."

Barely in control, Angel whispered, "*Leave.*"

"Leave what?" the Host asked. "The club? This place is my life."

"The planet."

CHAPTER SEVENTEEN

Lilith shook her head as she toured one of her few remaining safe houses with Balthezar, the youngest of her demon children, the most loyal of her lieutenants. Surveying the fiery expanses of the operational smelting plant, she stood leaning over a railing on the second-floor walkway, trying her best to revel in the cries of agony of the humans her soldiers had tormented below. Their pain provided little sustenance. Even the blazing heat from the fiery vats of molten metal provided small comfort for the chill she felt deep inside.

"It's come to this," Lilith said, barely restraining a crazed, frustrated urge to loose a mystical cry of havoc that would certainly leave all within earshot mad—or dead.

"The war has taken its toll," Balthezar said, his head hung low.

Clanks of steel meeting steel mixed with the screams of the damned, filling the yawning chasm of silence between them. Lilith was in hiding.

In *hiding*.

She found the very thought abhorrent, the reality of it even more so.

"Have our guests arrived?" Lilith asked at last, hoping to cheer herself.

"The lawyers from Wolfram and Hart?" Balthezar asked. "Oh, yes. Nearly a dozen have been captured and brought here for your pleasure."

"That woman, Morgan . . . is she among them?"

"Regretfully not," the demon whispered. "She was too well-protected."

Lilith shrugged. Yet another disappointment.

As she accompanied her child to a large room at the end of the corridor, she considered their attire. He was bare-chested, his beet-red scales and small, sharp black wings exposed, his lower body clad in black leather. She wore jeans, a black "Bad Kitty" crop-top, mirrored sunglasses, and boots adorned with buckles and straps. They weren't exactly dressed for company, but what the hell.

As they walked, she looked over the side at her minions. Though their numbers had been thinned, Lilith still had an army, and like any army, it needed to be fed. Those with perfect souls whom she had led to corruption, the ones who had received her brand would be called upon once she had the Hand, once the moment came when it might be used to its fullest potential. There was literally nowhere on Earth they can hide.

However, a fresh supply of those who had willingly given themselves to her and her message had to be kept to feed her demon warriors. These "stocks" were spread out among L.A. in various secret holdings like this one.

And, like her subservients, Lilith felt the need to feed. . . .

Lilith planned to finally interview the prisoner loyal Balthezar had brought her, but she didn't want to deal with the human while she was hungry. There was too great a chance that she might get . . . carried away.

Fortunately, a nice meal lay before her.

Guards stood before the door at the end of the corridor. They parted at the sight of her; one held open the door, while the other bowed and rumbled, "Your grace."

Your grace. She kinda liked that. Her minions were positioning to move up the ranks and fill the slots left vacant by the attacks of Wolfram & Hart—which had threatened her even before she came to Los Angeles, and had been sending squads of mercenaries against her holdings since the trouble began last night—and that bastard Angel.

Angel. In ways, he was so aptly named. His mission of redemption, of redressing his past wrongs, was pure, but, like her ancient enemies, he was proud, and that made him vulnerable.

She entered the stripped bare office. It was sweltering. The lawyers had removed their heavy jackets and ties, and each bore large, wet perspiration stains. Their fear washed over her in waves . . . and it tasted good.

The closest lawyer, a man who looked a little like a young Robert Redford, grinned as he took her in. "Jeez, Lily, what happened to you? I'd be embarrassed to take you for a glam shot at the mall. I guess what I read in the latest report is true, Lily Pierce and her New Life movement is nothing but old news. . . ."

Enraged by his insolence, Lilith punched through his chest and tore out his still beating heart. He grinned at the sight, then his eyes became vacant as he crumpled to his knees and fell over, lifeless.

Lilith tossed the heart away, annoyed at herself. He'd tricked her. He'd won. His death had been merciful and swift.

The others would not get off so easily. She took their souls slowly, enjoying every moment of their fear as she consumed their dark essences. These were not like her most devoted converts, the thousand willing lambs to the slaughter who would power the Hand and give her the ultimate prize she'd sought for so long. These were only for sustenance.

When she was finished, Balthezar approached. "We have new information. A way, I believe, of turning this whole situation around."

Lilith listened carefully as her child spoke, her smile growing wider and more brilliant with the demon's every word.

Wesley sat handcuffed to a chair in a small storage room of the smelting plant. He had been kept there, in near darkness, for hours, with no one visiting him once it became clear there was nothing he could, or *would* tell Lilith's people that would help them to track down Angel. Through the small glass window on the door, crimson light danced across the shadow-laden walls, the fires from below rising and falling with the suffering of Lilith's followers.

The moans and screams of the damned had been his sole companion, echoing through a high vent in the stuffy office. Their agony and perfect despair was palpable. Wes didn't care that these people all had, in some way, brought their torments upon themselves. He felt only pity and compassion for Lilith's victims.

He couldn't help but think about the hours upon hours he'd spent as a child, locked in a tiny, lightless closet by his father. That boosted his sympathy for Lilith's victims, yes—his heart truly went out to them—but it also lessened the trauma of his present situation, which by comparison wasn't actually so bad. Wesley sat, quiet and calm, waiting.

A key slotted in the door, and Lilith entered, reeling slightly as she looked his way.

"Balthezar, free him," she said, standing in the doorway, well away from Wesley. He was surprised by her reaction. What had he done to repulse her so terribly?

As he thought about it, focusing solely on his attempt to unravel the mystery, Wes remained still as the demon unlocked his handcuffs. Soon he was rubbing his wrists, stretching his arms and legs—and being led to his first audience with his enemy.

As he stepped out of the storage room and into Lilith's presence, he felt her siren call, the near intoxicating waves of temptation she projected pounding into him. She laughed, no longer uncomfortable, and worked her hands over the space between them, casting a spell he had never seen before.

"There," she said. "That should protect you from my charms. They are rather strong at the moment, since I just ate."

She laughed, turning as she beckoned him to follow. Balthezar fell in behind them to make sure Wes complied.

"So you're it," Wes said as Lilith led him downstairs and through the bowels of her safe house. The moans of the damned rose up from every corner, but there was nothing Wes could do for any of the sufferers. Even so, he was filled with contempt for the creature before him—and a deep-seated need to somehow make her pay for her crimes . . . if only a little. "The reason for all the misery humans have ever suffered. Ultimate evil."

Lilith shrugged. "I wish I *could* take credit for all of that, but humans have free will. That's the whole point. Still . . . there's never been a time, never a society, so *friendly* to my message."

"It's just that you seem to have fallen on hard times," Wes said haughtily. "No more galas planned?"

Lilith spun on him, arcane energies suddenly coalescing around her. Wes stumbled back as those energies became a swirling vortex of emerald and amber light flaring into life behind her, demonic hands manifesting from its reaches, clawing outward at Wesley . . . then it was gone. Lilith shuddered, her control restored, though her nostrils flared and her gaze was narrow and hateful as she studied him.

Take that, Wesley thought, but he kept his mouth shut.

"You think you're winning?" Lilith said. "You know absolutely nothing. A week ago I had a foothold into the mortal material world, I had holdings, I had an army that few could stand against. Now I have this."

She gestured at the squalor surrounding them. "It doesn't matter," she said. "In one moment, the balance can change again. And you humans are the cause. Your society is structured to cherish the chosen few as winners and dismiss everyone else as losers."

Wes looked away, thinking of how many times his father had used that word on him.

Lilith walked on, her confidence again evident. "Of course, there can be only a few winners. The top athletes, actors, entrepreneurs, and so on. Practically everyone else is left in the dust. Many blame themselves. They're not pretty enough, not smart enough, not lucky enough."

"We make our own luck in this world," Wesley said.

Lilith went on, ignoring him. "Resentment builds and is often turned inward, becoming self-loathing. For others, it's turned outward, resulting in explosive acts of mass murder and ultimate self-destruction. And that gives me a way in. It opens the door to what I have planned." She sighed. "It's almost perfect. Almost. But right now, it's spoiled by the same taint I feel within you. *Compassion.*"

Wes said nothing. He had hoped if he listened long enough, she might allow some critical bit of information to pass between them—and it had.

Compassion. That was her weakness.

Lilith took Wes to an office and gestured at a small desk bearing a speaker phone.

"I thought you might want to check your messages," Lilith said.

"Pardon?"

"Angel Investigations. My people have been monitoring your phone line, and a very interesting call came in not long ago." She ran her hand along Wesley's arm, causing a wildfire of sensation to spark along his nerves. Then she leaned in close to his ear. "I think you should check it out. You know you want to. . . ."

Startled, he drew back from her, feeling at once horrified and excited beyond belief at her lightest touch, the soft smell of her skin, the promise of her flesh.

"I'm not trying to seduce you," Lilith said knowingly. "The time for games is over. The call I'm speaking of is from your seer, the one you call Cordelia. She has something to say that you really should hear."

Thoughts of Cordelia in danger—or warning of something she saw in a vision—raced through his mind. Unable to stop himself, Wes dialed in and began to listen to Cordelia's frantic message, left from someplace noisy, a plane perhaps.

Yes, it was a vision, as he had suspected. As he listened to the details, his eyes widened in shock.

In Cordelia's voice, the machine said, "And David told me—" But Lilith punched a button on the phone, cutting the message off. "I think that's more than enough. Don't you?"

Wesley was in no position to argue. Besides, Cordelia's words, and her frantic tone, were burned upon his memory. His hand trembling slightly, he whispered, "My God."

Lilith nodded to the open office door. "You have two choices. You can wait here among the damned, or go and try to do something about the problem your friend described in her vision."

Wes hesitated, looking to the doorway as if it were some kind of trap.

"The way is open," Lilith said. "No one will try to stop you."

Yet you want me to do this, Wes thought. *That's reason enough not to. Still . . .*

"You *know* what I want," Lilith said. "And plenty of people are trying to stop me. What about him, and what he wants? What do you think the odds are of stopping *him?*"

Wes looked to the open door leading to freedom—and bolted.

Angel stood, hidden in shadows, watching the half-demons in the parked car. Their clothes and their hairstyles shouted *middle class*; they could easily be a couple of varsity football players and their cheerleader girlfriends. Police sirens wailed a few streets away, but Angel had no trouble ignoring those sounds to focus on the teenagers' voices.

The driver, Karen, a wholesome-looking blonde, said, "Brian, my stomach feels funny. Let's just go somewhere else, okay?"

The thickset boy in the passenger seat snorted and tugged on one side of his letterman jacket's collar. "Jeez, Karen, what? You wanna go rent another movie? I'm tired of sitting on the couch, all right?"

There were four of them, in a late-model Mercedes almost certainly bought by Karen's parents, all of them staring pensively at the huge house a few hundred feet away. Angel watched them. Listened to them. Studied their scents. The two in the back, a willowy, redheaded girl and her lanky, buzz-cut boyfriend, seemed to be waiting on Karen and Brian to decide what the group would do.

They were parked in the driveway of a massive Hollywood mansion, a gargantuan house with every single window lit up and trembling with bone-shaking bass. Angel figured the party had been going on for a few hours already and was just about to reach its peak.

Every single attendee seemed to be a demon or a half-demon.

Not fifteen minutes ago he'd seen two young men in their early twenties, wearing fraternity T-shirts and sprouting barbed horns from their foreheads, wheeling a keg up the driveway.

College-age demon party. Angel would have laughed at that, if the urge to wade in and kill everyone there weren't singing so deafeningly through every nerve in his body. He stayed where he was, hidden beneath the foliage of a tree, trying to decide what he was going to do.

Then these teenagers pulled up and parked practically right in front of him.

Brian kept talking. "Look, I've been wanting to go to one of these for how long now? And you know you'd like it." The couple in the backseat both nodded and murmured assent, finally weighing in with an opinion. "You know you'd *fit in* there. We all would." Brian's jaw muscles flexed, and suddenly his eyes grew large and red and compound, like a fly's, then shifted back again.

Karen giggled, but still wasn't convinced. "Yeah, but what if they find out we're still in high school? This is a *college* party."

Jason, the other boy, spoke up. "It's not just a college party. It's a party for *us*. For our kind."

"He's right, Karen."

All four heads swiveled around as Angel stepped out of the shadows. Karen's hand fumbled for the ignition, but Brian stopped her.

"You're . . . wait, *you're* one of us, aren't you?" He had to lean over Karen and crane his neck to look out the window at Angel. "You're like us?"

Angel's lips curled in a smile like cold marble. "After a fashion, yeah."

Karen and the other three exchanged brief glances at the cryptic comment. The teenager continued: "So, have you been up to the party? Is it—were there any—" He paused, visibly squirming at his own question. "Did you see any other high school kids?"

But Angel had stopped paying attention as the voice of the Serpent's Hand cried out: *Do it. Do it now. Kill them!*

Angel closed his eyes and turned his head away, the

pulse within his chest suddenly filling him with equal parts joy and shame, the excitement of its beating, the sheer rush of pleasure making it difficult for him to think through the red-hot haze consuming his mind.

"They're only half-demons," he whispered. "Half-demon, half-*human*. They've done nothing wrong."

Kill them, then kill the others in the house. They're all demons, Angel. All of them. Kill them!

The Hand bellowed the words, and abruptly its grip tightened on Angel's heart like a vise. He staggered, grunting with the pain, and caught himself against the side of the Mercedes. Karen and the other girl both screamed.

Angel almost cried out himself as the pain ravaged him, the Hand's clawed fingertips digging into his beating heart, crushing it, tearing it. With his face inches from Karen's, Angel manifested his vampiric features, and then the two boys shrieked along with the girls.

One of them yelled, "Go! Go! Start the car, damn it, go!" and Karen did manage to crank the engine, but with an inhuman howl, Angel crimped the metal of the driver's door in both hands and ripped it completely off of the car. As he turned and smashed the door into the pavement, his body wracked with excruciating convulsions, the teenagers abandoned the car entirely and rabbited away.

Go after them, the Hand hissed. *Chase them down, then come back to the house! Kill them all!*

"No!" Angel spun and bolted blindly, like an animal trying to outrun pain. "No! I won't take an innocent life! I *won't!*"

He ran and ran, directionless, unable to tell for how long, as the Serpent's Hand growled and raged inside him. Faces flashed past, lights and signs, and eventually the smell of salt and diesel fuel filled his nostrils—

And then the pain stopped.

The cessation of it was so abrupt, it felt like a blow in itself, a sudden ragged-edged hole where the pain had filled him up. Reeling, Angel brought himself up short against a metal wall of some kind; he realized he was slumped against a shipping container.

Close by, wavelets lapped against creosoted pilings.

He was in a dockyard.

Very good, the Hand whispered in his ear. His heart thumped in his chest, slow and reassuring.

Angel sat down hard, leaning his back against the container. Weakly he said, "What?"

You've just proven it, Angel. You're not an animal. You have compassion.

The realization startled him so badly, he didn't know how to react. He found himself laughing, almost but not quite hysterically. "That was a *test?*"

Of course. To see if you were a true hero. If you would risk death for what is right. If you would make the ultimate sacrifice to atone for the sins of your past— and if you could resist the temptation to become as evil as those you fight against. And you did, Angel. You proved yourself. Take pride in that. The way is now open. Don't you see? You are a true hero, as the prophecy foretold. Your path is now clear!

"You mean—you—I can . . ."

But before the thought had even gelled completely in Angel's mind, he caught a flash of movement out of the corner of one eye. Instinctively he threw himself to one side and rolled to his feet just as two needle-sharp, silver-tipped, trident-like weapons thunked into the side of the container where he'd been resting.

Some remote part of his memory identified the weapons as Chinese tiger claws. His brown eyes glittered and faded to yellow as his heart suddenly triphammered against his ribs and a rush of strength flooded him.

"All right, fellas," Angel said excitedly. "I know you're there, and I'm sure you've got me outnumbered. Why not come on out, and we can get this over with?"

No one spoke, but eight armored, helmeted demon soldiers crept forward out of the darkness. All of them held tiger claws, with extras harnessed across their backs. They moved to circle him.

"More anonymity, huh? Hide behind your masks. Make me doubt myself. Well, you know what I have to say to that?"

And before any of them could move—before he'd even finished pronouncing his last word—Angel sprang on the closest of the demons, drove the creature backward, and slammed it to the ground. Fingers scrambling around its neck, Angel located and burst open the catches on the demon's helmet, tearing it free.

He didn't immediately recognize the specific type of demon glaring up at him, but then, he didn't need to. All he had to know was that it was not Charles Gunn.

A sharp *crack* sounded, and Angel sprang back up, the essence of the demon he'd killed flowing into him. Its body began to decay, falling in around the splintered edges of its skull where Angel had smashed it open. Angel grabbed up the demon's weapon and held it across his body like a bo staff, the ugly purple of the dockyard's mercury-vapor lights flashing off his teeth as he grinned.

"I've got something for you, boys," he said, and then he was among them.

The tiger claw flickered out, both sharp tines and blunt end seeking and finding the mechanisms holding the demons' helmets tight to their heads. Within seconds, each of their faces was exposed.

Not one of them was familiar.

"Well now, this is something, isn't it?" Angel said as he vaulted over a warrior and landed on top of a large wooden crate. Seven faces scowled up at him. He grinned, twirling the tiger claw around him. "Any reason I might've had to spare any of you just disappeared. Guess what that means."

One of the demons spat contemptuously on the ground, glared up at Angel. "Soul or not, fang-boy, you're still just vampire trash."

Angel paused for half a second, genuinely amused. "Yeah? Well, that'll make this even more humiliating, then, won't it?" And he descended from the crates.

What followed seemed more like a vicious, cutthroat ballet than actual combat, a tribal war dance, a dervish at the center of spinning, thrusting death. The power of the Hand traveled out along the length of the weapon Angel held, so that with each stabbing lunge, each hammering impact, a demon's soul left its body, the corporeal shell crumbling to nothing. Angel was not slow to pick up on this . . . and so he decided to take his time.

As another demon unsheathed a wickedly sharp, ornate katana and charged at him, sword raised high and ready to slice downward, Angel considered and discarded three different ways to kill the creature instantly. Instead of anything lethal, he planted a foot in the demon's ribs and simply shoved it over, so that it sprawled gracelessly in the dirt at its companions' feet.

Angel felt the rage coming off Lilith's men like heat from a fire, particularly from the one he'd just humiliated. He flashed them the grin again. "What, you're not enjoying this? Come on!"

And come they did, rushing at him like a wall bristling with blades and tines, as he reveled in the power rising up inside him like magma in a volcano. The fight could have been over and done with in fifteen seconds.

Angel let it last a full forty-five, reveling the entire time in the warriors' suffering. And as he stood there, surrounded by the decaying remains of the demons' bodies, drinking in the last of the vaporous, ruby-red essences of their souls, he thought of the single best word to describe the skirmish—the single best word to describe what he had become.

Perfect.

In a rush of realization, two thoughts pounded at his brain: first, the window of time in which the Serpent's

Hand could be used for its ultimate purpose was almost upon him. Just a few more strikes of the clock and he'd have it. Second . . . he'd harvested the essences of enough demons now, he had enough power now to make the vision a reality. He could use the Hand, let its energies flow through him and out of him and into the world, remake all the horror and misery and pain and death into something good, something pure. Something *perfect*.

The vision unfolded before him; no darkness . . . no evil . . . no demon inside him.

No need for a Slayer. Buffy would be mortal . . . and so would I. The heartbeat he'd enjoyed so immensely since last night would continue, would become true and genuine and human, along with the rest of him. . . .

Angel glanced around him, giddy with the excitement and power and rush of what was coming. The dockyard hardly presented a dignified backdrop for this kind of thing, but he didn't figure that mattered, not really. All that this change, this world-bending transformation required was *power*, and he had that to spare.

Nerves jangling, body saturated with energy and anticipation and—he could scarcely admit it, with *happiness*—Angel scaled a stack of shipping containers with three smooth, limber movements. From that vantage point he could see out, far out over the Pacific, and then turn his head and stare into the heart of Los Angeles.

Nature and industry, side by side. The one feeding off the other, joined here where the world—which should be perfect—nurtured man, who so decidedly was not. Here in this coastal borderland, the two realms, natural and mechanical, met and intermingled and changed each other.

"I was wrong," Angel said quietly to no one. "This is *exactly* the right place."

He smiled up at the night sky, his face fully human, and raised his arms high, ready to begin. But—

"Angel!" a familiar, British-accented voice called from below him.

He dropped his arms back to his sides and turned to find the source of the voice. "Wesley?"

The Briton came out of the shadows, clearly noticing the decayed demonic remains littering the ground below where Angel had perched.

Angel bounded down to greet him. "Wesley, I'm so glad you're here!" He clapped his friend on the shoulder. "I wanted all you guys to be part of this, but I didn't know where anybody else was! It's almost time! I'm about to do it—I'm about to cleanse the earth!"

Wesley turned, then, so that Angel got a good look at his friend's face for the first time. If he'd had breath, it would have caught in his throat. Wesley seemed to have aged ten years since Angel had last seen him.

"Not so fast, Angel," Wesley said, his words slow and weary. "We have to talk."

CHAPTER EIGHTEEN

Angel's smile faltered, returned, then faded completely. Rarely had he seen his friend look so serious. "What's wrong, Wes?"

Wesley seemed to be groping for the words. He glanced down toward the end of one pier, then motioned with his head for Angel to follow. The two men walked slowly toward the ocean, Wesley's frown growing deeper by the second.

"Angel . . . please listen closely to me. You *cannot do this*. You cannot use the Serpent's Hand. You *must* not."

"Excuse me? Are you out of your mind?"

"I've never been more earnest. I have some information you need . . . information that'll change your mind."

"Not likely! I'm about to—" He broke off, eyes narrowing. "Oh, Wes."

"What?"

"She got to you, didn't she? Just like she got to Gunn."

Wesley sighed. "I'm telling you the truth. I'm telling you what's *real*. No one 'got' to me."

"No, she tried to take me by force with Gunn and all her little minions, and that didn't work, so now she's affecting your mind! Don't you see? She's filled your head with all these lies, because she knows she's losing!"

"She didn't fill my head with anything! Anything but what's true."

"Then she did talk to you? You admit it?"

"Angel, listen to me. Just listen. When you do this thing . . . when you use the Hand, when you cleanse the taint of demon-kind from the world and make all your dreams come true . . . what will that ultimate moment be like? What will that ultimate moment *feel* like?"

Angel stopped walking. "I'm sorry, I don't follow."

"It's a simple question. When you fully accept this destiny that the Hand is offering, and you become this, this *savior* of mankind, what will you feel? There's a word for it."

"I . . . uh . . ."

"Bliss. Perfect happiness, that's what you'll feel. And what will happen to you then?"

Angel's eyes registered shock, but only briefly. "No. This is different. It's—"

Wesley's voice grew stern. "What happens to you when you feel perfect happiness, Angel?"

Angel stood motionless for a few seconds, then closed his eyes and bowed his head silently.

"You lose your soul, Angel. What did Lilah Morgan say when she first told us about the Hand? It's the most corrupting artifact in existence, yes? If you do this, the Hand will corrupt you completely, with your willing help and cooperation!"

Angel looked up, his eyes human and full of pain. "But—no, it's, *no,* I'm telling you this is different! When I do this, it won't matter if Angelus tries to come back, because all the demons will be gone! I'm getting rid of all of them, him included, he won't be able to come back!"

"That's assuming nothing goes wrong. What if—"

"Wes, just, just slow down and think for a second, all right? You've read all the prophecies about me—you're the one who translated them in the first place! You know I'm supposed to redeem myself, and when I do, become human again! Right? And what am I doing here? Am I not redeeming myself? I mean, look at it, I'm cleansing the entire world of evil!"

Angel stepped forward and grasped Wesley by the shoulders, his face full of hope and possibilities. "Think of it, Wes! Just stop for a moment and let yourself imagine it. No more demons! No more vampires! We could all have normal, peaceful lives again. I . . . Buffy and I could . . ."

Wes frowned, and looked down at his feet. "This is not that prophecy, Angel. It won't work."

"Why the hell not?"

"Because what the Serpent's Hand wants you to do is like . . . it's like the prophecy *squared.* You're destined to perform some task, or play some role, that will redeem your soul, yes. But you do that on your *own.* Not under the influence of anything else, and certainly not under the power of something that we *know* to be a corrupting force! The Hand has changed you, Angel. It's made you feel things more intensely, more profoundly, hasn't it? And when you do this thing, when you 'cleanse the earth,' it's going to magnify your happiness so much that it'll rip your soul free and send it straight back to Hell."

Wesley shook him off and moved a few steps away. "Besides, even if it did work. Even if you did banish all of the demons, took every last trace of them out of the world, out of humanity . . ."

"Yeah?"

"Yes, of course, humanity would be pure. No one would be capable of violence, or even anger. We'd all be perfect, wouldn't we? Perfect . . . and perfectly vulnerable."

Angel blinked. "Come again?"

"Simply separating mankind from the demons won't get rid of the demons, Angel. Do you think, once Earth becomes pure, that all of the demon species from other worlds and other dimensions will simply leave us alone?"

"Well, I . . . well, I . . ."

I cannot believe you would even consider listening to this pathetic spy, the Hand hissed at him, venom in its voice. *I expected you to pitch him over the side of the pier once you realized he'd come from Lilith, but no! You continue listening. What is wrong with you?*

Angel turned his back on Wesley as he communicated with the Serpent's Hand. *What he's saying makes sense.*

Of course it seems to make sense! the Hand roared. *He's under the influence of the author of all evil! Lilith has been lying, cheating, and deceiving for thousands of years, and you must not listen to her!*

But . . . Angel struggled, his pulse quickening, his heart racing, his mind ablaze with the fever the Hand placed within him, his thoughts difficult to sort out. *But we were told . . . we were told you were a corrupter, and I didn't listen, and now . . .*

The Hand seethed. *You were told, yes—by your sworn enemies, Wolfram and Hart! I have shown you the true way, Angel. I have cradled you, nurtured you, empowered you. I can give you what you desire most of all! And now, rather than me, you'd believe a betrayer, an emissary of the mother of sin and a den of demonic lawyers?*

Angel gritted his teeth, squeezing his eyes shut and clenching his fists, then turned back to Wesley, silent. Waiting.

The two men stared at each other for the space of a few heartbeats.

"Your paradise can't last," Wesley said. "What allows humanity to survive is the touch of darkness, don't you see? Anger, outrage, violence—they're all part of self-defense, of self-preservation. The same thing that causes such misery among mortals also allows them the mechanisms they need for basic survival. The two can't be separated."

Angel wavered to the edge of the pier, sat down heavily.

Nonsense, the Hand said. It began gently massaging Angel's heart again, sending waves of pleasure out along his nerve pathways, demonstrating its good will. *You will be all-powerful, Angel. You could appoint guardians for the earth! Protectors that could turn away any demonic threat!*

After a few moments, Wesley joined him as Angel covered his face with his hands. "I don't know, I don't know," Angel said aloud.

Wesley didn't realize Angel wasn't speaking only to him, and gently asked, "Do you understand what I'm saying?"

A seagull cried out, gliding past them on a cool ocean breeze.

Angel said, "I almost . . . I . . ." Then, "How do you know about all this?"

"Cordelia had a vision when she was off with David Nabbit. She left a message on the machine at the office as soon as she could."

"And the—Wes, did she see—"

"I'm afraid so. Angelus, in all his glory, restored and gleeful amid mankind's death."

Angel groaned, shoulders slumping.

Lies! the Hand practically shrieked, seizing his heart, gripping it, turning pleasure to pain, then blinding agony. *What better way to turn you from the righteous path than to invoke your worst fear? Angelus will be gone forever, Angel! You'll destroy him yourself, simply by using me as you're truly meant to!*

"It's the Hand, Angel. It wanted Angelus to come out and play."

"And I almost let that happen."

No! the Hand screamed again, but this time Angel cut it off. *Shut up!* he commanded. *Just shut up and let me think a minute!*

"You wanted to make up for all you had done," Wesley continued. "That's understandable. But the Hand found your weakness, it recognized exactly how you could be manipulated. The Hand appealed to your—"

"Pride," Angel whispered bitterly. "Lilah said it. 'Such *pride*.'" His mind finally made up, and disgusted by his own indecision on top of the horror at the catastrophe he'd come so close to causing, Angel got to his feet and walked away from the water. Wesley stayed where he was, but watched closely.

"All right," Angel said, eyes closed again. He clearly wasn't speaking to Wesley anymore. "You had your chance, and you blew it. You're evicted."

For the first time the Hand's voice spoke audibly to more than just Angel. Wesley heard it and cringed involuntarily.

I offer you my gift, the most precious of all possible gifts, and you reject me? Think again, little vampire.

The sigil emblazoned on Angel's chest suddenly seemed to *erupt*, its fiery radiance blasting forth. Long fingers of flame reached out of it, circled him, encased him in a whirling maelstrom of dancing ruby-red power. Wesley stood nearby, powerless to help his friend.

"Get out!" Angel shouted, head thrown back and fanged teeth gritted.

No.

The Hand's voice came from everywhere, not just from within him. It rattled inside his bones, shook the pier itself. A crate fell beside Wesley, narrowly missing him. "You can do this, Angel," Wesley shouted. "You can be rid of this thing!"

Angel strained every muscle as he struggled to stay on his feet. He spoke to the Hand. "You almost did it, didn't you? Almost got your way. I won't let it happen."

Abruptly filled with blatant contempt, the voice hissed, *Pitiful, ignorant wretch. You talk as though you were human. Fine. Experience human agony.*

Angel screamed and doubled over, his hands clawing at his chest. "I said get *out!*"

The skin and flesh and bone of Angel's chest split open to reveal the Hand itself, glowing and evil, pulsing red and still digging its clawed fingertips into Angel's heart, which still quivered spasmodically.

No, no, NO! You're almost there, you've almost done it! An unmistakable trace of fear had crept into the unearthly voice. *Keep me, Angel, don't do this! We're so close! You can finally atone for all the wrongs you've committed. Redress all the hurts, take back all the pain you've caused! Only you can do this. The survival of this world is in your hands, no one else could rise to this challenge!*

It had been easy to believe that. Angel had wanted to think that he was the only one powerful enough in mind and soul to return humanity to the state of grace it so richly deserved, to take away all the world's pain and finally make up for his sins once and for all.

That it was his *destiny*.

It had only been lies.

Eyes glittering gold, Angel's vampiric features rippled and twitched with exertion and pain. Growling, crying, Angel cried out again as he thrust his hand inside his own chest—and ripped the Hand loose from his heart, which abruptly stilled, cold and lifeless once more.

You are weak, vampire. The voice dropped, began to diminish. *I will fulfill the function for which I was created long ago. I was made by beings whose very nature you could not even begin to understand. Harrowed by those who claim to serve good, my makers departed this realm and left me behind to one day gain vengeance for them.*

I will be utilized, and the world will be reborn into darkness. If not by you, then by someone strong enough to do it. . . .

Then the whispered words faded away altogether.

Angel found himself standing alone on the pier, a beautifully worked torque in his hand—and a gaping wound torn through his chest, its ragged edges glowing and burning like coals in a fire.

The torque clanged to the ground and rolled away as Angel collapsed.

"Angel!" Wesley called out, rushing to his friend's side. He nodded at the Hand. "Well. I heard what it said about where it came from. So much for the Serpent and the Garden and all that. It was all just smoke and mirrors to steer us away from the truth."

Angel moved feebly, his eyes open but glazed over with the pain. Wesley gasped as he saw the massive trauma caused by the Hand's removal. "Angel, don't move, all right?" Wesley whipped off his shirt, about to bundle it into a dressing, but then paused, confused. The wound's ragged lips had begun, very, *very* slowly, to close themselves.

In a tortured whisper, Angel asked, "Wesley . . . what's happening to me?"

Yes—yes, definitely, the damage seemed to be reversing itself . . . though at a maddeningly unhurried pace.

"I'm not sure," Wesley replied. "Is the, uh, is the pain getting any better?"

Angel made a guttural sound. "No."

"Well, I'll, I'll get you to, um, I'll get you to someone who can help, don't worry."

Another voice came to them from across the pier. "Oh, I don't know. I think a little worry might be in order here, truth to tell."

Wesley twisted around, and Angel turned his head just enough to watch Lilith, backed by a cadre of her demon warriors, stoop to pick up the Serpent's Hand where it had come to rest. They hadn't made any noise as they'd approached.

Lilith straightened, gazing down at the artifact, and smiled an intoxicating smile. "How nice. All powered up and everything. And just in time."

Angel tried to roll over onto his side. He only moved about half an inch before he collapsed back onto the pier—but then he groaned as he watched Wesley slowly rise to his feet. He tried to say, "Wesley, don't," but the words wouldn't take shape in his mouth.

Lilith cocked her head at the look on Wesley's face. "Oh, please. You're going to defy me? *You're* going to battle me for the Hand? You can't be serious."

"I can't let you do this," the ex-Watcher said simply. "I can't let you condemn the world to death."

"I'm only condemning *your* world to death, little thing. There are plenty of others. Open your mind, try to see the bigger picture!"

Angel attempted to move again as Wesley burst into motion, sprinting toward Lilith; the slender Englishman grabbed for the Hand, perhaps with the hope of diving off the edge of the pier and trying to lose the torque somewhere in the water. The weakened vampire could only watch as Lilith swatted Wesley aside as if disciplining a puppy. His friend hit the ground hard and didn't get back up.

Lilith strolled over to Angel and stared down at him disdainfully. She nudged him with the toe of her boot. "Can't move, can you? No? Then watch this."

Lilith raised her free hand and clenched it into a fist; immediately an energy-spear formed around it, and with a snarl she lifted it high over her head and slammed it down.

Angel jerked away from the spear, which Lilith drove into the pier less than an inch from his head. Some tiny bit of his strength had returned. But it was too little, too late.

Lilith laughed and let the spear dissipate.

"You see?" she asked. "You see what I could've done? You could be dead right now." She turned down the wattage of her grin a bit. "You aren't, though. And do you know why? Because you'll make an endlessly entertaining plaything. And your friend, slumped so heroically in a heap . . . I think, perhaps, I might make him a Watcher again. Let him chronicle the final moments of humanity. And the first of the new world."

After a couple of painful false starts, Angel found his voice. It came pitiful and wheezy, but coherent. "Lilith, listen to me. The Hand . . . the essences of your children . . . are inside it. If you use it . . . you'll destroy them."

She arched an eyebrow. "And?"

"But—but you can *release* them. Restore them to life."

Several of the demon warriors behind Lilith let out harsh, abrasive chuckles. She rolled her eyes. "When I reshape this world, that will happen, anyway." As she spoke the last few words, Angel got up to his elbows, then slowly, agonizingly, climbed to his feet.

Lilith's face became a study in skepticism. "Angel, please," she said with a sarcastic little laugh. "You think you can—well, I *know* you don't think you can stop me. What do you hope to do?"

He swayed, his knees almost buckling, his mind reeling, practically rebelling at the thought of what he had done. His beating heart had fallen silent, and the sensation in his chest, the cold core of emptiness, was terrible. Still, he could feel his strength coming back, little by little—and with it a monstrous, ice-cold clarity as the last of the veils the Serpent's Hand had draped across his mind slipped away. Everything he had done, everything he had said since accepting the Hand reverberated inside him and filled him with shame; likewise, the very absence of his cherished heartbeat wracked his soul with unspeakable pain.

The wound in his chest was little more than an angry red scar now. Angel whispered, "As much as I can."

Lilith shrugged. "If you insist." She turned to go, gesturing as she walked away to one of her warriors, who tugged sharply on a leash leading off to something behind him.

The warriors parted, freeing the Gunn-demon to rush straight at Angel, multiple sets of fangs bared and dripping.

Angel's hands and knees trembled as he faced the thing that had been Gunn. As soon as the creature came within range, Angel used a judo technique, pivoting to thrust the Gunn-demon past him so that it stumbled and fell, driven by its own momentum.

He could have landed at least one strike, if he'd been able to muster more than a fraction of his normal strength. But, as it was, the best he could do was keep Gunn away from him.

The demon got back to its feet less than a second after it landed, snarled, and charged again. Again, Angel shoved it away, and this time it almost went off the edge of the pier; it literally had to bite into the pier's edge with one pseudo-hand to keep its balance. Recovered, it circled Angel, crouched low, grinning its triple grin.

"I was wide open." The three-part voice grated like sand against glass. "Why didn't you hit me?"

Across the pier, Wesley made an indistinct sound and rolled over.

"You're my friend," Angel said, aware of how weak his voice sounded. "I don't want to hurt you. The demon laughed. "That didn't stop you or the other one back in the theater. My head still aches from the beating he gave me. I think I'll take that pain out on *you*."

The Gunn-demon started to rush in again, but paused, turning its head at a flicker of movement to one side. It grunted and staggered as Wesley smashed a crate slat right into its inhuman face. Wesley's second swing connected with Gunn's chin like a cricket bat and flipped the demon over onto its back.

"Wesley, go!" Angel said. "He's too strong for you!"

Before Wesley could reply, the Gunn-demon whipped one arm up and smashed the slat out of his hands, then drove a foot straight into the Englishman's chest. Wesley rolled to a stop several yards away, the breath driven out of him.

The Gunn-demon rounded on Angel. "You know what?" it asked, its grins growing wider. "I think you're too weak to hit me."

The creature who had been Angel's friend took one long, triumphant stride toward his victim—and stopped as a sudden bubbling sound from the edge of the pier distracted both him and Angel. The vampire risked a glance over toward the water.

A roughly circular patch of the ocean seemed to have come suddenly to a rolling boil, huge bubbles rising and breaking the surface—and within the space of two seconds, a brilliant silver-green light shone up from beneath the waves.

Angel and Gunn both fell back, stunned, as a column of water exploded up from the surface and arced over to touch the pier. Just as suddenly the water retreated, revealing the man it had set down.

Coronach's clothing had changed. Gone were the hooded sweatshirt and dark trousers, replaced by a long, silver-and-black cowled robe. The leather pouch was still nestled at one hip, but it stayed closed. He already held in one hand what he needed, his eyes gleaming with restored sorceress power.

The Gunn-demon growled, "You again."

Coronach didn't speak. He simply uncoiled the long, oil-black whip and cracked it at the demon's feet. A line of black fire sprang up from the pier and danced for a moment before it faded away; the demon didn't really have a chance to react to it, though, because by then, Coronach had properly gauged the distance between them. The whip cracked out again, this time coiling itself tightly around Gunn's neck; the mage let go of the whip, and it shivered and writhed like a living creature, springing from Coronach's grasp. The whip bound the Gunn-demon from head to foot before it could react at all, its arms pulled close to its body, legs tight together.

A wheezy British voice said, "Incredible," and Angel realized Wesley had come up to stand beside him. Wesley nodded a greeting to Coronach, who nodded back.

Angel took a trembling step forward and stared at the whip that had so efficiently entangled Gunn. It pulsed and breathed with a life of its own.

He turned to Coronach. "Good to see you."

"Good to be seen. Speaking of which, you look like hell." He flipped open the leather pouch, reached inside, and withdrew a vial of brownish liquid, held it out to Angel. "Here. Drink this."

Angel took the vial, regarding it skeptically. "How'd you know where we were?"

"I've been watching from a distance, keeping an eye on things as best I could. Go on, drink it."

Angel quickly knocked back the vial's contents. His knees, already trembling, gave in to a full wobble, and he almost had to sit down; his hand shook as he gave the vial back, but not for the same reason he'd trembled before. Angel suddenly felt as if he'd just slept for eighteen hours straight and then had consumed the vampiric equivalent of an eight-course meal. His blood *roared* in his ears.

Coronach said, "Well?"

"Thanks. That was . . . wow. I, uh . . . wow."

The mage chuckled as Angel looked over toward the Gunn-demon, which had flopped onto its back, unable to move more than that. "I hate to ask a favor on top of a favor, but do you think you can do anything for him?"

Coronach said, "Hmmm . . . ," and rummaged in his pouch as the three of them approached Gunn. After a few moments he pulled out a long, slim, silver tuning fork.

"What's that?" Wesley asked.

"It's exactly what it looks like." Coronach held out his own wrist and tapped the fork lightly on a bony spot right below the base of his thumb; a small, subtle, yet thrilling tone sounded out from the instrument. He stood there over the squirming Gunn for at least a full minute, but the quivering tone from the tuning fork never lessened. Then he stooped over and touched the fork lightly to the top of Gunn's head.

For a moment Angel thought the instrument's sound was growing louder, but then he realized the fork itself had fallen silent. The musical tone, increasing by the heartbeat, came from Gunn himself—and as its volume grew, Gunn's body shimmered, then throbbed with the sound. The grotesque maws at the ends of his wrists gave way to normal human hands, and as the three men watched, his skull blurred, shifted, then settled back into his familiar countenance.

The black whip let go of Gunn and wriggled lightning-quick across to Coronach, where it wound its way up his leg and slid into the leather pouch.

Gunn, fully human, got unsteadily to his feet and looked down at his body, then up at Angel, Wesley, and the mage. He grabbed Coronach's right hand in both of his. "Thank you. Thank you. I mean it. Thank you."

Coronach grinned. "You're welcome."

Gunn turned to Angel, a new light of understanding in his eyes. "Damn. That's you, every day, huh? What you're fighting back?"

Angel didn't say anything. He knew Gunn referred to the demon inside of him, the *beast* that he thought he could get rid of forever with the help of the Serpent's Hand.

The beast he had almost unleashed on the world again.

Instead of answering Gunn, Angel just said, "So. We're okay, Coronach's back, Lilith's got the Hand. We need a plan for how to fight her. Suggestions?"

Wesley cleared his throat. "I do know one thing from when she had me captive. Her weakness is compassion."

Coronach raised an eyebrow.

Angel said, "Compassion? Nothing more specific?"

"I'm sorry, no," Wesley said quietly. "The weakness is real . . . but I have no idea how to exploit it."

"Well," Gunn began, frowning, "I, ah . . . I remember something. From when I was changed."

"Yes?" Wes prompted.

"Uh, well, when the two of you guys came to the theater to try to bring me back, y'know? I could tell some of what was going on with Lilith. She got so angry, 'cause Angel killed her kid for one thing, but even more 'cause . . . well, because she had to *feel* something. She felt grief for the dead demon, and man, she *hated* that."

Angel furrowed his brow. "You're right. . . . She said as much to me outside the theater, but I guess I'd

307

forgotten about it. There's something there we can use," he said, groping in his mind. "I think . . . back in Lo-town, Peregrine told me that Victor was killed because he'd been 'tainted with conscience.' And that made him useless to Lilith."

"He was no longer one of her 'perfect' souls," Wes said thoughtfully. "Hmmm . . . her weakness is compassion—and the grief she felt for her dead child made her feel it! And conscience, what is conscience but applied compassion? Any kind of strong positive emotion can weaken her!"

But Angel shook his head. "That doesn't jibe. Elaine was supposed to have achieved perfect love, right? Lilith would've used her as one of the thousand if we hadn't gotten her away from there. So what gives?"

Just then an immense flare of light burst up through the sky from a point in the distance. More flares followed, and a glow of eldritch light sparked and expanded from the same place the flares had come.

"She's calling up the power of the Hand," Coronach said, his voice grave.

Wesley said, "How far away is that?"

"About ten miles from here." Angel squared his shoulders. "Come on."

The group raced down the pier.

CHAPTER NINETEEN

In the distance, a darksome palace burning with an eerie violet light rose from an abandoned lot overlooking the water. Dozens of jagged, honeycombed minarets, which looked more like angry spears stabbing at the stars, leaned in from each side, while gaping archways screamed and windows like dark eyes pulled monstrously out of shape wept with rivulets of glowing molten metal.

Angel sped toward the abomination in the late-model Toyota that Wesley had "temporarily acquired" after leaving Lilith's lair.

"What is that?" Gunn asked, awe mixing with disgust in his tone.

"She called it her 'Palace of Pandemonium,' according to the ancient texts," Coronach said. "It's where Lilith once reigned in Hell."

Wesley snorted. "We know better than that now." Coronach and Gunn gave him quizzical looks, and he explained what the Serpent's Hand had said after Angel had pulled it out of his chest.

"Smoke and mirrors," Gunn said. "I'll be damned."

Coronach simply nodded to himself. "She's still here, and she's got the Hand, and they're both very real, very dangerous."

Angel nodded. "She's using the Hand's power."

The muscles in Gunn's face twitched as he stared at their enemy's keep. "Guess she wants to feel right at home while she's remaking the world."

"But I don't understand," Wesley said. "Her mansion in Beverly Hills was an exercise in perfection. It was absolute symmetry, a joy to behold. This place—"

"Another kind of perfection," Coronach said. "Perfect madness."

A few more minutes and the Toyota stopped before the palace. All four fighters got out, staring up at the entrance. The central archway above the door looked like the yawning mouth of a terrible beast, with sharp, twisted teeth that could bite through stone or steel.

So, of course, that's where they were going. The stone steps were white marble, with the skeletons of things that were part-serpent, part-human twisting lazily in their depths.

As they entered the central hall, lit braziers provided flickering pools of amber light. It wasn't until they moved closer that each saw the candles were actually thrusting up from the mouths or eyepits of severed heads.

The whole effect within was that of a thing that had, at once, both grown organically from the depths of perdition to stab its way out of the earth and angrily toward the heavens, as well as a huge sculpture made of wax that had started to run and warp in the light of day, then had hardened once more in the cold chill of evening. A horrifying array of sculptures lined the walls, including skeletal hounds and winged demons reaching toward heaven for forgiveness.

Click-clack. Click . . . click . . . click . . .

Angel turned to see Lilith standing before them, fully empowered, and once again returned to her natural, blindingly beguiling state. Except she was not naked this time; she wore a flowing white gown and white high heels, her inner brilliance making her appear the perfect picture of an angel. Only her fiery red eyes and sharp teeth gave away her true nature.

"You know what I like about this place?" she asked. "Lots of room. No need to feel cramped when you're getting ready to have some fun crushing your enemies."

"I am so ready to dust this witch," Gunn said.

Lilith thrust her foot forward and set it down sensuously.

Click-clack.

"Are you sure you wouldn't rather lick my heels first?" Lilith asked. "You rather enjoyed it before . . . and you looked better, too."

"Angel?" Coronach asked, his hands dissolving into balls of white flame as he shrugged off his satchel, allowing it to fall to the ground with a slight crunch.

"Oh, go on, kill her," Angel said. "Or at least maim her as much as you want. Don't let me stop you."

"My pleasure," Coronach said, rising from the ground, lightning swirling around him.

Lilith laughed and wiggled her little finger. A wall of pure rippling force reached out from her, slamming Coronach into the far wall, pressing at him with such power that he suddenly couldn't move, couldn't breathe, and would, in seconds, be squashed like a bug.

Angel leaped into the air, propelling himself toward Coronach's bag. Rolling as he landed, he snatched the bag up and reached within. His hand slid deeply into its depths, the container far larger on the inside than without. Something touched his skin, something with a pulse, and it jammed the hilt of a sword into his grasp.

Spinning once more and kicking up into a standing position, he planted his feet and found himself face-to-face with Lilith.

In his hand was a sword of white fire.

Without taking even the barest second to question any of what was happening, Angel thrust the blade through Lilith's chest. She laughed, turning just enough so that the weapon did not pierce her heart.

Coronach gasped and fell to the ground, the waves of force vanishing.

With an arrogant backhand slap, Lilith propelled Angel halfway across the wide room. Then she slowly withdrew the sword and held it out before her. "Wow . . . an original Sword of Righteousness. Now that's something you don't see every day—oh, unless you've helped to stir up a fight or two between Heaven and Hell. Which I have."

Angel moaned, tried to rise, then lay still.

"So that was your plan?" Lilith asked, advancing on Coronach. "To distract me long enough to use this pitiful weapon to cleave my heart and separate me from the Hand?"

Coronach got to one knee and looked up at the ancient sorceress. "I'm open to suggestions."

She shrugged, and a fiery serpent with a head on each end appeared, curling around her arms and neck. Its maws opened wide and it *ate* the weapon, consuming it from both ends at once. Then it writhed out of existence once more.

"I suggest you go to Hell," she said, gesturing again and causing a swirling vortex of crimson energies to appear between them. "And I think I'll send you there personally."

Angel sprang up suddenly and yelled to Wesley and Gunn, "Now!"

The two mortals, who had stood away from the action, and had been all but forgotten by Lilith, drew the crossbows they'd been hiding beneath their jackets.

She set her hands on her hips as they fired in unison, a pair of silver bolts streaking across this unholy cathedral at her. "Fine. Hit me with your best—"

The impact wasn't pretty. It lifted Lilith up off her feet and split her chest wide open. Lilith landed hard, gasping for air, her eyes fixed on the *impossible* sight of her wounded flesh.

"Seems like I'm not the only one suffering from a little pride," Angel said as he leaped at her, his vampiric ridges and fangs extending, his hand curling into claws as he prepared to rip the Serpent's Hand from Lilith's exposed heart.

A sudden, crimson-fleshed, streaking form appeared and plowed into Angel in mid-flight.

Balthezar.

Angel and Lilith's child toppled to the floor, the demon's wings whipping wildly.

"Didn't think we'd leave our Lady unguarded, did you?" Balthezar hissed.

Angel struggled with the demon, and beyond him, saw dozens of Lilith's remaining soldiers manifest in the outer reaches of the room, weapons drawn. Wesley, Gunn, and Coronach were surrounded. Demons crowded around Lilith, many of them working magical spells of healing.

"Let them live," Lilith said, rising slowly, clutching at her rapidly healing chest. "Let them all bear witness to the miracle I will bring about, the reshaping of this world, that I might torture them each for decades with what I have done."

Balthezar rolled off Angel and sprang to his feet, drawing his sword as the vampire slowly followed. Looking to Coronach, who nodded slightly, his face grave, the vampire turned to Lilith.

Time for Plan B . . .

"Don't you want to know how we did it?" Angel asked. His only task left was to keep Lilith occupied while Coronach organized a great and terrible spell in his mind, one he would loose the moment it was ready.

"Those crossbow bolts contained the tears of mothers who gave their lives so their children might live," Lilith said. "I should have recognized the sting earlier. How ironic, coming from a child-killer."

She glanced at the mage. "Any movement, a single gesture, the first syllable of a spell, and my devoted will do *worse* than kill you."

Coronach was perfectly motionless. Angel knew that all he would need was a single gesture to release the spell he was forming, one Angel himself had recalled from a crisis many years ago and had suggested.

"That's another thing I like about this place," Lilith said, nodding toward the ceiling, which suddenly split apart to reveal the night sky. "The view's great."

"Me, I dunno," a voice said from the doorway. "I think this place is tacky as hell."

Angel whirled in surprise and saw Cordelia entering Lilith's palace, along with David and Elaine. The demons opened ranks only long enough to encircle and ensnare them.

His heart sinking, Angel looked away. "Cordelia . . ."

Lilith shuddered. "More *compassion* . . . I will make you regret that."

Angel ignored her. He had hoped Cordelia would be spared what they had planned as their final gambit for dealing with Lilith, or, if they failed, that she would receive a quick death like the rest of humanity. Now, unless they succeeded, she would suffer along with the others.

Coronach's eyes were flickering, the irises rolling back into their sockets.

The spell Angel had helped to engineer was almost complete.

"So, Lil," Angel said, hoping to distract her away from the newcomers. "You don't have a lot of time left, do you? A couple of minutes, that's all I figure. Then the power of the Hand is pretty much useless as far as reshaping reality goes—"

"The appointed time is upon us, it's true," Lilith said. "So I'll have to give you only a quick taste of the suffering you have to look forward to." Narrowing her eyes at Elaine, Lilith hissed, "And I'm going to save a special place for you, little one. You were almost ready . . . the self-absorption in your heart disguised as pathetic love was almost *perfect*. But now you've been tainted and lost your rank among my legion of souls filled with perfect corruption, perfect darkness, perfect *chaos*."

In a flash it all made sense to Angel. Lilah Morgan was only half-right about Lilith's plan: Lilith *had* been collecting perfect souls all this time . . . perfectly corrupt and evil ones. If there was even a taint of decency, of goodness, as there had been with Victor for a moment, then that soul became useless to her.

All this effort, he thought, *all this time spent finding a thousand perfectly evil human souls. . . .* He realized Lilith must not have been able to utilize humans who simply surrendered to their base natures, or sociopaths who lived outside of any rational sense of right and wrong. The evil she had to strive for was not the kind borne of weakness, and it wasn't the sort that grew out of madness, either. She needed to find a kind of conscious evil, done by someone fully aware of right and wrong, fully aware of the consequences for their actions; she needed to find a kind of dedicated evil that humans are not naturally predisposed to.

And if it's taken all of this to find a thousand souls like that, among the billions on the planet . . . maybe the human race is better off than I'd thought.

That was why grief, conscience, and compassion revolted Lilith, and perhaps even weakened her a bit; she thrived on negative emotions only. But . . . but if Elaine's connection to her was still open, and Elaine had discovered true compassion—

—He didn't have time to consider it. Lilith gestured at Balthezar. "The woman . . . kill the ugly one."

Elaine gasped and stepped back from Cordelia as the demons approached. David moved in front of Cordelia, but a demon knocked him down and out of the way with a single blow.

"Don't," Angel said.

Lilith raised a hand, and the demon who was about to plunge his blade into Cordelia's breast hesitated.

"More compassion?" Lilith spat in frustration. "Don't you even remember what pure anger and hatred is like?"

Elaine hugged herself, standing alone. "I do," she said softly. "But I remember compassion, too." She closed her eyes and concentrated—and the ward of protection Coronach had placed around her soul, invisible all this time, flickered once and fell away from her, the magic dissipating in a few tiny, fleeting motes of light.

Angel knew that the circuit between Lilith and

Elaine had just been opened once more—and Elaine's soul was once again ripe for harvesting. *Does Lilith realize what just happened?* Angel wondered, seeing Lilith focusing her attention to Coronach. *And what the hell is Elaine trying to do, anyway?* He was too distracted to analyze it.

Angel looked at Coronach, whose eyelids had slid closed. Any second now, it would happen *any second* now, and Angel's plan would work. . . .

"Oh, give me a break," Lilith said, loosing a bolt of violet and amber flame at Coronach's head. The mage screamed and fell to his knees, clutching his skull, as mystical rings of energy spun around him.

"Just a little something to scramble his brains for a while," Lilith explained. "I suppose he was going to loose one of those death spells that would have brought the whole palace down, burying us a couple of miles in the earth, making it impossible for me to use the Hand at the appointed time? With some provision to spare all our lives, of course, since you're not just some murderous thing like you used to be. That old ploy, right, Angel? And your idea, too, I would imagine."

Angel's nostrils flared as the fury Lilith had been after was finally upon him. He launched himself at her, but Balthezar doubled him over with a single blow and laid him out flat on his stomach, then placed his boot on Angel's back to keep him down. Much of Angel's strength had returned since he'd ripped the Serpent's Hand from around his heart, but not quite enough to overcome the demon, who, under normal circumstances, would probably be an even match for Angel in the strength department. He squirmed, pinned on the floor.

"Thought so," Lilith said. She tapped her chest. "Okay, it's showtime!"

A dozen feet away from Lilith, Elaine trembled. "You're not listening to *me*!"

From his awkward and painful position, Angel twisted his head just enough to make eye contact with Elaine—and began to understand what was happening.

Wesley had told them about Lilith's one known weakness, and Angel realized that Elaine was about to try to invoke it. And because of the pact she had made with Lilith, the "open circuit" she alone among them shared with the demoness, Elaine stood a real chance of doing true and lasting damage to her through some act of compassion, unlike the others who might only slow her down or bring her to anger with such a display.

But . . . that would mean Elaine had changed. She was no longer so self-involved, and that was proof positive in Angel's mind that humanity itself still had a chance of sorting through its own collective evils.

Yet—she was in danger and he didn't have the strength to help her. He struggled, anyway, and saw her watch his battle to regain his strength, all the while still pinned under the demon's boot. He saw Elaine's gaze flick from Angel back to Cordelia, her jaw set and her eyes filled with determination.

Lilith giggled, turning at last to face her former follower. "Not listening to you? Of course not. Give me one reason I should. You're nothing to me. You never have been."

"You're wrong." Elaine held her hand out to Lilith. "I'm someone you made a deal with. I owe you everything. It's time for me to pay the bill."

Lilith hesitated—then snarled, "This isn't the time or place."

Elaine moved forward. "You don't have a choice. A deal's a deal. And a pact, once made, may never be broken. Not by either of us."

Lilith faltered. "You don't understand what you're asking."

"I think she does," Angel said, his voice heavy with amazement as Elaine's resolve confirmed his earlier suspicions. She knew exactly what she was doing . . . and exactly what it would cost her: her life.

I can't let her sacrifice herself, Angel thought. *There has to be another way!*

But he was still not strong enough to help her.

"I can give you anything," Lilith said.

"You already have." Elaine looked to Angel again, then to Cordelia, and mouthed a silent, "Thank you."

Angel blinked once in momentary puzzlement, then understood. She was attempting to tell him that their compassion had inspired her, had overcome any last fears she may have had over what she was about to do. He could have forced her to stay, he could have used her as Lilith planned to use her, but instead he had sent her away to where she would be safe from Lilith—and the sinister designs of the Hand.

"I could kill you," Lilith said.

Elaine shook her head. Angel sensed that it was an empty threat, and they both knew it. Killing Elaine would only force a resolution to the issue between them that much sooner, and what Lilith needed now was time.

She loosed a spell on Elaine, an emerald cage forming around her. "Time for you will stop!"

Elaine strode confidently from the confines of the mystical cell, the bars passing harmlessly through her flesh. One last time she glanced at Angel, strengthened by the understanding she had achieved, thanking him with her eyes. Then she turned back to Lilith: "You have no power over compassion."

Lilith raised her hands to the sky, the violet light that came from the palace walls now dimming and flowing into her. "I invoke the Making!"

Above, the sky split asunder, and the primal pattern of the universe, the weave of eternity, was revealed. No mortal could look at it for more than a few instants without going mad, and no two beings could see it in the same way. For some, it was a crazy-quilt of colors and patterns; for others, it was every abstract notion in existence somehow given weight and form; while for still others, it was something else again.

"Take what's promised to you," Elaine said, weeping openly now. Lilith's warriors rushed at her, weapons held high, but their blows connected with empty air, bouncing off an invisible field of protection surrounding her. "My soul is yours. Take it *now!*"

Powerless to resist the demand, Lilith faltered in her attempt to connect to the pattern. She reached out to Elaine as the woman opened the front of her shirt, her hand touching the woman's chest. Both screamed as the brand of the serpent formed on Elaine's chest . . . and disappeared.

Lilith's warriors, Balthezar included, stumbled back, disoriented and weakened suddenly.

"Get clear of them," Coronach hollered, the spell of confusion fading from him.

"What's happening?" Cordelia screamed from David's side as a near-deafening wind howled through the chamber and a swirling column of violet and pure white light rose up from Lilith and Elaine, jetting skyward, toward the weave.

Angel and the others reached Cordelia quickly, drawing her and David away from Lilith's demon warriors.

"Elaine's soul is pure once more," Coronach said. "She found compassion, and that is Lilith's bane."

"How?" Cordelia asked. Then she looked to David. "You mean . . . just watching the way you treated me?"

"Maybe," David said. "Or just seeing you in action."

A shriek that was enough to sunder the souls of all present splintered the air, and jagged tendrils of light reached out from the column, consuming each of Lilith's demon warriors.

"My children!" Lilith screamed.

The demons died, one by one, their souls consumed. Balthezar was the last to fall, his body reduced to a charred, skeletal husk.

Within the column, Elaine threw her head back, her arms outstretched, and her body became pure white light that entered Lilith, piercing her chest. Angel stared as 1,000 wraith-like figures, the legion of perfectly corrupt, perfectly evil entities, were wrenched out of Lilith's body one after another. They rose up, shrieking silently, strange blue-white energies stabbing at them as they drifted high along the length of the column, and were torn to pieces by the white light long before they could reach the vortex above.

Elaine, Angel realized, *Elaine's doing this.*

Her willingness to sacrifice herself for others, for the world, had wiped the slate clean of the sins that had allowed Lilith to get her hooks in her; it was a weapon Lilith could not fight. Elaine died, all of the white light that had been her body disappearing into Lilith, showering her through the direct circuit they shared with such raw compassion that the Queen of Night, or so Lilith had been called throughout history, burned with a pure white flame.

Watching Elaine's incredible act of selflessness and self-sacrifice, Angel could scarcely believe it. Since the night of the horrendous car wreck, the night before Lilah Morgan had come to the Hyperion and told them about Lily Pierce, his faith in humanity had dwindled.

But now, watching a woman who had come so close to the edge of darkness yet managed to find her way back to the light of her own soul, Angel realized that the human race had just as much capacity for good in its collective heart as it did for evil. Possibly even more.

Mankind *can* fight its own inner demons, he suddenly understood. It can embrace love and generosity and, most of all, hope.

And even though Angel's heart had returned to its lifeless, inert state once the Hand had been torn away from it, he felt as if an immense weight had suddenly been lifted off of it.

The Serpent's Hand writhed and fled from Lilith's body, unable to coexist with the light. Lilith fell, and the Hand twisted in midair, changing, shrieking, expanding to the size of a silver python—then contracting in an instant to its former shape as it dropped to the ground with a sharp, high *plink*.

The palace and its supernatural protectors faded from existence, along with the rent in the sky and the column of fiery power extending to it.

"It's over," Coronach said, sighing with relief. "The time in which the Serpent's Hand could be used to its full potential—or destroyed—is over. It will be a thousand years before it comes again."

"Over?" Lilith asked, her voice trembling with near madness as she rose.

Angel stared at her, his feeling of triumph fading as he saw the hatred in her flaming eyes. This would never be over, not so long as she lived, and *that* would be an eternity.

With a scream of pure, animal rage, Lilith leaped at the Hand.

Angel stopped her. He came between Lilith and the prize, meeting her every punch and kick, blocking her attacks, forcing her back. A roundhouse kick sent her flying backward, and she eyed the statues of the skeletal hounds, smiling wickedly.

Even without the Hand, even weakened as she had been from her struggle with Elaine, she was a sorceress of incredible power.

"I bind you and keep you," Coronach yelled, throwing a vial of clear liquid at Lilith. It struck her like napalm, making her flesh burn and smoke. "You will work no magic so long as these waters of purity are upon you."

"How long does that last?" Gunn asked.

Coronach bit his lip as he gestured again. "Hopefully long enough."

Suddenly, a wide, swirling pit opened in the earth at the mage's command. A soft, blue-white light rose up from the deep, glowing well, and Angel was close enough to see that it appeared bottomless, nothing but an endless sky filled with clouds, that stretched on forever.

"The Well of Eternity," Coronach said. "We must—"

Angel was all over it. Gathering her by her hair, he hauled Lilith to her feet with one hand and struck her in the face with the other. He dragged her screaming and wailing to the edge of the pit, but, just as he was about to toss her in, she hissed and hooked her leg around his. Drawn off balance, Angel stumbled—and fell into the pit *with* Lilith.

Angel's hand shot out—and Coronach caught it as the wildly tumbling Lilith seized hold of Angel's leg. Wesley,

Gunn, David, and Cordelia helped to anchor Coronach so that the weight of the two fighters would not pull him over the edge and send all three to their fates. Then Wesley came around and gripped Angel's other hand.

"Please!" Lilith screamed, her fingers biting into his flesh in desperation. "I know what's down there! It's worse than death!"

Angel understood. If she fell, she would fall forever, immortal and alone. She'd go mad if she was lucky.

He thought of the hell she had planned to bring to Earth, the lives she had destroyed . . . then he looked in her eyes. He released Wesley's hand and slowly reached down for Lilith. Her terror seemed real.

"Angel," Wesley called, "what are you doing?"

She no longer cast a sheen of seduction—she looked nothing like an elder being, or the first woman, or the mother of all demons, or whatever she actually was. The creature of near limitless power he had battled appeared to have been broken. She was a frightened woman, and she had every right to be.

"Don't," Coronach warned, still firmly grasping Angel's other arm.

Angel held out his hand in a moment of compassion—and she nearly took it off with a long, curling blade she'd been concealing. He yanked his hand back just in time and kicked her loose, watching in horror as she plunged into the abyss. Lilith laughed wildly as she fell, her hatred of compassion damning her.

Coronach and Wes helped Angel out of the pit, and he fell over on his side, tired and worn. Cordelia went to him, kneeling and placing her arms around him. Wes and Gunn came and set their hands on his back, while David and Coronach could only watch.

This was power.

This was perfection.

Angel knew that, now. The power and perfection of the love they shared as a family was stronger than anything they might ever oppose.

Angel rose and nodded toward the Hand, which lay on the ground between him and Coronach. "Your employers want that damned thing."

"A damned thing, yes, an apt choice of words," Coronach said solemnly. "The bottom line is, I couldn't care less what they want."

"Well," Wesley said brightly. "Someone's coming around. And what are you going to say to Lilah when you see her?"

Gunn snorted. "Some bad-ass mystical version of 'take this job and shove it,' I figure."

"I don't intend on seeing her again," the mage said. He gestured at the dangerous mystical object as he locked gazes with Angel. "If you will allow me, I will take the Hand and ensure that it is never found again. As I told you before, there's nothing that foul thing has to offer that I could possibly want. But it's up to you. Do you trust me?"

Angel thought of how Coronach had proven himself to be an absolute man of his word, time and again. And trust and compassion went hand in hand.

"Take it," Angel said.

The mage quickly gathered up the Hand and placed

it in his satchel. He gestured over it and spoke quickly and quietly in an ancient tongue Angel recognized. Coronach evoked Spells of Sleep to still the Hand's hissing tongue and Wards of Warning to alert him if anyone nearby was feeling even a glimmer of the object's corrupting influence.

Gunn looked over the side of the quickly diminishing abyss. "Just one thing. Lilith is part demon, right?"

Angel nodded.

"She's not the sproutin'-wings, flyin' kind of demon, is she?" Gunn asked.

For a long moment they all looked at one another. Then Coronach quickly stepped forward and cast a spell to fully close the gateway to the abyss. "Hope gives us wings. Love, compassion, hope . . . these things are beyond someone like Lilith. Even if they weren't, even if she had the choice of reaching out for help, of embracing hope and redemption and finally taking flight— she'd choose to fall. This world was not meant for one like her."

They stood in silence for several moments. Then Angel thought he heard the barest echo of Lilith's screams—or her mad laughter—from the pit an instant before it vanished.

Or maybe it was nothing at all.

EPILOGUE

The cool evening breeze caressed Cordelia like the soothing touch of a perfect, lapping wave from a sandy shore. She carried a small bag of groceries, hugging them as the wind picked and pulled at her loose-fitting cashmere sweater and her heels clacked on the sidewalk. Her baggy jeans hung low, and long straggly locks cascaded into her eyes; she hadn't done her hair in a week.

Crossing a street about a block from the hotel, she heard a siren in the distance, and almost didn't notice the approach of the gorgeous guy who was chatting, facedown, on his cell phone, and nearly plowed right into her. Her gasp of surprise mere instants before their collision was all that made him look up as they met at the corner, under an amber streetlight that illuminated Cordy's "good" side.

"Whoa, hey, what—" He didn't finish. A look of absolute amazement came into his eyes as he drank her in, consuming her beauty hungrily. He clicked off his cell phone, smiling broadly. "Hey, sorry about that, beautiful. You, um . . . you need some help carrying that stuff? It's the *least* I can do. . . ."

Normally, a cheesy line like that wouldn't get a guy within a hundred yards of Cordelia Chase, but ever since the *incident,* she had hardly felt anything like a beauty. Right now this attractive man's attention seemed even more soothing than the touch of the chill night winds. He was a wiry Brad Pitt type, with a confident, slightly goofy smile, just adorable all around—plus, his Rolex told the time as well as the nature of his bank account. A real catch.

Shifting the groceries into one arm, she fell into an old nervous habit, brushing her hair back over her ear as she turned toward him, a faux shy smile on her face. She heard a sharp intake of breath and realized Mr. Wonderful had seen her scars. His phone rang, and he jumped. Face down, he answered it, hurrying off and mumbling an apology, leaving Cordelia feeling frozen and alone, unable to muster any warming anger to fuel a quick comeback. Even a slow comeback.

Hell, any comeback at all . . .

She walked on, and soon was back at the hotel.

In the office, Wes greeted her and handed her another message from David.

"Your gentle knight has again requested the pleasure of the lady's company," Wes said quietly, with no trace of sarcasm or irony . . . but possibly a hint of encouragement.

"Yuh-huh." Cordy glanced at the message and slipped it in a drawer where it could snuggle with about a dozen just like it.

Wes frowned slightly. "You're not going to call him back? He sounded very sincere. And more than a little worried."

"Look, Wes—"

The Englishman sighed before she could continue. "Sorry. None of my affair. Nor yours, either. I mean, not that I'm implying the two of you are having an affair. Or—relationship. How could it be an affair? Neither of you are married—"

"Please, Wesley, give it a rest, all right?" Cordy said, paging through a catalog she'd found in her desk drawer.

"Resting, yes," Wes said. "Sorry."

Cordelia's shoulders sank. She turned her gaze on Wes, who had his best hurt-puppy look firmly in place, his hands buried in his pockets, his weight going from one foot to the other as he studied the floor. She knew he was only trying to help, and that she'd been way too harsh.

"David says he doesn't care about the scars," Cordelia whispered. "But he knows I do. He says he's willing to pay for the plastic surgery, no strings attached."

Wes slowly lifted his gaze. He was such a good guy . . . he looked her full in the face and didn't flinch, didn't look as if he saw anything different than he ever did. And all she could read from his thoughtful gaze was his concern.

"How do you feel about that?" Wes asked.

"I don't know," Cordelia said softly, thinking about the look on the stranger's face only a short time earlier when he saw her scars. "Taking him up on what he's offering . . . what does that mean? What am I saying to him if I go through with it?"

"I don't know," Wes said regretfully. "I don't have any easy answers. I don't think there are any."

Suddenly, raised voices rang out from the lobby. Cordelia and Wes rushed out of the office and found Angel and Gunn with Lilah, who looked as proper and well-kept as ever, her stylish designer business suit fresh, her attractive features twisted up in a snarl of pure indigence.

"No, this is a simple question," Lilah said, her patience clearly taxed to its limit. "What happened to the Serpent's Hand?"

Angel shrugged. "It's gone."

"I believe it was dropped down the well, some time after Lilith fell," Wesley said.

"Is this what all of you are going to maintain?" Lilah asked.

The entire group exchanged innocent glances and bright upbeat smiles.

"Truth is beauty, beauty truth," Wesley said. "What else can any of us say?"

"Seeing the Hand go bye-bye?" Gunn added. "The thought of that thing never buggin' any of us again? I agree with Wes, it's a beautiful thing."

Cordelia shrugged. "Yeah, I mean—what dumbass would even want to go near that piece of junk in the first place?"

Angel cleared his throat.

"You don't count."

"Hey!"

"You know what I mean," Cordelia said. She put her hand to her throat in an exaggerated, theatrical style. "Oh, look. Here's my *snake torque*. How do you accessorize with something like that?" She frowned at Angel. "Okay, maybe with your feminine fashion sense you'd find a way, but that's not the point."

Angel's head snapped around as he set his hands on his hips. "Again with the 'hey!'"

Clearly frustrated, Lilah turned and picked up her briefcase. "Fine. Before your buddy Coronach took off for parts unknown without so much as stopping by the office to collect his payment, he gave the same story . . . in an e-mail."

"Might be something to that," Gunn said. "Y'know, like it's what *happened*."

"Yeah, like—what else do you expect us to say?" Cordelia asked. "Oh, gee, here's this object of ultimate evil and, darn, we should have tried harder to get it back for Wolfram and Hart. We're sorry . . ."

"Indeed," Wes added. "Things are how they are. Truth *is* beauty, and beauty—"

"Spare me," Lilah said. There was no way she would get any more out of any of them, and Cordelia could see the woman knew it. She took a few steps toward the door, then turned to look at Cordelia.

A strange glint came into the lawyer's dark eyes as she surveyed the younger woman's ravaged face. For a moment Cordelia felt as if she were under the scrutiny of a vicious predator who had just figured out how to get to her prey. Then Lilah's expression softened, and something like genuine concern appeared.

Could Lilah actually care about someone else? Cordelia wondered. *Could she feel someone else's pain? Now that's a creepy thought.*

Perhaps sharing that notion, Lilah shuddered—and her standard businesslike veneer crashed down over her attractive face like a stone door falling to seal off a tunnel. She stood up, her spine ramrod straight, her chin raised imperiously. Now, she would not look directly at Cordelia, would not meet her gaze.

"Wolfram and Hart will, of course, cover any expenses and damages sustained or incurred during the course of this incident," Lilah said, her tone making it clear the offer was not up for negotiation. "In terms of Ms. Chase's needs, we have a variety of mystical healers on retainer—human, nonhuman, whatever you people would be most comfortable with. Just let us know, and we'll handle all the arrangements."

"Now hold on," Angel said, pressing in on Lilah and causing her to take a quick, cautious step back in retreat.

Cordelia had heard enough. "Back off, buddy," she said, placing her hand on Angel's broad chest and easing him away. Then she got up in Lilah's face and forced her to make eye contact.

There was a twinge of sympathy, of compassion, in the lawyer's eyes—and Cordelia was certain now that Lilah hated revealing this side of herself.

"Let me break it down for you," Cordelia said. "I'm not going to end up owing you or anyone else. I'd rather spend the rest of my life looking uglier than brood-boy in full fang-face mode than have that hanging over me. Is that clear enough for you?"

Lilah hesitated a moment, then smiled. "No deals, then. I can respect that."

With what might have been considered a bounce in her step for anyone else, Lilah Morgan briskly strode from the office. The door managed not to hit her on the ass on the way out.

Darn.

"She doesn't come around nearly enough," Gunn said in a low, sarcastic growl.

"Brood-boy?" Angel muttered, his jaw clenched in a failed effort to disguise his pout.

"Oh, for heaven's sake," Cordelia said, heading back toward the office. "Doesn't anyone *work* around here?"

That night, Cordy fell asleep on the office couch. The guys gathered around her, moving swiftly and silently. Gunn gently removed her shoes, Wes put a blanket on her, and Angel kissed her forehead. Without waking, Cordy murmured, "Shoo. Scat. No, I'm sorry, Mr. Trump, we don't take those kinds of cases. Not for all the—really, *that* much? Sure, I'm free Thursday. . . ."

Exchanging smiles, her friends left her to her dreams.

Moments later, a shadow appeared on the wall. A cloaked stranger melted from the darkness—an inhuman, part lizard, part man, tall and gaunt, his pale skin covered with diamond-patterned scales. One long, supple hand reached for Cordelia's face. She stirred as his hand covered her scars, but only a little, and did not wake as a warm crimson and amber glow bathed her beautiful features, a lattice of arcane energies weaving itself around her.

Softly, the healer that Lilah Morgan had sent said, "No deals. No debt. A gift of our choosing, milady. For your courage, your compassion, your willingness to sacrifice, and your impeccable honor. If you and the vampire had not helped inspire the mortal Elaine with your displays of compassion, this world would be a very different place now. For that, we give you this gift."

When he took his hand away and drifted back to the shadows to take his leave, the wound was healed. Cordelia murmured once more in her sleep, a smile that would never again cause her pain appearing as she slept soundly and dreamed a perfect, blissful dream.

And outside, her friends chatted as though nothing had happened, no pain, no suffering, no divisions among them whatsoever.

All their wounds were healing.

Perfectly.

ABOUT THE AUTHORS

SCOTT CIENCIN

Scott Ciencin is a *New York Times* best-selling author of adult and children's fiction. Praised by *Science Fiction Review* as "one of today's finest fantasy writers" and listed in the *Encyclopedia of Fantasy,* Scott has written over fifty novels and many short stories and comic books. His most recent work is the Buffy the Vampire Slayer novel, *Sweet Sixteen.* He is also the author of *Jurassic Park III* and *Survivor,* the first in a series of original *Jurassic Park* adventures for young readers; *Anakin Skywalker: A Jedi's Journal; Captain America: A Winter's Tale* for Marvel Comics; and several original properties, some of which have been optioned for motion pictures and television. His first novels, *Shadowdale* and *Tantras,* written under the name Richard Awlinson, were published by TSR in 1989 and are still hot sellers across the world. His other works have been published by Random House, Simon & Schuster, Warner, Avon, Kensington, Berkley, and DC and Wild-Storm Comics, and more. He has written in a variety of genres including fantasy, horror, SF, historical, and suspense. He is the author of the critically acclaimed *Vampire Odyssey* trilogy. Scott lives in Fort Myers, Florida, with his beloved wife Denise.

DAN JOLLEY

Cutting his writing teeth in the comic book industry, Dan Jolley has worked for every major comics publisher in the country, and written stories featuring such popular characters as Superman, Batman, and the X-Men. With co-author Scott Ciencin, Dan recently had a *Star Trek* novel published through Simon & Schuster eBooks. He lives in Georgia, writes on a Macintosh, and could easily subsist on sushi alone. *Vengeance* is his second novel.

ANGEL™ IN PRINT!

Check out the full range of original novels based on the television series...

CITY OF...
Nancy Holder

The novelisation of the pilot episode which tells how it all began.

£4.99   ISBN 0 671 4144 4

NOT FORGOTTEN
Nancy Holder

A series of gruesome murders and a band of child pickpockets both lead to the same source: a rich slum landlord who conducts secret rituals to Latura, the Indonesian God of the Dead. Can Angel stop him before the immigrant gang he controls become the latest sacrifices in his quest for immortality?

£5.99   ISBN 0 671 04145 2

REDEMPTION
Mel Odom

Actress Whitney Tyler is the spitting image of a young woman warrior Angel encountered during his early days as the scourge of Europe. But who are the secret cadre of fighters sworn to battle creatures of the night? And what connects Whitney to someone that Angel once knew almost two centuries ago?

£5.99   ISBN 0 671 04146 0

CLOSE TO THE GROUND
Jeff Mariotte

Movie mogul Jack Willitts offers Angel
huge sums of cash in exchange for
guarding his overprivileged daughter,
Karinna. But Karinna's in trouble, and
suddenly Angel and company are being
pursued by an unidentifiable creature,
bent on destroying everything between it
and what it wants most in the world.

£5.99   ISBN 0 671 04147 9

SHAKEDOWN
Don DeBrandt

Doyle's latest vision leads Angel to a group
of non-evil, peaceful demons who are under
threat from another demonic clan who
have earth-shattering powers. Cordelia and
Doyle aren't sure their new clients can be
trusted – but Angel finds he has more in
common with this particular brand of
outsiders than he might think.

£5.99   ISBN 0 7434 0696 6

HOLLYWOOD NOIR
Jeff Mariotte

There's a new private investigator in town –
Mike Slade – who dresses and acts as if
he'd walked straight off the cinema screen.
Then Angel and his team find that Slade is
linked to some files that are strictly L.A.
confidential. But what do a cigarette girl, a
water commissioner and a slew of
disappearing demons have in common?

£5.99   ISBN 0 7434 0697 4

AVATAR
John Passarella

There's a trail of corpses across the city and it turns out that the victims all shared one thing: their fondness for online chatting. Evil has entered a new domain. A techno demon is on the loose, and he plans to extend his power far beyond the reaches of even the Internet...

£5.99   ISBN 0 7434 0698 2

SOUL TRADE
Thomas E. Sniegoski

To the junkies, gamblers and gangsters of the L.A. underworld, every soul has a price, and the soul of an innocent child is the hottest item in town. Until Angel appears on the scene and the dealers realise that there's another soul out there: one that is rarer and more valuable than they ever dared to dream...

£5.99   ISBN 0 7434 0699 0

BRUJA
Mel Odom

A madwoman is on the loose on the streets of LA. She seems to be a *bruja* – a witch. But is she real? Or is she a manifestation of La Llorona – the Weeping Woman of Spanish lore, eternally seeking her murdered son. Only one thing is certain: wherever the *bruja* goes, a trail of death will follow...

£5.99   ISBN 0 7434 0701 6

THE SUMMONED
Cameron Dokey

A stunner of a vision: Fear. Fire. Death...
and an ornately engraved amulet. When
Angel Investigations is alerted to a killer
who burns his victims beyond recognition,
they uncover connections with a
charismatic cult. Then suddenly Cordelia
finds herself in possession of an amulet
that looks frighteningly familiar...

£5.99   ISBN 0 7434 0700 8

HAUNTED
Jeff Mariotte

When Cordelia accepts a reality TV
challenge to stay in a so-called haunted
house she finds that the house hides more
than meets the eye. A participant
disappears and Angel, Wesley and Gunn are
on the case. But when Wolfram and Hart
are added to the mix, Cordy has to juggle
her chance of stardom against her very
life.

£5.99   ISBN 0 7434 4950 9

A new Angel novel is published every alternate month. Official
Angel and Buffy books published by Pocket Books are available
from all good bookshops or by post from Simon & Schuster
Mail Order, PO Box 29, Douglas, Isle of Man IM99 1BQ.
Telephone order line 01624 836000
email: bookshop@enterprise.net
Post & packing free within the UK. Please quote ref. ANGEL/SFX.